Bianca Gillam is a London- [...]
expert on 80s and 90s rom-c [...]
published in a variety of pul [...]
interest in asking people how they met their partner has
amassed an impressive collection of 'meet-cutes'. She
formerly worked in publishing, where she had the joy of
editing a wide variety of brilliant authors; she was inspired
by the books she published to write her own.

'A glorious debut. If you love a slow burn, enemies-to-lovers rom-com with plenty of chemistry and some deeper
themes that elevate it above the frothy, then this is the
book for you. Fans of Emily Henry books will adore *Bad
Publicity*' Sophie Cousens, author of *This Time Next Year*

'A beautiful story about grief, love and second chances,
Bad Publicity is a road trip romance that takes the reader
on an emotional ride. Filled with heart, humour and the
swoon-worthy moments every romance reader craves, this
book is a gorgeous debut for Bianca Gillam. I can't wait to
see what she writes next!' Laurie Gilmore, author of *The
Pumpkin Spice Café*

'*Bad Publicity* has all the hallmarks of a feel-good rom-com!
Full of twists and turns, Andie's love story with Jack sucks
you in from the start. A great rom-com read to cosy up
with!' Beth Reekles, author of *The Kissing Booth*

'A delightful blend of humour and heart. Gillam's enemies-to-lovers workplace romance sizzles with tension and
swoon-worthy moments' Bal Khabra, author of *Collide*

bad publicity

bianca gillam

BLOOMSBURY PUBLISHING
LONDON · OXFORD · NEW YORK · NEW DELHI · SYDNEY

BLOOMSBURY PUBLISHING
Bloomsbury Publishing Plc
50 Bedford Square, London, WC1B 3DP, UK
29 Earlsfort Terrace, Dublin 2, Ireland

BLOOMSBURY, BLOOMSBURY PUBLISHING and the Diana logo
are trademarks of Bloomsbury Publishing Plc

First published in Great Britain 2025

A catalogue record for this book is available from the British Library

ISBN: PB: 978-1-5266-7644-3; EBOOK: 978-1-5266-7643-6;
EPDF: 978-1-5266-7642-9; SPRAYED-EDGE EDITION: 978-1-5266-9056-2

2 4 6 8 10 9 7 5 3 1

Typeset by Integra Software Services Pvt. Ltd.
Printed and bound in Great Britain by CPI Group (UK) Ltd, Croydon CR0 4YY

To find out more about our authors and books visit www.bloomsbury.com
and sign up for our newsletters

'Fuck.'

Not a word I expected to come out of my mouth on the first day of my new job. In my first conversation with my new boss. From the look on her face, she wasn't expecting it either. My hand flies up to my mouth but it's already out there, in the air, floating around. *Fuck*, I say again, this time in my head.

'Is something wrong?' She's all wide eyes and concern, which is better than judgement, at least. I look back down at the list between us, squinting, making sure. The name is still there, clear as day. Jack Carlson. Jessica follows my gaze.

'Ah, I see. Nerves, right? He is a big name. I get it – I felt that way when I first started working on bigger authors.'

I open my mouth to correct her, then realise that explaining the actual reason would be infinitely worse. Five years ago at university, Jack Carlson screwed me over so catastrophically that I made a promise to myself I'd never have to be in the same room as him again. And until exactly this moment, I was pretty sure I'd sooner light myself on fire than break that promise.

'I thought he wrote non-fiction?' I say, trying to keep my tone neutral.

'He does, usually. But his editor persuaded him over to the dark side last year, so you'll get to be the publicist for his first novel. Once you're over the nerves it's actually a very exciting campaign!'

She starts telling me about the campaign, while I stare at the list of authors I will be representing in my first senior publicist role. The role I was so excited about until my big chance turned into my worst nightmare. I emerge from my stupor when I hear the words 'book tour'.

'What did you say, sorry?'

Jessica looks momentarily confused, then repeats herself without a hint of irritation. I like her very much. It's a shame I'll have to quit immediately.

'I said, you'll have time to get over those nerves when you accompany him on his book tour.' *Shit.* I grip the edge of the desk to hide my reaction, while Jessica tells me that there are a few events planned in New York, then a European leg.

'Europe?' I say, trying desperately to gather my thoughts. As Jack's US publicist, Europe is not my remit.

She nods and continues, her smile widening. 'He's extremely successful in France, Germany, the UK and Ireland, and our sister companies publish him in those territories, so we've arranged a tour.' I silently pray that this explanation isn't going where I think it's going. 'We did the same thing for Jack's last non-fiction book, but there were a few hitches on the tour – miscommunication between publicists in different countries, missed flights, etcetera. So this time, to keep things clean, his agent has insisted that we stick to one publicist. One schedule. One person to make sure things run smoothly.' She pauses, her expression expectant. 'That would be you.'

Oh, good. It can get worse. My knuckles are practically white from gripping the desk at this point, and Jessica waits as I force a smile which probably comes out more as a grimace and try to think of an appropriate response. I am sure she's expecting enthusiasm – and why wouldn't she? It's any book publicist's career dream, to run a global tour for a world-famous author. I should be excited – this should be the culmination of all the work I've done so far, an opportunity to show what I'm made of.

I manage to choke out a strangled 'Oh?' from my throat, which suddenly feels like it has closed up. Fortunately, Jessica smiles gently, interprets my response as concern about planning such a large tour, and reassures me that they have already handled the flights and accommodation, and nailed down the schedule. All I have to do is go and make sure the tour goes off without a hitch. Which would be fine, if there wasn't already a hitch: a fucking huge one. I excuse myself in a choked voice to go to the bathroom.

As soon as I find it, I lock myself in the nearest cubicle and let out a long breath. 'Fuck. Fuck!' I say, out loud, to no one in particular. It's been bad enough, watching Jack's stratospheric rise from a distance – *New York Times* bestseller this, literary award that. Historical documentaries, radio interviews. Viral threads about how hot he is, thirst traps, video compilations of him running his hand through his hair while he's describing some battle that happened 500 years ago. Now, not only do I have to be aware of his success, I have to *travel around Europe with him facilitating it.* There are not enough swear words in the world to do this justice.

I want to scream. But, somehow, I have to try and calm down. As disastrous as this reality is, it's not going away any time soon. *Come on, Andie. You can handle this.*

Can you? a small voice inside me asks, and suddenly I'm dangerously close to being pulled back to that last semester at Edinburgh. To telling Jack I never wanted to see him again, and meaning it. To the weeks afterwards, when my world was smashed into pieces. But I shut all that in a vault long ago. If I'm going to get through this, I have to keep it there, somehow.

I clench my hands into fists at my side and start doing the meditative breaths my dad taught me. A fresh pang of grief appears at the image of him in his yoga trousers on the deck of my family home, but then the breaths start to work, clearing the cloud of emotions into an almost-calm. My eyes flutter open, bringing me back to the present. I check my watch: it's been ten minutes. I'd better return to my desk, so Jessica doesn't think I've disappeared completely.

I take one more deep breath, and leave the cubicle.

As I navigate through the office, my profession-alism starts to take over, gradually replacing my earlier panic with a temporary resolve. For today, for this week, I need a plan. There are lots of other authors on that list. Perhaps until I can process this and strategise properly, I can focus on those.

Jessica is still at my desk when I return, sipping her tea as if I haven't just sworn at her and had a near-meltdown. I sit in my new swivel chair, at my new desk, and – for a second – feel a flash of pride. I've made it here, to senior publicist in one of the most prestigious publishing houses in New York. The Andie who moved here from London as an intern would hardly be able to believe this.

Unfortunately, this lasts about three seconds before Jessica starts talking about Jack again and I almost fling my pen across the room at the sound of his name. I'll have to get better at that.

'As you'll see there's quite a list of authors here, but most of them are under control – your predecessor lined up a lot before she left. So your focus will mostly be on Jack's campaign for the next few months.' I swallow the sound of frustration that moves up my throat and plaster what I hope is an excited expression on my face. So much for focusing on my other authors. 'The book publishes this week,' she continues, 'so we have events in the city spread over the next few weeks. The first event is this Thursday, actually. It would be a great chance for you to meet him.'

'This Thursday?' I say, my voice about three octaves higher than usual. I overcorrect my tone and my 'Great!' comes out in a baritone. *Jesus Christ, Andie. Get it together.*

'Wonderful,' she smiles, still seemingly unfazed. 'I'm sure he'll be delighted to meet you.'

Or he's about to get the shock of his life.

2

The evenings are bright at this time of year, so my walk home from the subway station to my apartment on the Upper West Side is bathed in soft dusk light. I usually love this part of my commute: everyone always seems to be out and about, on their way somewhere. The city feels quietly alive.

But with today's events, it doesn't have its usual effect.

By the time I reach my building, I'm covered in sweat and absolutely exhausted. I unlock the door and wait for a beat, half-expecting to hear Sara's voice greeting me, then remember for the hundredth time that she doesn't live here anymore.

The silence settles as I shut the door behind me, and I allow myself to feel her absence for exactly thirty seconds before throwing my bag on the sofa and watering all of my plants to distract myself. Andrew the ficas, Shirley the monstera, Sharon the cactus, Peter the succulent. Sara and I named them together when she first moved here – her arrival in New York, a year after mine, brought so much colour to the grey life I'd been struggling to build on my own. But now, three years later, they are mine. A few weeks ago, Sara moved into a new flat with her lovely investment banker boyfriend James, leaving me in our fifth-floor walk-up, alone. A part of me was delighted for her, but a larger part of me sometimes sits for hours in her old room because I miss her so much. Before I become too sad, I pull out my phone and call her.

'Big A, my babe!' Her voice is like a warm bath after the day I've had. I sink into it. 'How are you? How was your first day? Tell me everything!'

Relief washes over me at the question. The emotions I've been managing to keep in check all day flow out of me, drawn out by Sara's warmth and her total lack of connection to my job. 'On a scale of one to ten, I'm going to give it a three. And that might be generous.'

I hear rustling and footsteps – as if she's moving somewhere more private so she can give me her full attention. 'Oh Andie, I'm so sorry. Is your boss horrible?'

'No, she's delightful.'

'Were your colleagues mean?'

'Nope, they seem great.'

She pauses, groping for other reasons for my low rating. 'The office?'

'Marvellous. Beautiful.'

'Then what is it?' she says, finally defeated after we've covered the commute, the local lunch spots, the free office coffee, the view from my desk. All great.

'Jack Carlson is one of my authors.'

I hear her sharply exhale and wish she were here so I could see the expression on her face. She gets it. She's the only one who really does, the only one who knows what happened. The warmth of shared understanding is like a soft jumper.

'Jesus Christ.'

'I know.'

'Jesus fucking Christ.'

'Yep.'

'I'm so sorry.'

'What do I do?' I ask, and it's a genuine question. Sara and I have been inseparable since she threw a drink over a guy who wouldn't leave me alone in a bar in freshers' week: since then, she's always been my go-to person. So brave, so wise, so uncaring about the opinions of others. I could really use her help right now.

'I don't know, babe. It's really tough.' I feel momentarily panicked by the idea that even Sara, my problem-solver, can't figure this one out, but then she carries on. 'I think you've got to stick it out, honestly. You've made it this far.' Resolve enters her voice, and I feel the comfort of it wash over me. 'We're not in Edinburgh anymore. Don't let him ruin this for you.'

'OK,' I say, my voice smaller than I'd like it to be. At this moment, at my most honest and vulnerable, the thought of seeing him again is almost inconceivable. But Sara's voice reminds me of my own strength, and I lean into it. 'I won't.'

'Dinner this week as usual?'

'Always.'

'See you then. You can do this.' I savour the last of her voice before she hangs up, and I'm left once again with an empty apartment. I really need to get on with finding a new roommate – Sara, despite my protests that she didn't need to, has covered her rent for the next three months until the end of our lease. After that, if I don't find either a new apartment or a new roommate I'll be in some trouble, even with my new salary. Yet another spiral I don't need to go down today. I pour myself a glass of wine and turn to Andrew the ficas.

'I can do this,' I say. If plants could hear, he might be able to detect the fear in my voice. He might even tell me I was kidding myself. But his leaves hang silent, and I sip my wine in peace.

By the time Thursday arrives, I feel a little more settled in my new job. Despite the low-level nausea which has been swirling in my stomach since this morning, my panic from Monday feels further and further away. I have even allowed myself to entertain the thought that tonight's event might not be a total disaster. I'll just have to do everything I can to act natural, as if Jack is any other author. To keep the past in the past and focus on the present. I can't afford to consider any alternative scenarios. Plus, a large group of people from the company are attending, so I'll at least have a human shield around me.

As we're walking down the street in the warmth of the summer air, I tune in to the hum of the city, beginning to establish a tentative sense of stability, of calm. *Maybe I actually can do this. Maybe this will be fine.*

Then we arrive at the bookshop. Lost in my thoughts, I didn't recognise the familiar streets we

were walking down. I hadn't paid enough attention to the location of this first event, figuring
I was new enough that I'd just follow people
there. In this moment, I realise what a mistake
that was. As I look up, I register with horror the
gold lettering of The Lost Bookshop. My secret
haven from the overwhelming crush of New
York. I spent countless hours here when I first
moved, the comfort of the books around me dulling the loneliness of not knowing anyone in the
big city. I've become protective of it since, only
bringing people here if I really trust them. *Oh
God*. All at once, my feelings from earlier this
week resurge with full force, and I am no longer
anywhere near calm. In T-minus two minutes I'm
quite possibly going to either throw up on Jack
Carlson or scream obscenities at him in one of my
favourite places in the world, and I will never be
able to come here again. I inwardly curse whatever hell-demon is following me and arranging
for everything good in my life to be immediately
and decisively ruined. Jessica – interpreting the no
doubt horrified expression on my face as nerves,
again – gives me a sympathetic look.

'You'll be fine,' she says, resting a hand on my
arm. 'I'll be here to help, I'll introduce you. You're

really just here to meet him, everything else is already handled. Relax, have some wine, enjoy yourself.'

I force a smile and nod. Words aren't safe right now, with most of my vocabulary suddenly reduced to expletives. I take a breath to calm myself as we enter the shop, its warmth and familiarity dulled immediately by a tingling in the back of my neck. He is here, someone I thought I would never have to see again except by some huge misfortune. But now the huge misfortune is my life. I pull Sara's words of encouragement from earlier into my mind and wrap their warmth around me, a shield against whatever is about to happen.

I scan the room. There are people milling around, chatting, holding glasses of what looks like champagne. I raise my eyebrows internally – this isn't the usual standard for publishing events. Either we're pulling out all the stops, or Jack has contrib-uted to the alcohol budget. I grab a glass from a well-stocked table to the right of the shop floor. As I turn to find my colleagues again, I almost walk straight into an uncommonly tall man standing behind me. *Shit*. My stomach drops as I draw my gaze upwards past his shoulders, his immaculate suit, his edgy, slightly open-necked shirt, to a pair of expressive dark blue eyes which – for the briefest of seconds – seem to register as much terror as I feel. But then it passes, and a lazy smile spreads across his face, and my terror boils into furious hatred.

'Fancy seeing you here' he says in his perfectly deep voice, as British as my own, and for a millisecond the tingles on the back of my neck melt into something warmer which runs down my spine. *Get a grip.*

'I didn't want to come,' I blurt, then realise my words are a) unprofessional and b) nonsensical, considering I am both here and holding a glass of champagne. The fury bubbles up again and I hold his gaze with what I hope appears to be measured calm but which probably looks more like I'm trying to engage him in a staring contest. Just as I'm about to open my mouth and say something which will dig me into an even deeper hole, Jessica's voice floats across from my right.

'Hello, Jack. I see you've met your new publicist, Andie.'

If anything is going to make this evening, this whole situation, worth it, it's the look on his face as he glances from Jessica to me and tries to work out what exactly is going on. I can see in his eyes that

Jack is as unhappy about this as I am. At least we have that in common. But the look only lasts for a fleeting moment, and before Jessica can register what is happening the smooth veneer has returned. This isn't the Jack I knew – he's more practised, better at hiding his emotions.

'Of course. Andie, was it? A pleasure.'

I let out a small relieved breath – I hadn't realised until this moment how concerned I was that the game might be up, that even despite the negative implications for him he might reveal that he knew me and ruin the carefully constructed new life I've built here, away from all that. I turn to smile at Jessica and she gives me a knowing look as if to say, 'See? Not as bad as you thought.' She's right, but for completely the wrong reasons.

A few moments later I extricate myself from the conversation on the pretence of going to the bathroom. Once I'm out of sight, I take the half-hidden stairs to the next floor of the shop and make a beeline for the fantasy section. Up here, there is a hidden nook with an old, comfy armchair. I've come to think of it as my own: I've never seen anyone else here. I sink into it and sigh. I won't be bothered here, I know, but my time is limited. I can't spend the entirety of the first event in my new role hiding in a corner. I sit for a few moments, the cogs in my brain whirring as they process the situation I've found myself in, and don't notice the sound of feet on the stairs until it's too late.

'Andie?' *Fuck. Can I not get a second of peace?*

I wipe all emotion from my face and look up to see that it is, indeed, Jack. *Wonderful.* 'You followed me.' I say, trying and failing to keep accusation out of my voice. He shrugs and nods, his posture more awkward than it was downstairs, as if he's trying to make himself smaller somehow. I ignore it.

He goes to lean against the shelf next to him, almost knocks a book off it, then decides against it and straightens himself. 'I love this corner. I used to come here as a kid when I was visiting my dad and read books about dragons.' Frustration surges through me at this revelation – of course he's claimed this place as his, too. I cannot catch a break today. He shifts his weight from foot to foot, as if gearing up to say something. 'Listen, Andie—'

'Don't,' I snap, cutting him off. 'I really don't want to talk about it.'

He flinches slightly but carries on speaking. I plead internally that he's not going to go there, that he's smarter than that. 'I think I owe you—'

Apparently not. 'Nothing,' I say, interrupting him again. 'I don't want anything from you, Jack. Except turning around, walking back down those stairs and giving me a minute to myself. I'm going to have to see a lot of you in these next few weeks, so you'll forgive me if I don't want to start cosying up just yet.' The words flow from my mouth with ease, releasing some of my rage in his direction, and it feels good.

'Fine,' he says. 'If that's what you want.'

'It is.'

He lingers for a second too long, perhaps hoping I'll change my mind and let him apologise or say whatever it is he was going to say, which I'm sure he thought would instantly erase the five years of resentment. I remain silent, staring at my lap, and eventually he leaves. Once he's gone, I let out a breath, my calm exterior crumbling. *Fuck.* This is going to be a lot worse than I thought. *I can't do this*, I text Sara, hoping she'll know what I mean. *Yes, you can* she texts back immediately. *He is a stupid boy, and you are a boss bitch. Go get 'em. Don't let him ruin this for you.*

Sara's words are enough to remind me why I'm here: to do my job. To not let him ruin it. I take a deep breath and spend a few more moments steeling myself, then slip downstairs and find a spot at the back while Jack gives his talk. I replay our conversation upstairs a few times in my head, cursing myself for being so easily affected by him. But I couldn't help it: seeing him stripped away any professionalism, any calm I'd built up ahead of this evening and brought to the surface a myriad of feelings I thought I'd buried.

Through my thoughts, I catch snippets of his talk: about the shift from non-fiction to fiction, the importance of setting, his writing process. I tune it all out as much as I can – I'm going to be hearing a lot of this, in the coming weeks, so I can catch up. I only hope it doesn't drive me as slowly insane as it's doing right now. I glance around the room at the audience: about a seventy-thirty split between the public and my colleagues (at least, the ones I recognise). Tonight was a sold-out event. People love Jack, from what I've been hearing all week from Jessica as I've desperately tried to keep a lid on my past while learning the ropes. His books are bestsellers, and this one no different: it hit the top 100 of the *New York Times* bestseller list this morning. This is going to be a challenge, too – watching someone I hate be so openly adored by everyone else, when I know who he is deep down, know what's lurking behind that charming veneer. Someone who would sell someone out, wrecking their life without a second's thought, just to protect themselves. It's enough to make me want to just leave, right now – walk out the shop doors and never come back, leaving this entire mess behind. But I swallow, taking a breath and digging my nails into my palms. I can't do that, can't let him win.

When the talk ends, I find a spot on the other side of the room from Jack and do my best to throw myself into meeting colleagues and social-ising, making the most of the human shield. But with each moment that passes the pretence becomes more and more draining, as if just being in the same room as him is sucking the lifeblood out of me. Eventually and fortunately Jessica finds me, mistakes my pale complexion for first week exhaustion, and tells me I can head home.

It's a cool evening, and the fresh air outside is welcome. I gulp it in, relieved, my lungs suddenly expanding – as if there had been something press-ing on my chest while I was in there, making it harder to breathe. I let it out in a long, slow exhale, the harsh reality of my current situation hitting me all over again. I've been keeping it together so well up to this point: one foot in front of the other. Don't look back, don't dwell too much on the past. I thought I'd built a life far enough away from it all that it didn't have any power over me anymore. I put an ocean between us, for God's sake. But seeing Jack this evening came very close to unravelling all of that. His presence makes me feel out of control, vulnerable in ways I haven't felt since I left the UK five years ago.

When I get home I can't stand the sight of my empty apartment, so I climb out onto the fire escape, the first place I go when I need some space to organise my thoughts. I sit for a while, looking over the blinking lights of the city, and take some deep breaths, hoping they'll bring a moment's relief. In the space between breaths, a thought rises to the top of my mind, as true as it is terrifying. If this evening is anything to go by, Jack Carlson could be the undoing of me. And I can't let that happen. This time I might not be able to put myself back together.

4

The next evening, at dinner, Sara and I have an argument. We're in the flat she now shares with James: a glossy two-bedroom in Tribeca with a lift and windows so large they look like glass walls. From the table where we're sitting, I can see the High Line. I still can't get used to it, though I'm now a regular guest here. It feels too clean, too flashy – distinctly un-Sara. But maybe I just feel that way because I miss her.

'Hear me out,' she says, in a tone so reasonable it makes me momentarily want to stick my tongue out at her.

'No. You weren't there. It was awful. Terrible. A hundred times worse than I thought it would be. The worst—'

'I think you've established that it wasn't a roaring success.'

'I hate him, Sara.'

'I know.'

'He makes me furious.'

'I know.'

'He—'

'Trust me, I know. I was at Edinburgh too, in case you've forgotten. Will you just listen for a second?'

I stop talking but arrange my face into the expression of a grumpy two-year-old so she knows I'm not happy about it.

'It's a free trip. To Europe. Come on, Andie. Doesn't the prospect of Berlin, Paris and Dublin excite you even a little? And you could see your mum while you're in London—' I knew she'd play that card, and I hate how well it works. I flinch at the reminder of the miles between us that seem to increase with every year I live here. I applied for my first publishing job in New York a few months before my dad died, a graduate scheme at a big five publisher. It was a long shot, so I was barely checking my emails, sure I'd been turned down. Then one came through, telling me I'd got a place, in the week of his funeral.

My plan was to turn it down; to stay with my mum and get a job in London. But when I told her, she pushed me to ask if they'd allow me to defer entry for a few months. 'It's what your dad would have wanted, love,' she said. 'You have to

24

go and live your life.' They agreed to defer my place, and so – after six months with my mum, helping her get my father's affairs in order and trying not to fall apart at the seams – I went. I figured it would help, to be away from the pain for a while. And at first, although in some ways I was lonelier than ever, it did. The vibrancy of the city was a constant distraction from the grief which in London felt like it was always pressing down from above, threatening to crush me. I could breathe a little easier. No one here looked at me with an expression of pity that reminded me of everything I'd lost, that defined me, stamping a label on my head as the girl who'd just lost her father.

I had always planned to go home when I was feeling better. Once I'd got some CV points and a foot on the corporate ladder. But then my career advanced, and Sara moved out here, too, and what started out as a holiday from my grief started to feel more and more like a life. Things felt lighter, like I'd left behind everything that was weighing me down. And the more I stay here, the more that rings true: the prospect of returning home is like a force of gravity back to a heavier, sadder version of myself. I'm determined to resist its pull. But I can't help but feel guilty for being so far from my mum,

for so long. Bi-yearly visits to the UK and fort-
nightly calls have been nowhere near enough to
stem the steady feeling that I'm letting her down.

'It's a month, Sara,' I continue. 'A month with
him. I'll kill him, or I'll lose my mind. I can't do it.'

She raises her eyebrows at my dramatics but
reaches for my hand across the table.

'A, I think this could be good for you.' She stares
me down, her gaze kind, her grip on my hand
firm now.

I don't respond, stunned into silence by her
words, so she continues. 'Ignoring what happened
hasn't made it disappear. Maybe…' she pauses, gathering herself. I hold my breath. 'Maybe this will be
a chance to realise that he is just a human being,
that he doesn't have as much power over you as
you thought. Maybe – and I know you'll hate me
for saying this, but I'm going to say it anyway –
maybe this is what you need, to finally move on.'

I close my eyes – I can't deny that I expected
this, from the moment I brought this to Sara. She's
always so logical. And, usually, I trust her logic. But
this time, the hundred-pound lead weight in my
stomach would seem to disagree.

'I just…' I hesitate, trying to find the right
words. 'I don't know if personal growth is enough

of a motivation for me to spend a month with Jack Carlson. My career, maybe. But I'm not interested in giving him a free pass for what he did. He doesn't deserve it. Besides, I'm here, in New York, with you. Isn't that moved on enough?' She raises her eyebrows and opens her mouth to speak again, but I interrupt her before she can. 'And don't you dare start talking about forgiveness.'

Sara throws up her hands in surrender on the other side of the table. 'This is an F-word-free zone. Except fuck, of course. Just think about it, Andie. That's all I'm saying.'

I must still seem unconvinced, because she gets that look on her face that tells me she's about to pull out the big guns. 'Remember what your dad used to say?'

Yep, she went there. I level a furious glare at her, but she ignores me and ploughs on, saying the only words she knows will absolutely guilt me into agreeing with her. 'The only way out is through.'

'Fuck you.'

'Well done for making use of the F-word-free-zone addendum.'

I continue to glare at her, and she waits, arms crossed, in the smug silence of someone who knows that she has won.

'Fine.' I say, finally, and a slow smile of victory spreads across her face. 'I will think about it.'

And I do think about it. Every day when I'm at work and an email lands in my inbox from jscarlson@gmail.com, in the excessively formal tone he has adopted since the event at The Lost Bookshop. When I'm out for lunch, when I'm at the shops, when I'm walking the fifty million stairs up to my front door. Every minute of every day, Jack Carlson is on my mind, and I wrestle with the idea of spending a month with him. Eventually, in a bid to get him out of my head, I decide to defer the decision until the day before the trip. That way, I can have a few more practice runs in New York to see whether I can be around Jack without throwing things before I decide whether I'm capable of sitting on a plane with him for seven hours.

The next event is a book signing on the Upper West Side, a few blocks from my apartment. I work from home and walk straight there when I finish, making use of the journey to get my head straight. Thankfully, this particular bookshop – Albertine – is not one I have ever entered before, and, judging by the furious French man behind the counter, not one I will be in a hurry to visit again. Which is a shame, because it's really beautiful – all oak shelves and leather armchairs and a celestial painted ceiling, gold stars scattered into constellations across a deep, vivid blue.

This time, I feel more resolved – committed to the experiment of spending time with Jack, again. There are fewer attendees: Jack's editor, Daniel, is here, but unfortunately we don't have much in common – his conversational topics of choice are restricted to grammar and obscure architecture, neither of which I can claim to be an expert on. Oh well, I think, as he lists off his favourite uses of the Oxford comma, at least I won't have to worry about the evening descending into dramatics: this man's energy is so gently soporific it could neutralise a tense situation in ten seconds flat.

Mostly, I am right not to be concerned. To my immense relief, Jack is distant and polite and professional, hardly speaking to me beyond greeting me and asking whether I had a pleasant journey. As the huge queue of customers waits patiently, I flip the book they've purchased each time to the right page for Jack to sign it, then pass it to him. About half way through the pile, our thumbs accidentally brush as I'm handing one to him, and I jerk my hand away, an electric shock running up my spine. But apart from that minor incident, and the occasional urge to throw whichever book I'm holding across the room when he addresses me to ask for a new pen, we put on a decent performance of a recently acquainted author and publicist for the signing audience and a mostly oblivious Daniel. It is only at the end of the evening, when I have wrapped up thanking the shop manager and have somehow managed to charm him out of his French ennui into discussing some further potential events, that things almost come apart.

'I gather you were both at Edinburgh.' Daniel says, gesturing to Jack and me as we're standing by the door about to say our goodbyes. For a second, my heart drops to the floor, and I flash Jack a glare which makes him look like he wants to step away in case it burns a hole in him. His eyes, though, betray his confusion – he's blindsided by this comment, too. I search my brain for the conversations I've had with Daniel so far this evening and dredge up a memory of him talking about the stonework in Edinburgh, and me mentioning that I went to university there. It seems reasonable that Jack would have told his editor that he was there, too. We're about the same age; he probably put two and two together.

'Not together.' I say, quickly. 'Just at the same time.'

Daniel looks at me, bemused. 'That's what I meant, yes.'

'But we never met.'

'Understandably, in a university so large.' Jack chips in, slightly recovered from my glare but still looking pretty apprehensive. Thankfully, the conversation ends there and Daniel, still oblivious, starts discussing his favourite typefaces with Jack. I take my leave, and I can see Jack trying to catch my eye as I go, but I ignore him.

By the third event, I'm feeling more confident. I'm starting to find my feet at work: I called in a favour with a friend at the *New York Times* and managed to get Jack's book into a 'Top 5 Reads This Summer' round-up, as well as pitching him for a few last-minute interviews. A particular win was discovering that a presenter on a New York radio show that's notoriously hard to book was born in the exact part of Ireland where Jack's book is set. He was so thrilled about the home connection that he's doing a special ten-minute segment on it. Jessica was delighted, and Jack's email was restrained but grateful.

If I still wasn't 100% sure whether Jack would play along before, the Edinburgh slip-up at the last event has gone some way towards reassuring me that he's not going to dredge up the past. It's the closest we've been to discussing it in public, and he seemed as keen to avoid it as I was. And with each event I feel a little calmer, a little less on the edge of losing my cool. If I can keep my interactions with him minimal and professional, then the tour might not be impossible. But I'm certainly not telling Sara that until I'm sure.

I arrive at a bookshop in the East Village which also appears to be a wine bar. Excellent, I think – I can avoid the warm cheap wine which is usually offered at these events and get myself a glass of something good. When I get there, I realise I must have arrived a little early: the shop is mostly empty, and its owner greets me enthusiastically. Once he realises I'm here for Jack, not as a customer, he launches into an effusive speech about how excited he is to have *the* Jack Carlson in his shop, and tells me the event sold out within hours. I manage to nod along for a few minutes, then take the excuse of a customer arriving to politely excuse myself and head straight for the bar. *Nice, Andie. Really professional.*

As I'm browsing the wine menu with my back to the door, I hear the bell of the shop trill to announce someone's arrival, and the scuttle of the owner's excited footsteps behind me lets me know that it's Jack. I continue browsing the menu, hoping to enjoy a moment's more peace, until I hear someone approaching. Praying it's the owner but knowing from the cadence of the steps that it's not, I wait until Jack is leaning on the bar next to me before I turn to look at him.

'What can I get you?' he asks, as if we're back in Edinburgh, in a pub, and this is a normal interaction. Despite my best intentions, this immediately sends irritation surging through me.

'Nothing.' I try to restrain myself but fail to keep all the vitriol out of my tone. There's something about him arriving so suddenly and acting so casual that's setting off every nerve ending in my body right now. I feel like a grenade with the pin yanked out. So much for my earlier calm, my hope that things between us were beginning to feel almost normal. He blanches slightly.

'Come on, Andie – at least let me buy you a drink.' I take a deep breath, but it's not enough to stem the rage now surfacing at him acting like he can just buy me a glass of wine, like it's nothing.

Like it would make up for anything. *Maybe if I threw it over him*, I think, imagining red wine splashing down the front of his crisp white shirt. I struggle to keep my voice at a normal volume, aware of the bookshop owner hovering behind us.

'I said no. This is on the company, anyway. It should be me buying you a drink, not the other way around.' My voice is shaking, despite my last-ditch attempt to remain professional. 'Besides,' I continue in a lower tone, the words flowing out of me before I can stop them. 'You don't have anything to prove to me. I know who you are, Jack. A glass of wine isn't going to change that.'

I can see the damage, each word a wound I'm inflicting, and I can't deny that a large part of me enjoys it. He looks crushed, but only for a moment. Then the bookshop owner flutters over and asks Jack if he wants to go through to the back room which he's set up as a green room of sorts. Relieved to have the interruption, I tell them to go ahead, that I need to make a quick phone call – really, I just need a moment to compose myself, to reset my professionalism. As he's ushered away, I can feel his gaze burning into me, but I turn to the bar, determined to tune it out.

As the bookshop fills up, I do my best to breathe through the adrenaline coursing through me – *Jesus Christ, why can't I keep myself together around him?* – and instead focus on the people arriving. For the first time, I notice that there are *a lot* of women here. That makes sense, I suppose – despite being a backstabbing arsehole, Jack is an attractive man who, thanks to a few viral social media threads, has become something of a heartthrob in the historical documentary community (not much competition there, I'd wager). He was on the swim team at Edinburgh, so was pretty much de facto considered hot, and was also actually hot. High cheekbones, messy dark hair. The kind of boy-pretty that makes you angry – why does he get to have such long eyelashes when I have to wear mascara all the time? I've spent the years since hoping he'd get ugly. Unfortunately, the universe has let me down in that respect. The bastard is just as handsome, just as charming. Edinburgh Andie would fall for it all over again. My wine glass trembles in my hand and I drag my thoughts away from that extremely dangerous avenue. We do not need to think about Edinburgh Andie this evening. New York Andie has enough to worry about as it is.

I make it through the talk, his voice washing over me as I focus on the books on the shelf to the right of my seat, playing my favourite game of 'spot the publisher' by examining the logos on their spines. I've scanned the room three times for other colleagues who might have unexpectedly shown up, but I can't see anyone here. I'm on my own.

Once Jack has offered many smiles to many adoring fans and signed their books, no doubt about to become treasured possessions, the queue eventually dissipates and we're alone in the shop with the owner. I keep a pleasant expression plastered on my face while Jack tries to extricate himself from possibly the most grateful man in the world. Eventually, I interrupt and tell him that it's us who are grateful to him for so kindly hosting Jack at his bookshop. This almost makes him cry, and I usher Jack away before he starts.

'Thanks,' he says, retrieving his jacket from the coat rack by the door. I open the door and step outside, and he follows.

'I didn't do it for your benefit. I want to go home.' I'm tired of the wounded puppy expression my dismissal of him causes, so I avoid looking at his face, instead busying myself searching for my MetroCard in my handbag.

'Look, Andie, if you don't want to come on the tour—'

I look up, sharply. 'What are you talking about?'

He gestures between us. 'This clearly isn't working for you. I'm grateful for everything you've done so far, but it's obvious you'd rather peel off your own skin than spend a month with me. If you don't want to come, I can handle it.'

Furious that he's read me so easily, but intrigued by his proposition, I frown. 'What do you mean, handle it?'

'I mean, I know a freelance publicist who I've worked with in the past. I can make up some high-maintenance author excuse that I want to work with someone I already know, then you won't have to go.'

The rage which has so far been simmering inside me comes to a boil. I've never understood the meaning of the expression seeing red before, but I do now.

'So you're going to kick me off your campaign?'

He baulks at my tone and takes a step backwards. 'I didn't mean it like that—'

'Really?' I seethe, eyebrows raised sarcastically. 'Because that's exactly what it sounds like. You know how it looks when an author hires a freelancer to replace someone. I'd be totally screwed.' I ball my hands into fists at my side, digging my nails into my palms and desperately taking a breath before I say something I regret. But, even as my heart-beat slows slightly, a realisation dawns which sends my rage levels right back up. 'But this isn't about me, is it?' I say, each word laced with venom. He looks confused, but I press on, sure that I'm right. 'I bet it would be convenient for you not to have me hanging around all the time, reminding you of what you did. So convenient you'd be happy to tank my career to get rid of me. Fuck you.' Though I'm still furious, I can feel each word expunging some more of the anger I've kept balled up inside me for so long, and it feels great. It courses through me, an electric current finally released.

He runs a hand through his hair. His posture is deflated, a hint of exasperation passing across his features. I clench my fists again. *What the fuck does he have to be exasperated about?* 'I thought it was what you wanted,' he says, still looking wounded. 'I'm only trying to help.'

This triggers another surge of rage so strong I struggle to remember to breathe. Is he an idiot? How can he have misread this so horribly? It was what I wanted, of course it was, but not like this.

A broken leg, maybe, or a family emergency – not a high-profile author kicking me off my first big campaign, risking my chance of ever getting another job like this one. And – I realise, anger suddenly sharpening into clarity – it's not what I want anymore. If before I was hoping not to let him ruin this job for me, now I'm determined. If Jack Carlson doesn't want me on his tour, if he's willing to risk my professional reputation to get me off his campaign, then I'm fucking going.

5

'I'm proud of you, A,' Sara says over the banquet she's cooked for us to mark our last dinner in New York before I leave.

I'm not exactly sure she should be: I am, after all, mostly going out of spite. But I haven't exactly been explicit with her on that, so I smile, pretending to bask in her approval of my journey of self-discovery. As far as she knows, I am as zen as a Tibetan monk, ready to achieve peace with myself and the situation. In reality, it's going to take every bone in my body not to deliberately sabotage every single event I have to attend with Jack, or accidentally-on-purpose push him off a cliff. I feel a twinge of guilt at that last thought. *Alright, perhaps attempted murder is a bit far.*

I pile some more tabbouleh onto my plate and try not to think about how much I'll miss this. It's only a month, but I'm going to hate being so far away from Sara. On top of my less-than-ideal travelling companion, when I get to London I'll be back in Hampstead, surrounded by memories of my dad. It will be all I can do to get through it in one piece.

As if she can see what I'm thinking, Sara says 'You'll be fine. I know it. We'll text the whole time.'

I must look unsure, because she reaches for my hand and says 'Remember when that guy grabbed my bum in the student union, and you kicked him in the shin?'

I laugh. 'Yes. He deserved it.'

'From what you've told me so far, you've given Jack a hard enough time that he's probably feeling a *lot* worse than you at the prospect of this trip.'

I imagine myself giving Jack a good kick in the shins with my largest platform Doc Martens, and smile to myself. Sara, yet again, reads my mind. 'I'm not suggesting that you *kick* him, just that if he says or does anything … unexpected, you'll be able to handle yourself.'

I think about the dressing down I gave him a week ago, his nervousness around me, the look on his face every time I say something cutting. It's pretty obvious that Jack is terrified of me, so far. Perhaps, if I can keep this up, the trip won't be a complete disaster.

The sound of someone swearing loudly in frustration in the next room cuts through our conversation, and we both turn instinctively to the door. Sara's boyfriend, James, is working in their spare bedroom. Her face tells me that this isn't an uncommon occurrence.

'What's that about?' I whisper, feeling momentarily guilty that I have been so focused on what's happening in my own life that I've barely asked about hers.

'They're pushing him so hard at work. I barely see him at the moment, and when I do he's horribly stressed, on edge all the time.' She looks downcast for a second, then looks up and smiles. 'Not as fun a flatmate as you.'

I smile back, even as my heart sinks. A few weeks ago, on our last night in the flat before Sara moved out, I had a few too many glasses of wine and said some things I didn't mean about her leaving to live with James. I was feeling lonely and sad, and I didn't think through my words properly. I felt awful and apologised the next day, but it's still a little shaky between us when the subject of her relationship comes up. Right now, I can see that even as she's trying to make light of the situation, she's worried. James is usually so calm, so carefree – the human equivalent of a golden retriever. I want to console her, but I don't know how.

'Can he quit?' I say, but as soon as the words leave my mouth I realise how naive they sound. This seems grown up and difficult, a problem not easily solved. She shakes her head, tight-lipped, and I squeeze her hand. Clearly, the just-moved-in-together bliss I've been imagining for them isn't as idyllic as I thought.

A few seconds later, there are footsteps in the corridor and I watch Sara tense up as the door opens and James enters the room. Immediately, the atmosphere changes. He looks awful: his hair is sticking up in different directions from where he's been running his hand through it, and his shirt looks like he's been sleeping in it. Even from this glimpse, I can see what Sara means: his stress is palpable.

He stares for a few moments as if he's confused by my presence, then seems to remember himself.

'Hi, Andie,' he says, some warmth returning to his features.

'Hi, James,' I say. He smiles, and turns to Sara, who is regarding him with concern, getting ready to speak.

'Don't,' he says. 'Please. I'm just getting water, then I need to get back.'

'Babe—' she says, getting up out of her chair as he moves over to the sink, but then she cuts herself off, glancing at me. I get the sense that she doesn't want to say too much, to risk having an argument in front of me. He finishes filling his glass and moves past Sara, touching her tenderly on the shoulder as he does so.

'Later, OK?' he says, softening. 'Let's talk later.'

She nods, but her expression is defeated as she watches him move towards the door. My heart contracts for her. I get the sense that they've already had this conversation a few times. Again, I'm moved to try and help, to say something to make her feel better, but I don't know how. Once he's left the room and the door is safely closed, I place my hand over hers. 'Love you,' I say, because it's the only think I can think of to say.

She squeezes my hand affectionately. 'Love you, too.'

A few days later, I meet Jack at the airport at 4 a.m. He looks infuriatingly good for the early start: not a hair is out of place, not an eye bag in sight. I, on the other hand, look atrocious. But then, I don't really care what he thinks. My focus is on getting through this trip in as professional and detached a manner as I can, and I am absolutely determined not to let him get in the way of that.

The trip through the airport to our terminal is strictly business: checking our bags, grabbing a sandwich for the flight, going through passport control. I am all efficiency and professionalism. I even help him lift his bag onto the conveyor, startling him so much he almost drops it. *Good*.

We sit three seats apart by the gate – I put my backpack on one and my jacket on another, in case he gets any ideas, but he seems to get the message.

As we board the plane, he places himself a few people behind me in the queue, but I'd have been stupid to hope (I am stupid, I did hope) that Jessica wouldn't be able to find seats next to each other. I end up boxed in by the window with Jack beside me. *Fuck*.

It's OK, I think, I'm prepared for this. And I am: I've meticulously chosen the book I'm going to read on the plane. I wanted to read the next instalment in the fantasy series I've been enjoying, but Jack's comment about reading books about dragons in The Lost Bookshop has rendered this dangerous territory: he might take it as an opportunity to bond, and I can't have that. So instead, I've gone for the grisliest thriller I could find. If

Jack glances over, it will be all dismemberment and disembodied feet and gore and murder. A fitting message, which will hopefully encourage him to keep his distance for the next seven hours. With other authors, I might spend a flight this long doing some press-prep. But right now, I'd just like some peace.

About two hours into the seven-hour flight, he glances over. 'L. R. Brown is one of my favourite authors.' *Double fuck*.

'I hate him,' I say, closing the book.

'But you've been reading—'

'I said what I said.' I'm being petty, but in this moment I don't care. He can't just talk to me like this, pretending that everything is fine. That's not how this trip is going to work. I will do my job, but casual conversation is firmly off the table.

He sighs and, though I'm not looking at him, I guess from my peripheral view that he's pinching the bridge of his nose. 'Andie, I'm just trying to make conversation.'

'I don't want to make conversation, Jack. I'm here to do my job, and that's it.' I say, my tone firmer than before.

'Could you try and be a little less hostile?' he says, and this sends a spike of irritation up my spine. He has no right to police my tone, even if a small voice in the back of my mind is telling me that perhaps this isn't the veil of professionalism I was hoping to display on this flight.

'Could you try and be a little more silent?' I retort, then open the book again stare at the pages intently to indicate the conversation is over.

A few hours into reading my book, I start to drift off to sleep, and before I know it the pilot is announcing that everyone needs to put their seatbelts on and tray tables up, and telling us that the time in London is 6 p.m. I take more pleasure than I should in elbowing Jack awake, and we both watch as the city appears beneath us. A surge of familiarity hits me all at once: this great, sprawling mass was my home for eighteen years, and I hadn't realised until now just how much I've missed it. Jack catches my expression and opens his mouth to say something, then shuts it again. Good. He's learning.

I close my eyes as I disembark the plane, the sun hitting my face, the London air refreshingly familiar despite being thick and humid. For a second, I allow myself to forget that Jack is here, instead enjoying my surroundings as we move through the airport: the concentration of British accents, the familiar newsagents we pass on our way out of departures. The overwhelming feeling of belonging that seeps through me, almost without warning. Though somewhere in my mind there's still worry about Jack, and this trip, I can't deny that – right now – it feels good to be home.

6

Our hotel is tucked away in a townhouse, a few streets away from Angel tube station. My first summer home from Edinburgh, I interned at a small publishing house around here. I spent long summer evenings in old red-bricked pubs, or lazing on the green with colleagues. Every lunchtime, I'd head out with the other assistants to one of the local markets, trying all the different foods and making sure our salaries never went far. I still think fondly of that office, especially when I'm cooped up in a grey cubicle: from every window, you could see trees. From my window in New York, it's just buildings.

The driver helps us with our bags, and we drag them up the steps into the foyer, which is beautiful: all period features and antique furniture, crown moulding lining the ceilings. A Jane Austen dream. I don't know how we managed to book this and stay on budget – Jessica must have used some serious powers of negotiation.

I get up to the room, which has a claw-footed bathtub I'd give my left foot to be able to spend the evening soaking in. But we have to leave for the first event in under an hour – a private party in a rare bookshop in Bloomsbury Square hosted by Jack's UK publisher for industry people and journalists. So instead, I splash some cold water on my face and pull on the beautiful red chiffon dress Sara lent me. I risk a glance in the mirror and what I see is not half bad: Sara was right that this dress would suit me. I text her: *Miss you so much it hurts. Thank you for the dress!* She texts back immediately: *Miss you, too. Enjoy the dusty old books!*

Before I forget, I text my mum, too – to let her know I've landed safely. Her reply also comes in swiftly, in a tone so effusive it chokes me up immediately: *My Andy Pandy is in the UK!! Lunch booked at Gino's at 2pm xxxx.* Gino's is our favourite restaurant, around the corner from the house I grew up in. We used to go there with Dad for my birthdays.

I swallow the lump that has suddenly appeared in my throat and text back *Can't wait!*, carefully matching her four kisses, then shove my phone in my handbag and head downstairs a few minutes early to wait out front for the car which has been scheduled to take us to the event. It's a beautiful evening – not cold enough for a jacket, but mild. The waning light hits the buildings across the street, turning them a soft orange. I breathe in, allowing myself a moment of reflection. Here, on this empty street, the soft buzz of London traffic in the background, I feel almost calm. And through the calm, a flutter of excitement appears: a car is arriving shortly, to take me to a high-profile event for a famous author. Objectively, a part of me can acknowledge in this moment that Sara was right: this is cool.

Unfortunately, Jack arrives a few moments later, ruining the illusion. He's dressed sharply, in chinos and a navy jacket. When he sees me, I could swear he does a double take. My momentary excitement is immediately replaced by irritation. *Ugh*.

'You look—'

I hold up my hand to tell him to shove whatever compliment he's about to offer back down his throat. 'Got it,' he says, shaking his head as if he's annoyed with himself. 'I'll shut up.' He stops short of me, so there are a few metres between us as we wait for the car to arrive in a now-awkward silence. I'm not willing to break it, so instead close my eyes and take a few breaths, trying to shift into professional-Andie-mode for the evening. The car arrives, and I climb in the front to avoid sitting next to Jack, slightly startling the driver.

The drive is short and traffic-free, which is a relief: the longer I'm in the car with Jack, the more difficult I'm finding it to breathe easily. I'm too aware of his presence behind me, pulling my attention towards him even as I focus on reapplying my lipstick in the mirror and try to engage our driver in polite conversation. Eventually I give up and focus instead on the streets as we pass them: Georgian sash windows, white Victorian architecture. The familiarity of spotting local cafes, pubs and bookshops I used to frequent. But even this isn't enough: in the back of my mind, I am aware of Jack's every breath, every movement, and it's driving me slowly insane. A good sign, given the number of car rides we're going to have to take on this trip. *Get it together, Andie.* Ten agonising minutes later, we arrive at the square and I almost run into the path of a bus, I'm so focused on getting out of the limo as fast as possible.

I make it to the pavement of an old square, a neat patch of green bordered on each side by a row of townhouses, all equally grand. When I used to dream about working in publishing, this is what I imagined: Bloomsbury Square (I was crushed when I realised that Bloomsbury is actually located in Bedford Square) and champagne-laden author events. I'm getting both this evening, which would be magical if not for the fact that I'd like to kill the author I'm here to celebrate.

I steel myself, allowing Jack to go ahead of me, and climb the steps to the entryway, where a young assistant is taking peoples' coats. She's so eager and achingly reminiscent of my past self that I almost want to tip her – a reactive impulse, based on five years of tipping culture in the US. But – as much as I'm aware that she's definitely not being paid enough – it would be a bit weird to hand her money in this context. So I hand her my coat instead, and take her directions up to the second floor.

The room is spectacular: oak panelling lines the walls, and the floors under my feet look to be at least a hundred years old. There are glass cases everywhere, filled with books of every description: illustrated tomes, gold-leaf-rimmed and beautifully bound religious texts, even a few first editions of Emily Brontë, in perfect condition. I spend a moment taking it in, then scan the room for Jack and find him in the corner, deep in conversation with two men wearing tweed jackets who look to be in their seventies. I make my way over, not exactly enthused about talking to him, but supporting Jack at these events is a large part of my job here. And, much as I'd like it to, sitting and scowling in a corner won't accomplish that.

'Hello,' I say, breaking up an intense debate about who was the true mastermind behind the discovery of the remains of King Richard III. *Oh God, I hope they don't expect me to join in.* Jack's two companions look at me, visibly irritated at first, but as they slowly move their gaze down my dress in a way that feels invasive, the irritation disappears into a sort of faint bemusement. 'I'm Andie, Jack's publicist,' I say, trying to make sure my voice doesn't falter.

'Hello, love,' one of them says eventually, extending his hand. 'Bernard Smith. I wrote—' he pauses, assessing me again '—ah, never mind, you probably haven't read it.' I probably *haven't* read your *boring fucking book*, I think, but I'm stung nonetheless by his comment.

The other aims a watery smile at me. 'George Richards. I used to publish this star's non-fiction here in the UK before he deserted us for fictional shores.' He chuckles in Jack's direction, and I'm just beginning the process of settling in for an evening of this man's self-important drivel, when he turns back to me and gestures to the other side of the room. 'It's great that you're here, actually. You couldn't man the drinks table, could you?' *Thank God* is my first thought – he's given me an out. I'm about to say 'Of course, I'd be delighted,' in my politest and most formal tone before scurrying away as quickly as I can when the kicker arrives: 'We're in need of someone pretty to pour wine.' He gives me a quick wink, then turns away, indicating with his posture that I am dismissed. I freeze in place, momentarily immobilised by his comment, and through my shock hear Jack's voice.

'I don't think—'

I spring into action. I can't have him rescuing me. 'It's fine.' I say, giving George and Bernard my sweetest smile and mentally wishing them both incredibly painful deaths. I turn away before they can see how bothered I am and move resolutely to the oak table on the other side of the room. The assistant who took my coat earlier is standing behind it, looking a little nervous and out of her depth. I've had the luck of being pretty sheltered from attitudes like this in my career so far, and have usually been afforded immediate professional respect in most rooms I enter: mostly because they're full of women. Clearly, none of that matters here – to those men I'm just a pair of hands in a nice dress, without anything resembling a brain behind my eyes. I take a deep breath and steel myself, determined not to let them ruin my evening; they're not worth it.

I text Sara, to make myself feel better: *Old boring twats making me man the drinks table.* Her reply pings through immediately: *!!!! Fuck them!!!!.* Her rage warms me through, and I pick up a glass of champagne from the table, take a sip, and take my place next to the assistant. She looks at me like I might be about to give her orders, or tell her off for the crime of standing there and doing her job, so I soften my expression and hand her a glass.

'Perks of the job. If they're going to stick us back here the least we can do is enjoy it.'

She looks a little terrified still, so I wink at her, pick up my glass and take another sip. This gives her confidence, and pretty soon we're three glasses deep and accidentally-on-purpose pouring Sauvignon when people ask for Chardonnay and vice-versa. Nobody notices.

About half way through the event, I hear the sound of a glass clinking. I look up from my wine pouring duties and accidentally catch Jack's eye – for half a second a warmth moves up the back of my neck at the intensity of our eye-contact, then he turns to look at George and breaks it.

'I'd like everyone here to raise a glass to this young man, if you would,' George says, his deep voice carrying across the room and silencing everyone still talking. Jack smiles, seemingly at ease, but there's an undercurrent of discomfort to his expression I can't quite place.

'I hope you don't mind me saying, Jack, that I rather feel I discovered you – fresh out of university, you produced an account of the British monarchy that was absolutely astonishing. I still remember the day it landed in my inbox. I was stunned that one so young could write so vividly, so expertly. And not only that, but lend a fresh perspective to such a well-covered topic. And look what's happened since – a stratospheric rise. Documentaries, three more non-fiction books, and now a novel. Of course, all of this is down not only to your talent but to my excellent publishing skills.' At this, he smiles and pauses for a little too long. 'Though I jest. Through the years, I've been proud to guide you as you have become historical publishing's brightest star. May you continue to breathe new life into everything you touch, my boy,' he says, clapping Jack on the back, whose expression is becoming more fixed by the second. To be honest, much as I'm enjoying this, I'm not surprised Jack seems to be struggling – this speech is cloying and slightly patronising, the kind of false flattery that settles over you like something sticky that you can't quite wash off. 'Though I'm loath to release you, our young superstar, to fiction with your new novel, I can't help but feel – if you'll permit me one last liberty – that if I were your father—' he turns to address the crowd, and I suppress an involuntary shudder at the thought. Much as I hate him, I wouldn't wish such a fate even on Jack. '—who I'm sure you all know is a well-known historian in his own right and a dear friend of mine, I'd be immensely proud of all you've achieved.'

Wow. I didn't think I could like this guy any less, but he's rapidly securing himself a place in line for least-favourite editor I've ever met. His words are ostensibly in praise of Jack, but their intention is clear: to increase his own standing with the crowd. The ending to his speech feels overly personal, patronising. Conceited. All qualities he seems to possess in spades. And it seems I'm not the only one who thinks George has crossed a line: at this last statement, Jack looks as if he might actually throw up for a few seconds.

'Thanks very much for the kind words, George,' he says, his facial expression carefully controlled. 'And for this wonderful party.' He clears his throat, looking around the room, then continues. 'I am so grateful for your continued support. Now enough about me, let's let everyone get back to enjoying themselves!'

At this, a brief cheer is raised and everyone disperses, returning gradually to the conversational clusters they were in before. Jack waits until George is comfortably back in conversation with Bernard, then slips out of the room. Perhaps it's because the wine service is slow for the moment, or because I still can't quite wrap my head around why George's final remark, patronising as it was, seems to have had such an impact on Jack, but something has me watching the door for his return. When he appears a few moments later, though, his face is back to its normal colour: as if nothing happened. I must have been imagining things.

By the end of the evening, the intern Jenny and I are getting along swimmingly. I've seen pictures of her two cats: Mabel and Molly, both of the ragdoll variety. I know where she grew up, which university she went to, how many times she's broken bones (twice: her wrist and her ankle), and her dreams of being a sci-fi/fantasy book editor. We've covered a lot of ground in the last four hours, and all of it has been infinitely more interesting, I am sure, than any conversation I might have had about Bernard's stupid book.

I've used the time to keep on top of a few things work-wise, too: drunk party guests make excellent book customers, and I've confirmed our schedule for the next few days and sent out a few more pitches for last-minute radio interviews once we get back to New York. The thing they don't tell you about the more glamorous parts of the job like being on tour is that everything else carries on while you're there, and it's still your job to handle it: I might be in London, and a different time zone, but my inbox will stop for no-one.

When nearly everyone has left and Jenny and I are beginning to stack glasses back into the boxes they arrived in, Jack floats over to us. Jenny freezes as he arrives, the look of terror from the beginning of the evening returning to her face. Oh right, I think, I'd forgotten the effect his appearance can have on people.

'This is Jenny,' I say, gesturing to her. He aims a smile in her direction, and she almost drops the glass she's holding. *Bless her. If she knew what I knew she'd go running.*

'Can I help you?' I ask, after a few seconds of him staring at me, expectant.

'What time did you say we were being picked up?'

Ah, right. I check my watch, and realise the driver is coming in ten minutes. But there's no way we'll be done with the glasses by then. 'He'll be here in ten, but you go ahead. I'll get an Uber when we're done clearing,' I say, and go back to my previous task. Jack leans towards me, out of Jenny's earshot, and speaks in a low voice.

'It's not your job to help clear up.'

'It's my job to make sure the events run smoothly.' I say, my tone firm. This is the second time he's tried to rescue me this evening, and it's really starting to get on my nerves.

'I'm really sorry about George—'

'I don't want an apology, Jack,' I say, cutting him off before he can make this worse. 'And I'm not leaving Jenny to clear up alone when she's already worked really hard this evening and is probably paid about ten pounds a week.'

He sighs, exasperated. 'Fine,' he says, then walks off. *Good riddance.*

I look down at the table, focusing on the task at hand, and when I look up again Jack has returned, carrying about eight wine glasses.

'What are you doing?' I ask, as he starts putting the glasses into boxes.

'Helping.' If he hadn't irritated me so much already, I might be touched. As it is, it reads like another attempt to rescue me from a situation that I am handling *just fine* on my own.

'We don't need your help,' I say, turning away from him to collect some glasses from Jenny. 'Why don't you go outside and wait for the car?'

'I'm not just going to go back to the hotel like an arsehole while you clear up,' he replies, shocking me with how firm his tone is. 'Plus, with an extra pair of hands we'll probably make it to the car in time.'

'Ugh. Fine,' I concede. I've had enough of bickering with him, so I return to stacking glasses and resolutely ignore him.

I'm making my way back across the room with a final stray champagne flute which was hidden behind a giant antique globe, and I see Jack standing close to Jenny and talking to her, their heads bent over something on his phone. Without warning, my protective instincts kick in. *Don't do it, Jenny,* I think, willing her to telepathically hear me somehow.

'What's going on over here?' I ask, trying to keep my tone light.

'Jack has booked me a taxi home.' *Oh.*

'I couldn't let her get three buses across London,' he says quickly, his tone defensive.

I feel the tension leave my body. 'That's, uh, very nice,' I say, and Jack looks at me like I might have had a personality transplant.

All of a sudden, I feel bone-tired – this day has been long and exhausting, and all I want to do is crawl into bed and never get up again. On top of everything else, I'm seeing my mum tomorrow, and I feel suddenly and unbearably unprepared for the emotions that might bring up.

Jack observes me, concern flashing momentarily across his face. 'Let's get back to the hotel,' he says, 'I don't know about you, but I'm exhausted. And—' he pauses to glance up at the clock '—the car should be outside by now.' I search for the irritation from earlier, and find only a deep well of exhaustion. I give the smallest of nods, hug Jenny goodbye and follow Jack out of the room, down the stairs and back into the cold night air.

'I love this square,' he says to no one in particular, and I'm about to tell him that I love it, too, but remember just in time through my present exhaustion that I want him to burn in the fires of hell. As I'm descending the steps behind him, my brain fuzzy, I don't pay enough attention to the ground below me and my heel gets caught in a gap between paving stones. I lose my footing, stumbling forwards. To my surprise, and horror, Jack reacts quickly and catches me, gripping my arms to slow my momentum. For a moment, as his hands brush my skin, the strangest sensation spreads through me, like an electrical current running through my veins. The next second I'm upright again and he lets go, leaving a ghost of warmth where he was touching me. I turn and give him a small and polite 'thank you' smile.

What the hell was that?

7

I wake up the next day to a pounding headache and a few texts from my mum. I check the time: 1 p.m. I'm meeting her for lunch at 2 p.m., across town. *Fuck.*

I scramble out of bed and fling on the first thing resembling an outfit that I can find in my suitcase. Orange trousers and a bright red jumper – not exactly a stylish combination, but it'll have to do. I drag a brush through my hair, splash some water on my face, grab my handbag and head for the door, rushing straight into Jack Carlson.

'What the fuck are you doing here?' I snap. He scared the shit out of me, creeping outside of my door like that. Who does he think he is? And why does he always have to look so effortlessly put-together, especially when I'm looking my worst?

'Good morning to you, too.'

'It's 1 p.m.'

'So it is.'

I stare at him. 'I repeat. What are you doing here?'

'I was working up the courage to knock on your door, if you must know.'

'Why?'

'You're quite scary.'

I roll my eyes. '*Why* were you knocking on my door? It's our day off. I'm not contractually obliged to spend time with you today.'

'I have a message for you.'

'Email it to me, then. I'm running late.' I say, moving past him and heading down the corridor.

'Have a nice time with your mum!' he calls after me. I stop in my tracks and turn slowly back towards him.

'How do you know I'm having lunch with my mum?'

'She called the hotel, and they gave her my extension. She was worried that you hadn't replied to her texts yet, and asked me to check if you were on your way.' He pauses, and an ever-so-slight smirk crosses his face, which sends rage up my spine. 'She's quite a nice lady.'

'You don't get to have an opinion about my mum,' I snap, folding my arms. 'Or anything in my life, for that matter.' *You revoked that right a long time ago.*

He holds his hands up in mock-surrender. 'I was only trying to help.'

The irritation from last night surges again, more powerful this time. 'I don't need your help, Jack,' I say, my voice cracking slightly.

I watch him deflate, shrinking into himself like he did on that first night. 'I'm—' he starts, but I've already turned away and am halfway down the corridor before he can finish.

'I'll see you tomorrow,' I call back, without looking.

I get out of the tube station in Hampstead and am hit by a wave of familiarity so painful it makes me nauseous. I grew up here, but I have spent very little time here in the last five years. Its streets serve mostly as a painful reminder of the life I had before my dad passed away – the café we used to frequent for Saturday coffee; our favourite bookstore. it's what I moved to New York to get away from, unable to bear the constant reminder that he was gone. I shut it out, making my way across the road to the restaurant as quickly as possible.

My mother is sitting at our usual table, by the window. She's dressed, as always, impeccably and simply in a red wool jumper and jeans – we accidentally match, though where I'm clashing, she's chic. She wafts towards me in a breeze of bergamot perfume.

'Andie! My love. It's so good to see you. I've missed you.' She pulls me into a hug, and I bury my face in the softness of her jumper. Freshly laundered, as always. She's clutching me like I might run away, and she suddenly feels so much smaller than me. A wave of guilt hits me at how little I've spoken to her recently, at how delicate and easily breakable things have felt between us since I moved an ocean away.

'Missed you too, Mum.'

We sit down and the waiter sweeps over and takes our usual order – carbonara for Mum, pizza for me, a bottle of red wine for us both. There's a bit of an awkward silence at first, but that's how it has been since my dad died: so much lies unsaid between us that we have to grope for safe conversational land.

'Jack seems delightful,' she says. I choke on the water I've just gulped. This land is not safe. Very much not safe. If it were an island, it would be full of snakes.

'Mmhmm,' I say, as noncommittal as possible. She doesn't know about any of my history with

Jack. It was so close to my dad getting sick that I kept it from her at the time. I shielded her from my grief when Dad died, too. I'm very good at shielding my mother from things.

'Very nice indeed. Such a deep voice. Is he good looking?'

'Mum!' I roll my eyes.

'Just asking, darling. There might be a prospect there, you never know.' *You have no idea.* And there's, you know, the fact that he's now *my author.* I won't even get into how inappropriate that would be.

'Please can we talk about something else?'

'I have something to ask, actually.'

'Sure,' I say, taking a large sip of wine. Whatever it is, at least it'll steer the conversation away from Jack.

'Do you think he'd be willing to come to my book club on Friday?' I almost drop my wine glass in shock.

'Have you lost your mind?' I say without thinking, momentarily forgetting that she has no idea how I feel about him. She looks confused, then sad, and she covers it up by pretending to examine her napkin. My heart drops.

'I knew it was a silly idea. Of course it would be unprofessional to ask, love. Forget I said anything.' Guilt surges up again at how incapable I seem to be of being a good daughter, even when I'm not on the other side of the world.

'Sorry, Mum, I didn't mean—'

'It's OK, Andie. I shouldn't have asked. I just thought it might be nice, that's all. See a bit more of you while you're here, too. But I can see now that I shouldn't have said anything.' She looks down at her lap, again, twisting her hands. She seems so small, so vulnerable. *So lonely*, I think, and suddenly my throat feels thick.

'I think he'd love to come, Mum.' The words are out of my mouth before I can consider the implications, but I can't let her down, especially not when I'm already in competition for the *World's Worst Daughter* award.

'Are you sure?'

I reach across the table for her hand. 'Of course. I'll ask him. Promise.'

The rest of the lunch passes uneventfully – my mum retired a few years ago from her job as a solicitor, so now spends her time between local committees and volunteering. By the time we've finished our food and moved on to coffee I've heard about Victoria's outburst at the local council meeting, the scandal of twenty dildoes being donated to the charity shop down the road, and what sounds like a lengthy and vicious back-and-forth over whether they're going to install steps at the local tennis club. I listen intently to all of it, determined to give her my full attention.

Just before we get the bill, Mum shifts in her chair like she's about to say something important. *Here it comes*, I think, a slow sense of dread pooling in my stomach. Every time I see my mum, she tries to get me to open up about dad. I think she's concerned by how little I talk about him, perhaps, that I haven't fully processed my grief. And she's not wrong, judging by the deep well of loss that opens every time I come home, every street I pass that reminds me of him opening a new, fresh wound. But I made my choice, I've built my life: I don't see what can be done about it now. Talking about it this far on feels too painful. And either way, it's not going to bring him back.

'Love, I need to talk to you about something important.' She pauses, folding her napkin neatly and setting it on her plate, not meeting my eyes. 'You know I've been going to a grief group? Well, I—'

Ah, the therapy angle. We've had this conversation a hundred times before, where she tells me about the benefits of therapy and tries to convince me to go. I went to see a therapist once, a few years ago, and it was awful. We talked about my dad for all of five minutes and I came out feeling like Pandora's box had been opened. I couldn't get the lid back on for weeks. Safe to say it's not for me, and in any case I don't feel like having this conversation again. Not today, at least. I reach over and place my hand over hers, gently interrupting her before she can go any further.

'That sounds great, Mum,' I say, squeezing her hand. It's soft: she's been using the hand cream I got her for Christmas. A lump forms in my throat at the thought of her applying it, thinking about me. Missing me. 'I'm so sorry, though – I'm a bit jet lagged. Can we talk about this another time?' She looks disappointed, and my heart contracts with guilt. I almost relent, getting ready to send myself to the place I usually go to when she starts these conversations – where I can listen to her words from a safe emotional distance, without being overwhelmed by the feelings they bring up. But after a few seconds she nods, and I feel myself relax, letting out the breath I'm holding.

'OK, love.'

8

At 4 a.m. the following day, Jack and I are up, dressed and waiting to travel to a TV studio for a breakfast interview. To add insult to ungodly hour, it's raining. Hard. And we arranged to meet our driver around the corner from the hotel. And he is running late. And I left my umbrella in my hotel room.

Jack extends his, keeping his usual safe distance of a few metres away from me, and I can't help but glance towards him.

'Do you want to—'

'No,' I say, immediately, folding my arms as the downpour increases.

'Suit yourself,' he says. I last approximately thirty seconds until I feel the rain starting to soak through my jacket. He looks over at me and gestures subtly, offering his umbrella as shelter again.

'Fine. Yes. Please,' I say, moving to stand next to him.

The proximity is immediately uncomfortable. I can feel the warmth of him next to me; the rise and fall of his breath. I tense up and turn my back to him, busying myself scrolling through emails on my phone, then reach one that makes me exclaim aloud.

'What?' he asks.

'You're number one on the *New York Times* bestseller list!' I say, excitement building inside me despite myself. I've never had an author go to number one before.

He looks bewildered for a moment, then his bewilderment disperses into a smile so dazzling it stops me in my tracks for a second. 'You are kidding me,' he says.

I shake my head, swept up momentarily in his joy, and before I know it he's pulled me into a hug. For the briefest of seconds I lean into it instinctively, then I come to my senses, my stomach dropping. *Oh God. What the fuck is happening?*

I immediately stiffen, and he does, too, seeming to realise his mistake. He pulls away and I extricate myself, stepping out into the rain again.

'Sorry,' he says. 'Got a little carried away there.'

I choke slightly, still struggling to find words.

'I just – I've never had a number one, before,' he says, and his tone is so soft and vulnerable it gives me pause.

'It's OK,' I say, eventually. 'No harm done,' I reassure him, even as mortification moves through me. 'And – congratulations.'

'Thanks, Andie.'

The TV studio is in central London, and we make it there in good time – 5 a.m. is not exactly peak time for city traffic. The building is flashy, its glass exterior jutting out onto the street below. It's the only one on the street that seems awake, so far.

The studio is busy, runners and producers bustling around us and shouting instructions at each other. For the second time this morning, I feel a thrill of excitement. Another first: my first time in a TV studio with an author. Though I'd much rather be here with anyone but Jack, this is a career highlight for me. We sign in and they whisk Jack away to the make-up department almost immediately. I wait, soaking in the atmosphere for a few minutes, until Jack reappears, scaring the living daylights out of me.

'Here,' he says, holding out a takeaway coffee cup.

'What's this?'

He looks at me like I might have lost my mind. 'Coffee, Andie. I had the runner pick one up for you, too.'

'I don't want it—' I start, but he presses it into my hand.

'It's 6 a.m., and we have a long day ahead of us. Take the caffeine.'

'But—' I go to protest again, but it dies in my throat. I am exhausted. 'Fine,' I say, closing my hands around the cup. 'Thank you.'

'You're welcome,' he replies. 'Besides, it's the least I can do—'

These words send a ripple of dread through me.

'—after jumping you this morning.'

Oh. That. A wave of nausea comes up my throat at the memory, my face heating with embarrassment. I could have done without *that* reminder.

'Well, thanks,' I choke out, mortified. 'Again. For the coffee.'

'You're welcome,' he says, scratching the back of his neck. 'Again.'

Lord please save me from this conversation.

A producer comes and grants my wish a few moments later, taking Jack to the green room. I wait in my allocated area to the side of the set, watching Jack's performance live. He's impressive: clearly well-honed from the documentaries he's done. I should be pleased and proud that my author is doing so well, but instead I can't help but feel the injustice of it all. That he should have turned out *so* attractive, *so* successful. Could karma not have given me a bit of a break?

I'm so lost in thought that when someone taps me on the shoulder once Jack's segment is over, I jump and throw my coffee half over them. *Fuck.*

'I am so sorry,' I say, surveying the damage: the man's crisp white shirt is now a shade of brown. He looks down in slight horror, before returning his face to a polite expression and reaching out to shake my hand.

'I'm Aaron, the director of the show. I thought I'd introduce myself.'

Oh good. I've just thrown coffee over the most important person in this room.

'Andie,' I say, shaking his hand and realising a moment too late that mine is still damp from throwing my coffee everywhere. I watch him notice this, then pretend not to notice this, and subtly wipe his hand on his trousers before pulling out his wallet. If a hole in the ground could open me up and swallow me into it right now, that would be great.

'I wanted to give you my card,' he says, handing it to me. 'We'd love to have Jack back at some point.'

'Back?' I ask, still reeling from how catastrophically I've screwed up this interaction.

'Yes,' he says, slowly. 'We do a book segment every week. I think he'd be great for it.'

I stare at the card for a few seconds. 'That's, uh—' I say, eventually. *Words, Andie. Use your words.* 'Great. Lovely. I'll be in touch.'

He nods, looking slightly bemused. 'Wonderful. Now if you'll excuse me,' he says, 'I'm going to go and find a new shirt.'

After the TV segment, we travel back across London for a print interview. We're meeting the journalist in a local cafe, about ten minutes' walk from the hotel. I spend most of the taxi journey recovering from my interaction with the director – at this rate I'm not feeling hopeful that he'll reply to my follow-up email.

The café is fairly classic for central London: plastic tables that customers have to squeeze past to reach the counter, music playing just a little too loud and pastries that are on the pale side of cooked.

We cram around a table in the corner, almost knocking a bag off the back of someone's chair, and I make the introduction. I've been in touch with this journalist for the last few weeks: she seems nice, if a little green. She's written a few think pieces, but nothing to write home about. As far as I can tell, this will be a fairly standard interview.

She opens with a few questions about Jack's writing process, and the differences between fiction and non-fiction. I watch him relax into the interview, turning on the charm. I silently praise myself for the briefing I gave him on the way here – he's already asked her about a book she gave a rave review a few weeks ago, and this seems to have created a great rapport between them. *So far, so good*, I think, zoning out briefly while they discuss the intricacies of plotting a historical novel.

But then, all of a sudden, Jack tenses up opposite me and I return abruptly to the present, the conversation coming into focus again.

'Your father,' she says, looking at him pointedly, 'is a well-known historian and regularly writes reviews of historical literature. Is there a reason why he's never reviewed any of your books?' My stomach curdles, my attention suddenly and inescapably on them both, praying that Jack somehow finds a way out of this and doesn't accidentally rise to the bait.

'We, uh,' Jack falters, suddenly looking lost. 'We prefer to keep things separate. Nepotism and all,' I flinch internally. *Oh god*.

'Interesting you say that,' she says, leaning forwards with a triumphant expression on her face. My stomach drops to the floor. 'When your father is close friends with your UK non-fiction editor, George Richards. Is there any connection between that relationship and your route to publication?' Jack has, at this point, turned a shade of puce. *Fuck. Fuck. Fuck.*

'No,' he says, slightly stammering now. 'My father and I – our relationship – it's complicated,' he falters again, sinking, and guilt seeps through me. I am suddenly reminded of Jack's response to George's speech. Judging by that, and his reaction now, his father is a no-go zone for him. So not only is this interview going south for the purposes of the campaign, it's ventured into a personal sore spot. *Excellent job, Andie.* Normally, I'd have asked an author more carefully about any pressure points they specifically wanted to avoid, and helped them with strategies to do so. But in this case, I've been so focused on keeping Jack at arm's length that I've not done my due diligence.

'Complicated how?' she asks, with the look of someone that's about to get the scoop she wanted. A flash of protective anger suddenly kicks in. She doesn't get to pin an author of mine to the wall like this – even if that author is Jack Carlson.

'That's enough,' I say, before Jack can answer the question. 'We made it very clear in our briefing that you were not to ask personal questions outside what had been agreed. Jack's father was not on that list.'

'But—' she protests.

'I think that we are done with this line of questioning,' I press, my tone firm. I watch her shift in her seat, her assuredness slowly dissolving into light panic. While I might have underestimated her desire for a scoop, I did read her correctly earlier: she's too green for this. She doesn't have a plan.

'Now,' I say, leaning in to drive it home. 'Do you have everything you need, or would you like to ask Jack any further questions about his book?' I say, enunciating the last three words carefully.

'No,' she says, gathering her papers and standing up. 'I think I'm done here.'

'Thanks very much for your time,' I say, shaking her hand. We might not be getting the best coverage from this journalist, but I'd like to at least try to leave on civil terms. From experience with these situations, it could be the difference between a three-star review and an absolute disaster. I look at Jack and plead silently that he understands that now is the time to put on a show and turn the charm back on.

'It was wonderful to meet you,' he says, standing up and now successfully knocking the stranger's bag off their chair. *Smooth*. He puts it back apologetically and reaches across the table to shake her hand: he's trapped in the corner, and it would be too awkward at this stage to extricate himself. It's not quite the put-together performance I was hoping for, but it's strangely more than that. A glimpse at his human side, which might endear him to her.

The journalist takes his hand, breaking into a slight smile. She then slings her bag over her shoulder and nods at us both, her posture now more closed, and heads out of the café. As soon as she's gone, Jack lets out a long sigh, his composure crumpling. He puts his face in his hands, and looks at me through his fingers.

'How bad was it?' he asks.

'I've seen much worse,' I say, looking down at my phone to hide how flustered I am.

'Come on, Andie,' he says, removing his hands from his face. 'Hit me with it. Scale of one to ten, with ten being a one-star review?'

Despite myself, I smile a little. 'Solid five, I'd say.' I relent, and he relaxes. 'But let's not hold our breath about that write up being glowing.'

His face falls, slightly. 'I'm so sorry, Andie. I don't know why I got so flustered—'

I hold up my hand to stop him. 'Jack, stop. It wasn't your fault. It's mine. I should have seen that coming, or prepped you better. It's on me.'

'But—'

'Stop, or you're going to annoy me,' I say, in a warning tone.

'OK,' he says, sitting back in his chair. 'It's just – I've had questions like that before, just none quite so—' he pauses, bewildered, and I watch him shake his head briefly as if trying to rid himself of the last ten minutes. When he looks up at me again, he's smiling tentatively, the Jack Carlson veneer mostly back up with only a small crack through to the vulnerability underneath. 'Usually I'm very charming, you see.'

I suppress an eye roll, ignoring the flash of something else that lights up inside me at his words. 'I can tell you're feeling better,' I say, my tone laced with sarcasm.

'Maybe. Anyway, thanks for saving me out there, Andie,' he says, leaning towards me with an expression suddenly so earnest it makes me squirm inside.

'I was just doing my job, Jack,' I remind him, gesturing for a passing waiter to bring me the bill. They bring it over, and I pull my company card out of the bag to pay. 'It's why I'm here, after all.'

'Right, of course,' he says, and when I catch his eye he looks strangely disappointed.

9

The next day I wake up to a voice note from Sara. It could not be more welcome, after the night I've had: one of my other authors got themselves into a social media controversy yesterday, and I was up until three in the morning detangling it. It took me a good hour of back-and-forth to eventually convince them that our suggested strategy of going dark for a few weeks was for damage control purposes rather than a personal attempt by me to limit their free speech. Eventually I won them round, but I got about three hours sleep as a result.

'Hey, champ! Checking in. How are things?' she chirps, her voice a balm to my exhausted mind. Hearing her speak is like the sun shining through curtains, immediately brightening my day. I drink it in: her descriptions of New York in the summer – too hot and crowded, but alive with people – and an update on her job. She's been offered a promotion. The news buzzes through me like caffeine.

I send a voice note back, telling her how thrilled I am and how much I miss her, promising her a celebration when I'm home. But when I get to myself, to the question she asked at the beginning of her message, I find myself stumped. 'Things are, objectively, fine,' I say, thinking out loud. 'But there's not much more to say than that. Jack annoys me, we get through the day. It's – fine.' The word sticks in my throat as I say it. I lift my thumb off the recording button and hit send, then press it again. 'Love you! See you soon,' I say, then drop my phone on the bed and lie back, staring at the ceiling.

I turn my answer over in my mind, an unexpected heaviness falling over me. I should be pleased that things are going OK so far – my expectations for this trip were on the floor. I haven't yet pushed Jack into traffic, or screamed at him, or ruined any of the events we've attended. Aside from a few slip-ups, which are to be expected considering I'm mostly focused on not losing my mind, there haven't been any disasters yet. So I'm not sure why I feel disappointed. But I don't have long to mull on it. I have to get up and get ready for the day.

After dragging myself out of bed and throwing on a pair of my most comfortable shoes, I meet Jack outside the hotel and run him through the schedule. Today is a bookshop tour, which means I spend the day as Jack's chaperone – transporting him safely to each venue and keeping us on schedule while he meets booksellers and signs books. No driver, today: it would be inefficient with London traffic. Just us, our feet, and the tube.

Unfortunately, the day doesn't get off to a good start. I'm so sleep-deprived and focused on getting into professional-Andie mode so I can keep it together around Jack that the tube journey ends up being two stops too long. We have to travel back in the other direction, and show up to our first stop ten minutes late, throwing off our schedule for the rest of the day. Fortunately, the booksellers are understanding, but I have to rush us slightly, leaving five minutes early so we can make up some time and calling ahead to the next shop to tell them we're running late.

The rest of the day goes mostly smoothly, from an outside perspective, at least. I manage to make it through the morning, fuelled by caffeine and vague delirium, but by the afternoon I'm barely standing, and not just because of the hours of traipsing around London: everyone, without exception, loves Jack, and it's a special kind of hell to hear so much praise about someone you hate. By the afternoon,

I'm really having to work hard to hold a smile while a seemingly never-ending convoy of booksellers, all of whom appear to be Jack's biggest fan, talk about how great he is. 'You write so presently,' one bookseller says. Another compliments his form, a third his smooth transition from the more serious tone of his non-fiction to the engaging style of his fictional prose. The worst, though, is when a female bookseller compliments his intimate understanding of the female psyche. At that, I grip the book I'm holding so hard my knuckles turn white.

'Andie?' he says, waving a hand in front of me.

'What?' I look up, sharply, and realise that the bookseller has drifted off, and we're alone on the shop floor.

'Thanks for today,' he says, and I flinch at his gratitude. 'I know it's been a marathon.'

'You're welcome.' I say, but I can't help but add. 'Though, as I have told you a few times now, it is my job.'

'You're good at it,' he persists.

'I don't need your praise, Jack.'

'I know you don't. I just wanted to say, I've had a lot of publicists over the years, and for one who absolutely hates my guts you're very professional. The booksellers loved you, today.'

I want to tell him to shut up, but something about what he's said doesn't sit quite right, giving me pause before I respond. I think back through the day. All I can really remember is trying to keep my mood in check, but I suppose I did put on a good performance: keeping us firmly on schedule, introducing him to the booksellers by name, handing out up-to-date press releases. Making sure each book was open at the right page for signing, keeping a supply of pens going. And, generally, looking after people – the most important part of the job. It's all become second nature to me now, such a familiar routine that I don't really notice when I'm doing it. But then, all of a sudden, a thought comes out of nowhere and hits me like a punch in the gut. Jack is wrong. I might be good at my job, generally. But I'm not good at this one.

On tour, your job is to be the eyes and ears of the trip, the source of calm and composure. So far, I have neither been calm nor composed: I've been jumpy and irritable, far below my usual standard of professionalism. Yesterday, I threw coffee over a TV director and missed a key point of preparation for Jack's interview. Today, we were late. Minor mistakes, perhaps, but rare ones by my usual standards. And they're multiplying. Besides, if that's just the first few days of the tour, what might happen in the next few weeks, in Berlin or Paris or Dublin?

And then it clicks: the reason I felt heavy this morning when I told Sara things were 'fine'. Momentary shame floods through me: until this moment, I thought my priority for this trip was just to get through it without causing a huge disaster. But I can see now that it's more than that: I'm disappointed in myself, in my performance so far. I don't want to just scrape by for the next few weeks, content that I only made a few slip-ups here and there. That things were 'fine'. I want to do a good job. I want to feel proud – of myself, of this campaign. Quite apart from anything else, if I'm going to spend three more weeks with the person I hate most in the world, the bare minimum I want from it is some job satisfaction. And to achieve that, I have to *actually* find a way to be around Jack without wanting to tell him to get fucked every five seconds.

After a few seconds of silence, Jack clears his throat, bringing me back to the present. 'Did I say something wrong?' he asks, with a slight furrow in his brow.

'No, you didn't,' I say, shame suddenly hardening into resolve, an idea forming in the back of my mind. I might hate Jack, and that's not changing.

But I'm here, and so is he. If I want this trip to be a success, to meet my own standards of professionalism and prove to myself that I deserve this job, that I'm capable of doing it well, no matter the hurdles – I need a new plan. 'Listen, Jack – we're done for the day, can I buy you a coffee?'

'So,' I say about twenty minutes later, sitting opposite him, awkwardly staring into my latte. We're in a coffee shop a few doors down from the bookshop, and he still looks absolutely bewildered as to why I've gone from *leave me alone* to *let's go for coffee* in the space of an hour. 'I don't think this is working.'

He sits back in his chair, his expression hard to read. There is a long pause. If I didn't know any better, I'd say he looks disappointed. But that can't be right.

'Okay,' he says eventually, nodding slowly and stirring some milk into his coffee. I hold my breath as I wait for him to continue, and eventually he looks up at me, his eyes startlingly blue, and breathes out a small sigh. 'So we'll need to work out how to spin this, I guess. Any ideas?'

I frown. 'What are you talking about?'

He looks at me sideways, confused. 'You're leaving, right?'

'For God's sake, Jack. Would you stop trying to kick me off your trip?' I say, rolling my eyes. 'I'm not leaving.'

Another indiscernible expression passes across his face – relief? But that would also be ridiculous.

'OK,' he says, carefully, as if he doesn't want to make another misstep. 'I'm confused.'

'What I'm suggesting,' I say, leaning forwards, 'is a truce.'

'What sort of truce?'

I take a deep breath. *Here goes.* 'I think you and I need to agree to *actually* act as if nothing ever happened between us. Like, for the purposes of this trip, we have a clean slate. You have nothing to make up for, I have nothing to be angry about. We're just two people who have never met, on a tour together for the first time.'

He sits back, processing what I've just said. 'Isn't that kind of what we're doing already?' he asks, eventually. I shake my head.

'Do you think I normally tell authors to get fucked this often?'

He laughs. 'Well, probably not.'

'And you can't honestly tell me this is how you usually behave around your publicists, Jack,' I say, raising my eyebrows slightly. 'You're jumpy as fuck.'

He smiles, his expression turning slightly sheep-ish. 'Perhaps I have been a little skittish around you,' he says.

'Exactly,' I say, my assurance that this is an excellent plan increasing with every word. 'Every interaction we've had so far has been setting me on edge, and I realised today that it's because we haven't set the terms of this trip clearly enough.' He purses his lips, slightly and I continue, lean-ing on my resolve from earlier. 'So let me be clear now. I don't want to discuss what happened. I don't want you to apologise, or try to make anything up to me. I want – I *need* us to agree to act as if there's no past between us, and you're any other author. It's the only way I'll get through this trip.' My voice grows a little thick – this is the closest we've been to talking about Edinburgh since the first night in that bookshop. I feel suddenly vulnerable, exposed.

'OK,' he says, eventually. 'I guess I hoped—' he pauses and runs a hand through his hair, then changes track, his jawline setting. 'But that doesn't matter, now. You have a right to keep the past in the past, if that's what you want. I'm willing to agree to whatever terms you ask for.'

At his words, relief washes over me. I hadn't real-ised how exhausted I had been until this moment.

From the moment I saw Jack's name on Jessica's list, a part of me has been on edge, worried one wrong move might send us irrevocably back to that night five years ago – the article, and the car park, and everything unravelling around me. By agreeing to these terms, he's promising that's not going to happen, and I see the sincerity on his face and hear it in his voice. Against all odds, I believe him.

'OK,' I say, taking a sip of my coffee. 'So I'll stop being so hostile, and you'll stop being so weird. And we'll just get on with the trip as if everything is normal. Deal?'

'Deal,' he says, and I let out a long breath, exhaling all the tension from my body.

'Thank you,' I say, the first genuine words I've spoken to him since we left New York.

Unfortunately, though, when I call her that evening, Sara doesn't seem quite so on board with the idea.

'Hmm,' she says, when I've finished explaining the truce to her and asked her what she thinks.

'I thought this was what you wanted!' I say, incredulous. 'You told me this would be good for me, that it would help me find a way to be free of this.'

'This wasn't what I meant, A.'

'What did you mean?'

'I thought you'd talk to him about it maybe. Finally address what happened, finally put this all behind you. Instead you've just buried it even deeper than before.'

'I haven't buried it,' I say, hurt. Why can't she see what a great plan this is? 'I've just – put it to one side, for a while. I need to be able to interact with Jack without being one comment away from kneeing him in the balls the whole time.'

She laughs at this, but it's ever so slightly forced: she still doesn't agree. A knot of doubt forms in the pit of my stomach. Her disapproval stings more than I thought it would – I thought she'd be proud of me for sorting something out on my own for once. Besides, it's not like I'm *not* addressing the problem – I'm acknowledging our past is there, still. But it's better, for the purposes of this trip, that we don't drag it into the present.

I take a deep breath. *It's Sara. She loves you. She just wants what's best for you*, I remind myself. *She's your best friend*.

'How are things with you?' I ask, changing the subject. 'How's the promotion?'

'Oh it's so great, A. I'm working harder but the work is fun, and we had a party the other day to celebrate. I wish you could've been there.'

'Me, too,' I say, guilt seeping through me for missing it. 'Promise we'll celebrate when I'm back,' I say, and a brief silence falls. I hesitate, feeling suddenly and inexplicably awkward. I never run out of things to say around Sara, but I find myself scrambling in this moment, unsure how to close this weird distance I'm suddenly feeling between us – how to ask her the question I really want to ask, without making it sound loaded or strange. 'And how's James?' I say, finally, my voice coming out a little overenthusiastic.

'Um, fine, thanks,' she replies, her tone shifting slightly into the one she uses when James is in the room with her. My suspicion is confirmed a moment later when I hear him shout from the kitchen in the background, letting her know that their DoorDash delivery has arrived. My stomach drops – I can always tell when she's lying.

'I'll be there in a minute,' she calls back, holding the receiver away from her. Then her voice appears in my ear, soft and Sara-like again. 'Listen, A – if you think this is a good plan, then I think you should go for it. Just – be careful, OK?'

The knot loosens slightly at her words. 'I will,' I say, feeling suddenly and inexplicably tearful. I want to be in New York, not here. To reach for her hand and ask her what's really wrong. 'Love you,' I say, willing the force of it to reach her through the phone.

'Love you more,' she says, then hangs up. I imagine her walking over to the kitchen, sitting down to eat with James, the city lights blinking around them through the sterile glass walls. I stare at the wallpaper of the London suite – a William Morris print, I think – and try my best to stay in the present. A flower here, a leaf there. *Don't cry, don't cry.* For a fleeting second, I find myself deeply and inexplicably missing my mum. I wish I could hug her, right now. I scroll through our recent texts, and find one I'd somehow missed – checking that Jack is still happy to come to her book club on Friday. *Fuck.* I've been so caught up in my job the last few days, I almost forgot about it.

'Andie?' Jack's voice comes from outside the door, quiet and tentative, jarring me out of my feelings. His sudden arrival makes me jump, but it's perfect timing – if there's a time to ask him this, it has to be now.

'Yes?' I call, desperately trying to plan how I'm going to ask him at this short notice to give up his only free night in London.

'I, uh – I ordered way too much room service. Do you want some fries?'

'That would be great, thanks,' I say. I'm not hungry, but it gives me an excuse to open the door. I walk over to it, nerves swirling in my stomach, and find him standing outside in his pyjamas, his posture awkward. The sight is startling – vulnerable, somehow. I recognise the plaid of the trousers from a pair he offered me to sleep in, a million years ago, and my heart stutters for a second. *Fuck. Not the time to be thinking about that.* I shove the image out of my mind and fix my gaze firmly on his face. He hands me the bowl, and moves to turn away.

'Jack, wait—' I say, trying to dredge up some courage. I curse myself for not being a better daughter, so I wouldn't have to ask this of him. The irony does not escape me that after all my talk today of not wanting Jack to do me any favours, I'm about to ask him for one.

'Yes?' he says, turning back towards me.

I blurt it out all at once, suddenly feeling incredibly nauseous. 'Would you come to my mum's book club tomorrow?'

He looks momentarily startled by the question, which deepens my embarrassment. 'As a guest of honour, I mean. It's just – she's a big fan of yours—' I start, stammering, to fill the silence. But he cuts me off.

'Sure. Tell her it would be my pleasure.'

Thank God for that. I let out the breath I was holding. 'Are you sure?' I ask, relief flooding through me.

'Of course,' he says, a slow smile spreading across his face. 'I like your mum. She seemed lovely on the phone the other day.'

Ah, right. They've sort of met. I roll my eyes and, despite myself, start to smile back, but as per usual he immediately ruins any charitable feelings I have towards him. 'And you should know,' he smiles at me, a glint in his eyes, 'being fawned over by older ladies is my forte.'

'Yeah, yeah. I'll believe it when I see it,' I say, waving him away. He shrugs and starts back down the corridor. I pause, watching him walk away. 'Thanks, Jack,' I call after him.

'You're welcome, Andie,' he says, then disappears into his room.

10

At 6 p.m. the following evening, after a long day of radio interviews, we meet in the corridor to travel to my mum's house together. I'm wearing a soft pink dress and a navy cardigan she made me a few years ago when she went through a phase of knitting prolifically – mostly, I think, to keep thoughts of Dad at bay. It lasted for the time it took to knit three scarves and four cardigans, and just before she started knitting jumpers her friend Barbara asked if she wanted to join the local council. I was glad, obviously, that she was spending her time doing something a bit more social, but did feel a little sore that my consistent supply of hand-knitted clothes suddenly stopped. I'd started to look forward to the packages – always arriving unexpectedly, lumpy and soft and wrapped in far too much tape.

'You look very – smart,' I say, and I mean it: he's dressed the part of star author, in jeans and a blazer and a white shirt with the top button undone.

'I didn't really know the dress code,' he says, grimacing. 'Is it too much?'

I shake my head. 'They'll love it.'

And they do – we can barely get through the door of my mum's house when we arrive. Jack is immediately swept to the corner of the room where an armchair has been set up for him. My dad's old armchair, I realise with a pang as he sits in it, but I keep my expression carefully blank as he smiles at me through the crowd, shrugging as my mum's friends compete to offer him a beverage or some crisps. I spot my mum on the other side of the room and move to stand next to her. She's enjoying this, warm with the company. She's always loved it when the house is full. Which it's probably not very often, these days. My stomach twists with guilt. If I lived in London, I could visit her. But I can give her this evening, at least. *It's going to be a good one, Mum*, I promise internally. Jack looks up at me from the crowd of women and raises his eyebrows as if to say 'Help me.'

'Mum, is there an order to this evening,' I ask, 'or is Jack just going to be suffocated by your friends for three hours?'

She ignores my question. 'He's even better looking in person than in photographs,' she says.

She winks at me, and before I can say anything in response, she taps her glass with a spoon.

'Ladies, can you give Jack some breathing room?' She waits for them to move away from him, then continues. 'Now, I believe I asked you to each come with a question for our special guest. Who would like to start?'

And so begins a portion of the evening where Jack is asked everything from what his main literary inspirations are – Stephen King, John Steinbeck and Frank O'Hara – to whether he'd ever consider writing the next *Fifty Shades of Grey* – 'Never say never'. He weathers it well, answering every question respectfully, even when the questions themselves are not respectful (several ladies take it upon themselves to ask in increasingly direct ways whether Jack is romantically attached – he dodges each one expertly, my favourite being: 'Unless you ever find yourself single, Elizabeth, I'm afraid I shall remain married to my writing.').

When the questioning ends, Jack takes advantage of the brief lull to make his way across the room and approach my mum.

'Thanks so much for having me tonight, Deborah,' he says, his voice kind. Mum lights up as he offers his hand.

'It is I who should be thanking you, young man,' she says, and I blush at her use of the words 'young man' to describe Jack, but he only smiles wider.

'It was my pleasure,' he says.

'I hope you're taking good care of my Andie on this trip,' she replies, squeezing my arm.

'Mum,' I start, mortified by the turn this conversation has taken. 'That's not how it works—'

'Actually, it's Andie that's taking good care of me. She's an excellent publicist. You should be very proud.' *And if I didn't want to die before, I absolutely do now.* I stare intently at my shoes, unwilling to make eye contact with either of them.

'I am,' my mum says, putting her arm around me now. And all of a sudden, I find myself very close to tears. Jack seems to notice, shifting on his feet and changing the subject.

'Deborah, I've noticed you have an impressive collection of vintage lamps in this room. Is there a story there?'

'Do you know, you're the first person who's noticed that they're vintage,' she says, and launches into a lengthy description of her process of winning eBay auctions. He flashes me a smile as she leads him across the room to one of her favourite pieces, and a warmth starts to spread through my chest, followed by a flash of warning. Truce or no truce, this feels dangerous. *It's just a favour*, I remind myself, but I can't deny it feels like more. He's given up his night off, and made my mum happier than I've seen her in ages. Conflicting emotions swirl through me, gratitude blending with dread at how vulnerable this all suddenly feels.

'Thank you,' I say to Jack as we head for the door half an hour later. We've finished saying goodbye to everyone. My mum hugged me for a minute longer than was comfortable, so I found myself unable to leave without promising to meet her for a walk through Hampstead Heath tomorrow morning, before we leave for Berlin in the afternoon.

'That sounded almost sincere, Andie. Are you feeling OK?' he jokes, giving me a sideways glance.

'Seriously, Jack,' I say, resting my hand on his arm to turn his attention back to me as he opens the door. 'I really appreciate what you did tonight.'

As the cool night air hits us both, an emotion crosses his face that I don't recognise. 'You're welcome,' he replies, his tone soft, then turns away and we both head out towards the waiting car.

11

I meet my mum at 10 a.m. in our favourite patch of the Heath – there are three benches, each with a panoramic view of the park, and I take a seat on our usual one. From here, trees rise on either side, giving way to a deep valley that extends to the city below. London looks like a painting from here – only half-real, blurred by the city haze. It's busy today: a Saturday morning. Londoners have descended, as they always do on weekends, to get their allocation of leaves and grass. From here, you can almost pretend you're in the countryside – I breathe a little easier, my feet firmly planted on earth rather than pavement for the first time in a while.

My mum sits down next to me and reaches for my hand.

'It's been so good to see you, love,' she says. I keep my gaze on the park: if I look at her for too long my heart might explode with guilt and I'll promise to move back to London.

'You, too, Mum,' I say, squeezing her hand.

'That man Jack is *really*—' she starts.

'—Mum, please, don't start talking about how good-looking he is again.'

'I was just going to say that it was very kind of him,' she says. 'Taking time out of his schedule to be fussed over for hours.'

'It was,' I agree, ignoring the twinge in my stomach.

'I think the ladies appreciated it – it was nice to have a man there who actually wanted to be there, for once. I invited Elizabeth's husband Tony last month, and he asked if he could watch the football on my television.'

Dad would have wanted to be there, I think, suddenly – he always came to Mum's book club events, serving drinks and refilling the crisp bowls and being his endlessly charming self. Everyone loved him.

'Well, since your father,' she says, as if she's read my mind. 'But he was special.'

'He was,' I agree. My throat suddenly feels thick, the waves of grief crashing in the near distance. We're in dangerous territory, now.

'Mum—' I say, ready to cut her off but, mercifully, she returns to talking about Jack.

'There seemed to be something going on between you two, pet,' she says, and my mouth dries up. 'Mother's instinct, I suppose. It isn't just a business partnership, is it, darling?'

A jolt of frustration hits me that I haven't covered it well enough; that, somehow, my mum has seen through me. For the briefest of seconds, I consider opening up and telling Mum what happened between us. How much it hurt, how out of control everything felt. How desperately I tried to keep it together – for her, for dad, even as everything else fell apart. I imagine resting my head on her shoulder and letting the tears come. But even at the thought, my chest clenches in fear.

'It is, Mum,' I insist, turning to her. 'Just business.'

Concern passes across her face, as if she can tell I'm lying to her, then it's gone. 'I'd just like to see you happy, love,' she says, squeezing my hand.

'I am,' I say, aiming what I hope is a convincing smile in her direction. She sighs and looks out at the view.

'Your dad used to love this place,' she says, and this time I don't get the defence mechanisms up in time. Memories of my dad flash through my mind without warning – playing hide-and-seek in the trees behind us, chasing him across the grass.

Racing him to the bench we're currently sitting on.

'Mum—' I say, not trusting myself to say more, hoping she'll understand from my tone that I need this not to go any further.

'No, Andie. Please don't stop me – I need to tell you this in person.'

I have a sudden, desperate urge to end this conversation, but she's holding my hand and looking at me with her wide blue eyes, and I'm about to leave her and I don't know when I'll see her again. So I stay quiet, and she tells me how she's been going to a grief counselling group for the last year. How it's helped her to process the loss.

My throat feels like sandpaper, but I squeeze her hand tighter, forcing myself to listen. My own grief sits like a lead weight on my chest.

'I still love your father,' she says, looking at me, now. 'But for the first time since he passed I feel a little less weighed down by it all. Ready—' she pauses, taking a breath. '— Ready, perhaps, to think about moving on.' Her words land like a stone – it sounds so final. Like she's describing a job, or a house, not a living, breathing person.

But he's not, anymore, I think, and it knocks the breath out of me. Then she says a name: Nigel.

'He lost his wife a few years ago, so our situations are similar,' she starts. They've been meeting outside the group, having coffee, sometimes dinner. At first, they mostly talked about their spouses, but now it's turned into something more. 'I think you'd like him,' she says, squeezing my hand. And I want to reply, but my words are trapped in my throat, drowned out by the memories which now come thick and fast: my parents, dancing in the kitchen. My mum, suddenly laughing at something my dad said. She was always laughing when my dad was around.

'Andie?' my mum says, my silence now noticeable. She looks worried.

'That's great, Mum,' I say, 'really great. I'm happy for you.'

She can hear in my voice, can see in my face, that I'm not OK. She reaches for my hand again, her eyes soft and sad. 'I know it's big news, love. But I thought – well, I hoped you might like to meet him before you left. I wanted to tell you at our lunch, then bring him here today. But we didn't get a chance to talk about it, so I hope it's not all too fast.'

Oh God. I can feel what's coming. She looks over to her right, and I follow her gaze towards a man walking up the hill. The hill my dad used to walk up, to join us on this bench. The parallel is too much, too painful. I'm under water now, being dragged deeper and deeper. 'Of course, that's fine,' I hear myself saying. Then he reaches the top of the hill, and Mum stands, and so do I, my heart pounding in my chest. I'm operating on impulse now, as if pushed by some force outside myself.

'Hello, Andie,' he says, reaching out his hand. His voice is so warm, so kind. I take his hand and shake it, his grip firm. *Hold it together, Andie. For Mum.* 'It's so wonderful to finally meet you,' he says. 'I've heard so much about you.' Of course he has: I'm sure my mum has sung my praises, like she always does. Praises I don't deserve.

'I—' I start, struggling to find the right words. He's so tall, so warm. So gentle. So much like my dad, even from this brief first impression, that it almost brings me to my knees with grief. 'You're so much like him,' I say without thinking, and in the silence that follows the grief overwhelms my every sense. 'I mean—' I start, panicking now, the tears I've been suppressing starting to come. 'I'm so sorry,' I choke. I want to be happy for my mum, and a part of me is, soaringly so – that she's found someone, that she won't be alone anymore. But a much larger part of me is overwhelmed right now by a pain that colours everything around me, turning it to grey.

'I thought we might go for a short walk,' Nigel says, kindly. From here, I can see his eyes are grey with flecks of blue. His face is lined, softly creased as if from years of laughter. He seems gentle, his energy soft and unintrusive – just the sort of person my mum deserves. Sadness and guilt spill through me all at once.

I desperately try to make sense of the warring emotions inside me. But I can't. Even looking at his face for a second longer feels like it's going to tear me in half. I hide my expression by looking at my watch. 'I'm so sorry,' I say, trying to keep my tone light even through the thickness of my throat. 'It appears I'm running a little behind schedule. It's wonderful to meet you, Nigel. But I—' I clear my throat, hitting my stride now, my voice sounding more normal. '—have to leave soon for my flight this afternoon.' He nods, disappointment colouring his expression, and it makes me feel so sick I can barely breathe.

'Of course,' he says, raising his hand to touch my shoulder then changing his mind and letting it hang by his side.

'I'm sorry to leave in such a hurry, Mum.' I say, turning to her. 'But I have to go.' I squeeze her hand, trying to take a mental picture, one last glimpse of her – so beautiful, so soft. So deserving of a daughter better than me.

'Call me when you land, love?' she asks, her tone softly laced with concern.

'Of course,' I say, pulling her into one last hug. 'I'll see you soon, OK?'

She nods, and I gently brush her arm. Then I turn away, my heart in my throat, and I walk down the hill without looking back. Once I'm out of sight, I start running, and I don't stop until I reach the edge of the Heath. When I'm far enough away from it all, tears streaming down my face, my breath coming in short, harsh gasps, I pull out my phone and book an Uber back to the hotel.

12

When we get to the airport, I'm a wreck: wracked
with guilt about how I handled things with Mum.
When we're through security and Jack goes to get
himself some food for the journey, I try to do my
dad's breathing exercise to calm down, but it only
pulls me deeper into the memories, into the vast
sense of loss spreading through every part of me
within reach.

I pull out my phone and call Sara. I need
the solid feeling I have when I hear her voice, the
sense of coming back to myself. I need her to tell
me what to do. But it rings through to voicemail:
it's still early morning in New York. I send her a
text asking how she's doing, and if she can call me
when she has a moment, followed by seven flower
emojis – our code for 'love you'. For a fraction of
a second before I put my phone away, my thumb
hovers over my mum's number, but I find myself
blocked from calling her, unsure what I'd even say.

I start when I feel a hand on my shoulder, whipping round to see that it belongs to Jack. Where, usually, my response would be mild irritation, now something surprising happens. His sudden presence jolts me into my emotions, and before I know it, they rise up my throat and release into tears. *Fuck.* It's mortifying, and exactly the opposite of the new standard of professionalism I was aiming for. But I can't seem to stop it.

'Are you OK?' he asks, looking slightly terrified.

I shake my head, the tears still falling, because I can't reasonably tell him that I'm fine. I go for a half-truth: 'I haven't been sleeping well,' I sniff, wiping the tears from my face.

He nods, with an understanding expression. 'I've been really struggling to adjust to the time-zone change, too.' He looks down and we both notice his hand is still on my arm. He gives my shoulder a brief squeeze, drops his hand and takes a slight step backwards. 'It's hard, functioning on so little sleep.' I nod, glad that my excuse has been accepted.

'Our gate number is up,' he says, pulling out his passport and fiddling with it, to give me a moment to compose myself. 'Are you OK to go?'

I take a deep breath, willing myself to get my emotions under control, and after a few seconds the waves are more manageable, the flow of tears beginning to abate even as a tightness settles in my throat. I nod, not trusting myself to speak in case it starts again, and grab the handle of my luggage, following him through the terminal. The plane, as it happens, is already boarding when we arrive, and we catch the back of the queue. Jack keeps quiet as we wait, his back to me – I sense he's giving me some privacy, and I'm grateful for it.

By the time we're seated, I feel mostly normal, the worst of it past, the tightness in my throat gradually fading into a lump that I can ignore. I'm glad to be on a plane, taking me away from London and all the memories it holds. About half an hour after we take off, once the seatbelt signs have been switched off, Jack pulls two sandwiches out of his bag and places them on his tray table, followed by two packets of crisps. I frown, calculating. Two of each item. The maths is clear: one of each is for me. A second later, I spot a familiar blue and squint – one of the crips packets is salt and vinegar. The same flavour Jack brought me once, a million years ago in a lecture theatre I'll never visit again, because they were my favourite. A shiver moves up my spine at the memory, at the thought that he might have remembered such a small detail, after all this time.

He looks up at me, slightly sheepish. 'I don't exactly know where sandwiches fall in the terms of the truce,' he says, 'but I figured an author getting his publicist some lunch for the plane wasn't too much of a stretch.'

'Thank you,' I say, shaking off my emotions. There's no way he'd have remembered a detail so small as my favourite flavour of crisps. I'm sure he just grabbed the first two bags he saw. In any case, my hunger wins over. I take the sandwich and eat it quickly, then almost immediately fall asleep, not waking again until the announcement that we are landing in Berlin. I feel better: I slept deeply and my emotions feel further away than they did before.

After a taxi journey through the centre of the city, we arrive at a hotel built inside an old factory, its interior all open space, clean lines and exposed concrete. Artful triangular cushions are strewn over industrial-looking leather sofas. Not for the first time, I have the sense that I am reaping the benefits of travelling with a priority author. The last tour I went on, through the US, we stayed in budget hotels only: one had bed bugs, forcing us to relocate at 11 p.m. – not exactly the four-and-five-star standard I'm getting on this trip.

The elevator is in use and we're on the first floor, so Jack wordlessly picks up my suitcase as well as his, carries them both upstairs before I can protest, and drops mine outside my room. 'I hope you get some sleep,' he says, with a brief smile, before disappearing into his own room.

We have Sunday off to recuperate and prepare for the following week, which will be busy – it's split down the middle between Berlin and Paris, so we're only here for a few days before flying to Paris early on Wednesday morning. Jack knocks on my door at about 8 a.m., to briefly tell me he's heading out sightseeing, and there's a pause that's a little too long before I tell him to have a nice time, and that I'll see him tomorrow. It's only after I've shut the door that I wonder whether he was about to ask me to join him. Either way, I don't see him for the rest of the day, spending it mostly holed up in my hotel room catching up on emails, only emerging to eat in the hotel. I'm incredibly behind – the constant onslaught of things to deal with in a different time zone is really starting to pile up, but I do my best to clear it, taking advantage of the fact that it's a weekend so at the very least no one is likely to be emailing me, today. By the time I glance back up from my screen, it's 9 p.m., so I decide to get an early night.

I wake up early on Monday morning, feeling suddenly terrified of spending the day with Jack again after my outburst in the airport on Friday. The point of this truce was to solidify that I should be buying Jack lunch, I should be the one to call the gate number, I should help him with his bags. Not cry at him in the middle of the airport, like some pathetic loser who can't keep it together for more than a day at a time.

After a few attempts to go back to sleep, I get up and pull some clothes on, deciding instead to wander down the street in search of a cafe. It's 7 a.m., so Jack will be up soon – I'll pick us both up some coffee. That feels like a fair exchange for the lunch he bought me yesterday – and it'll make me feel better. The streets in Berlin are such a welcome change to New York and London: wide, tree-lined. There's so much space, and the pace is different. In New York, I often feel compressed, funneled forwards through the streets of the city by crowds all moving towards their destination. Here, I can stop and breathe; it's a nice feeling. I find one almost immediately, open for the early morning commuters, the sound of soft techno music spilling through its doors into the street.

I pick up two flat whites and a pastry, and on the way back to the hotel I run through the day's itinerary in my head: this bookshop at 11 a.m., that one at 12 p.m., break for lunch, interview at 3 p.m., occupying my mind until I reach Jack's room. I raise my hand to knock on his door, but feel unexpectedly nervous about seeing him. What if he's asleep? I don't want to wake him up. Perhaps I haven't quite thought this through. I hover for a few seconds, then decide to leave them outside his door, with a short note: 'Thank you for yesterday. I don't normally cry like that in front of authors. Won't happen again. A.' I knock quickly before I go, then head back to my room.

Two hours later, I'm browsing the large selection of books in the hotel lobby and waiting for Jack to arrive so we can get going on our bookshop tour, when a voice sounds from behind me, scaring the hell out of me.

'Interesting hotel we're staying in,' Jack says. I whip round.

'I suppose so?' I agree, still a little alarmed. It's a weird opener, but I suppose we're still working on the whole small talk thing.

'Have you noticed that the doors to our rooms open outwards?'

'Uh – I hadn't given it much thought,' I reply. *What is he on about? If this is normal for Jack, he's weirder than I thought.* Then his meaning hits me all at once. *Oh. The coffee I left outside his door.*

'Mine got stuck this morning, actually,' he continues. 'I had to really shove it open.' He leans towards me. 'Hard.'

'Did you?' I ask, still affecting ignorance.

'I'm afraid I couldn't save the coffee,' he says, his expression faux-serious, with a hint of a smile underneath. 'The receptionist was not happy – something to do with the carpet recently being replaced.'

'Ah,' I say, struggling to suppress my own smile now.

'The pastry was lovely, though it did have some carpet fibres attached.'

I smile at this, a laugh bursting out of me unexpectedly. 'I don't accept any liability for carpet-fibre poisoning.'

'Thank you,' he says, returning my smile. 'It was a nice gesture.' Then he pauses, twisting his hands, and looks up at me, his gaze surprisingly intense. 'But you have nothing to apologise for, Andie.'

I look down at my feet, my face burning.

'Thanks,' I say, my voice suddenly quiet.

I look back up at him, expecting the intensity of his gaze to still be there, but it's gone, fading into a smooth, neutral expression that gives the impression that he's already thinking about other things. I breathe out, relieved that the moment is over. He clasps his hands together. 'Now, where are we heading again?'

We leave the hotel and make our way to our first stop on the tour this morning: a bookshop called Another Country. The door rings with the sound of vintage bells when we open it, tied in a tangle to its back. I feel immediately at home, like I'm *in* someone's home. Its interior is eclectic, filled with objects which wouldn't be out of place in an antiques shop, a mixture of second-hand and new books strewn across colourful shelves.

I greet the shopkeeper – a gentle older man, who shakes Jack's hand with great enthusiasm and gestures him towards a pile of his books they have stacked at the back of the shop, ready for him to sign in advance of an event they're holding this evening. Jack organised the event himself: a writers' discussion group he's leading, so he's given me the evening off. But having entered this shop, I'm almost tempted to ask if I can come – it's so warm, so comforting. Like a well-worn pair of shoes, or a conversation with an old friend.

I browse the shelves as Jack chats away to what I have assumed is the shop owner, leaving them to their conversation, but pause in my tracks when I hear something that makes my heart stutter: the man tells Jack that he is not, in fact, the owner of the shop, but it belonged to his friend, who passed away last year. He is a member of a community of volunteers, who have been keeping it afloat in her absence. I stand still, my ears suddenly and inescapably attuned to what he's saying, my heartbeat in my ears. The shop got a little messy, he says, when she was sick, and they've left it this way to keep a piece of her alive. I think of my home, my dad's armchair. My mum's quiet vigil to his absence. A vice clamps across my chest. She was trans, the owner. She started this shop as a community space for the people of Berlin who just wanted to read. It was more than a shop for her, it was a safe haven for those that needed it. She'd rent people books for two euros when they couldn't afford to buy them, or even lend them out for free, sometimes.

She gave people jobs, gave them somewhere to go. Somewhere to belong. *No wonder it's so special in here*, I think as I hear the man's voice catch.

'Thank you for asking,' he says to Jack, referring to a question I didn't hear. 'It's good to talk about her again.'

The weight of loss in his voice is almost too much to bear, and a wave of grief moves up my throat, tightening it. I hear Jack say something softly, something like 'Thank you for telling me about her,' and I turn away so he can't catch the tear that's escaped as he moves back towards the front of the shop. I wipe it away, close my eyes and take a quick breath to steady myself, just as his footsteps reach me.

'Andie?' Jack asks, and I open my eyes.

'Let's go,' I say, quickly, saying goodbye to the shopkeeper and stepping out onto the street.

The rest of the day passes without event, through bookshops and sampling of some of Berlin's excellent coffee, which Jack lightly teases me about not having tried yet due to most of his first sample still being soaked into the hotel carpet. We get an early night, still both exhausted from travelling so much, and the next morning, we head out on a press day, starting with a radio interview at the Haus des Rundfunks – a purpose-built broadcasting house, dating back to the 1930s. Inside, red and white angular light fittings hang from a giant skylight, latticed balconies running along each of the four floors. Its architecture is unlike anything I've seen before. I'm so caught up in its appearance that it's a second before I can get my bearings and find the right floor for Jack's interview.

When we get up there, there's a bit of a drama unfolding – the radio is on-air, and we're about fifteen minutes out from Jack's slot, but the host appears to be having a heated argument with his assistant. I leave Jack in the waiting room, and try to find someone who can tell me what's going on. After a few seconds the assistant spots me and waves, and the argument stops. The host sits back down in his chair, returning to air after a music break, and the assistant escapes from the booth and comes to talk to me.

'You must be Andie,' she says, introducing herself as Anneliese, the person I've been corresponding with about this interview. 'I'm afraid we have a bit of a problem,' she says, and I baulk – from the tone of her voice and the scene I've just witnessed, this doesn't sound good. She explains to me that the host got his schedules mixed up and thought Jack was arriving next week, and that this week he was interviewing a romance author. Consequently, he has not done his research and knows nothing about either Jack or his book. *Excellent*, I think, as her facial expression grows more and more concerned. 'He's going through a terrible divorce,' she whispers to me. 'A lot of mistakes at the moment. And he is never in a good mood. He shouts, a lot.' Oh, good. *Even better – not just an unprepared host, but a hostile one, too.*

'How long do we have before he's on air?' I ask.

She looks at her watch, then grimaces at me. 'Ten minutes.'

'OK,' I say. It's clear this assistant is too young and inexperienced to come up with a solution to this, and I'm sure the host will be useless. So this is on me. I think of Jack, waiting in the corridor to be thrown into a situation that will likely be disastrous, if I don't act fast. *Think, Andie. Think.* I frown, taking a breath and forcing the switch on my creative brain. A few seconds later, an idea comes to me – it could be insane, but it also might just work. 'Right,' I say, turning to Anneliese, who looks up at me with an expectant and hopeful expression. 'Here's what we're going to do.'

After I've explained my idea to the assistant, I step out into the corridor to retrieve Jack and give him a very brief run-down – that this interview might be rough, but he's just got to stick to his aim of promoting the book, and do the best he can to illustrate his work and sell it to the listeners. Everything else, I'll keep under control.

'But how—' Jack starts, but I interrupt him, pushing him towards Anneliese, who is waiting to lead him through.

'No time to explain,' I say. 'Just trust me.'

He looks panicked for a second, but then he locks eyes with me and a calm comes over his expression. 'OK,' he says, then turns and enters the booth.

I take a deep breath and ready myself as Jack settles in the chair and the host speaks to him briefly, introducing himself while the music track plays. I catch Anneliese's eye and she gives me a subtle thumbs up, telling me she's prepared the host and let him know the plan. The notepad and pen I asked for are in front of me, and I position myself behind the glass in the host's eyeline.

I count down from ten in my head as the song finishes, and the host readies himself in his chair to introduce Jack. I write down the first question, my hand moving fast across the page. The host glances towards me, and I give him a nod.

'Good afternoon, everyone!' he says, swiveling back towards Jack. 'I am delighted to welcome Jack Carlson, a bestselling author, to our studio today for our afternoon interview. Welcome, Jack.' I breathe a sigh of relief that the host got Jack's name right, and ready the paper.

'Thanks very much,' Jack says, 'I'm delighted to be here.'

'Now, tell me, Jack,' the host says, glancing sideways and quickly reading the paper I'm holding up against the glass. Jack clocks him and glances at me, too, surprise passing across his features before he turns back to the host. 'You are a celebrated non-fiction author,' the host continues. 'How was it, writing your first novel?'

I let out another breath as Jack starts answering, his flow miraculously un-disrupted by the weirdness of this situation. *Thank God for his professionalism*, I think, quickly scribbling down the next question. I've worked with many authors who would have completely choked in a situation like this, but Jack seems to be handling the pressure fine.

The next question is a little stilted, because I'm not in a position to follow on from the previous answer – I just have to get them out as fast as I can. But it's better than nothing. 'Place is a very import-ant aspect of your book,' the host reads, frowning slightly to decipher my handwriting, which must have become slightly scrawled. Luckily it doesn't trip him up: his tone is smooth as ever. '– its own character, almost,' he says, turning back to Jack now he's finished reading. 'What inspired you to set the book in Ireland?'

Jack leans in, enjoying the question. He flashes me a quick glance, smiling as he's talking. But I can't get caught up – I have to focus on the next question. I write down and hold up a few more in quick succession, all focused around the subject matter of the book – its exploration of family dynamics (obviously steering away from the father-son angle), the discovery of the self, the way present blends into past. And, to finish, a question that's open enough to allow Jack to say anything he might have missed so far.

'And if you could summarise the book for a reader picking up your work for the first time, what would you say?'

'It's about love,' Jack says, eventually. 'How it fills the gaps between people. The distances that emerge without us realising. The past we hold on to, that weighs us down. And how you find your own way out of that.'

As he speaks, for some reason my mum comes to the forefront of my mind, and then Jack looks up and catches my eye. For a second I'm frozen in place, my breath in my throat, eyes locked on him. But a second later he finishes the interview, the host thanks him for coming and shakes his hand.

'Well done,' Anneliese whispers, from the other side of the booth.

'Thanks,' I say, putting the pen down, the last of the adrenaline fading and being followed by a familiar and welcome feeling, one I haven't had so far this trip. The satisfaction that I'm perform-ing at my best, that I not only avoided a disaster but did a good job. And so did Jack: the interview was excellent. Nuanced, interesting and engaging. Even the host, who at the beginning looked less than thrilled to be there, seemed to want to read his book by the end. Hopefully it will have had the same impact on anyone listening.

'Good job,' I say to Jack, after we've left the studio and are descending the steps outside. The sun is out and the city is vibrant. I feel lighter than I have so far on this trip – buoyant, almost.

'Thanks,' he says. 'You, too. I didn't realise you moonlit as a radio interviewer.'

'Very funny,' I say, following him down the steps.

'"Location is almost its own character",' he says, with air quotes. 'A brilliant line, by the way. Inspired. They should give you a job.'

'Shut up,' I say, but I can't entirely hide my smile. I was pretty proud of that question.

'Seriously, Andie,' he says, placing his hand on my arm. 'Thank you. That's the most interesting interview I've had about the book so far. I felt like you really understood what I was trying to do with it. And I know it's just because it's your job. But I've not had that level of understanding from a publicist before. I'm grateful.'

My breath catches in my throat. 'It's no problem,' I say, because what he's saying is kind and might be true, but I'm overwhelmed by it, even as a part of me tells myself that this is why I do what I do – for moments like this, especially with someone I wouldn't have expected it from. 'You're welcome, Jack.'

He gives me a quick, final smile, with an edge of some concealed emotion beneath the surface. But before I can consider what it might be, he removes his hand from my arm and we continue down the steps, my heart still beating a little faster in my chest.

That evening in my hotel room, I pull out my phone to find a text from my mum in bold at the top of my messages. I realise with a jolt that I forgot to call her when I landed, yesterday – too focused on sleeping off my emotions.

Hello, love. Tried calling, but you must have been on the plane. Just to say Nigel loved meeting you, and I hope it was all OK that I brought him along. Would love to call in the next few days. I love you very much. Missing you already. Lots of love, Mum xxx

She always signs off her longer texts like emails, and the sight of it almost makes me cry. I momentarily consider calling her, but the same instinct from the airport earlier stops me. I push through it and tap my thumb to her name anyway, my breath catching as I listen to it ring.

'Andie, love!' she says, answering after two. My heart contracts at the sound of her voice.

'Hi, Mum,' I say. 'Sorry I forgot to call yesterday.'

'No worries, my darling,' she says, her voice warm. I lean into the warmth, even as the sadness starts to reemerge.

'Nigel seemed lovely,' I say, working to keep my voice as steady and calm as I can.

She breathes out what sounds like a sigh of relief, sending a wave of guilt through me. 'I'm so glad to hear that, Andie,' she says. 'I was afraid – well, that doesn't matter now.'

'Really, Mum,' I say, pushing through the tears that are threatening. 'I'm happy for you. I'm sorry I had to leave in such a hurry. Perhaps –' I pause, gathering myself. 'Perhaps we can all have dinner together, next time I'm in London.'

'That would be wonderful, love,' she says, and I hear a voice call from behind her – Nigel's voice. 'I'm so sorry but I have to go, pet,' she says. 'We have a lunch booked, and I don't want to be late. Talk soon?'

'Sounds great,' I say, a boulder landing in my stomach.

'Bye, love.'

'Bye,' I say, and hang up, the tears starting to fall.

13

Early on Wednesday morning we depart Berlin, and a few hours later we're dragging our suitcases through Paris Orly airport. The early nights haven't been helping: the jet lag just about wore off in London, but has now been replaced by a dull, constant headache. I move through the airport like a zombie, using all the faculties I have to keep us on schedule, figuring out which trains to get and double checking our hotel check-in time. Underneath it all, though, there's a jolt of excitement. It's my first time in Paris, and I can't wait to experience what Sara calls 'the Paris effect' – the romanticism, the rose-tinted glasses. The joy of being in a city so historic and beautiful. If I weren't so tired, I'd be buzzing with it. It's incredibly cool that I'm here.

We take public transport this time, and I find the right line of the Paris metro, surprising myself with my enjoyment of the novelty of a new city's transport system. The sight when we emerge from our stop takes my breath away momentarily: stunning architecture, balconies, café after café with patrons sitting outside and smoking, drinking wine and enjoying their day. We drag our luggage over cobblestones and through narrow streets to another beautiful hotel, tucked away in the Quartier de Louvre: centrally located, near all of the sights. There's a café on the same street, mismatched colourful chairs and tables scattered over the cobbles, each adorned with a chess board. It's delightful, but I'm too sweaty from the walk to dwell on it for too long.

Jack has an event and a few signings this afternoon, so after a quick shower and outfit change I make my way down to hotel reception and settle into a velvet armchair to wait for him, taking the opportunity to answer a few emails on my phone. The social media fire from last week has died down – the author took my advice and went underground for a few days, and it all seems to have blown over. I then pull out my personal phone and light up at the sight of a few texts from Sara. New York is still hot, she still misses me, she wishes she could be in Paris with me, right now. James is 'fine', which yet again gives me pause, sending a knot into my stomach – she's usually much more effusive about her relationship with him. I don't know why she's shutting off about this – or, actually, I do: she doesn't trust me. I can feel it, and it hurts. I text her back to let her know I've landed in Paris, covering my sadness with a million Eiffel tower emojis and twelve kisses to tell her how much I miss her. I feel it overwhelmingly in this moment: I miss her, I miss her, I miss her, thrumming through me like a heartbeat. Despite my excitement at being in Paris, I'd give anything to teleport back to New York in this moment and check that she's okay – it seems weird to ask over text, when she hasn't actually told me anything is wrong. I scroll down to see that my mum has also texted, which tightens the knot further:

Lovely to talk yesterday. Are you in Paris yet? Xxx

I reply immediately: *Love you lots. And yes I am! Xxx* I send her a picture of the hotel lobby, and some heart emojis. Another wave of sadness moves through me as I hit send, but I push it aside, forcing myself back into the present, and look around: I didn't get a proper chance to take in my surroundings when we checked in earlier because I was in a rush to get showered and unpack. The hotel is beautifully decorated: ornate and Rococo-style, with gold trimming everywhere and delicate crown moulding on the ceiling. I feel pretty plain by comparison, in my jeans and white shirt, but Sara – who studied French, and did a year abroad in Paris – advised me that if you don't want to be stared at too much by Parisians, it's best to keep your outfit simple. Too much colourful clothing offends their sensibilities, apparently. I look up to see Jack coming down the stairs in an almost identical outfit: white shirt, blue jeans.

'Great minds?' he says, gesturing to our clothes.

'Mm-hmm,' I say, still not recovered from the thought I've just had – that we're going to look like a matching couple.

He gestures towards the door of the hotel and I stand up and walk towards it, holding it open for him and stepping outside into the cobbled street below. It's a gorgeous day: the sun is shining, and the street is full of tourists.

There are people of all descriptions sitting outside the next-door cafe, engaged in games of chess when we pass. At the sight of a little girl playing with her father, I'm transported suddenly to a memory of my dad, teaching me at seven years old. It stops me momentarily in my tracks, and I wait for the jolt of grief, like missing a step on a staircase, but it doesn't come. Perhaps because I hadn't remembered it until now, I haven't had a chance to colour it with loss. I let it pass, enjoying its warmth for a moment, then turn my attention back to the day ahead.

The event is fairly standard – a short reading, followed by an author Q&A. But, to my surprise, it's in French. The events and interviews in Germany were all in English, and I must have missed the brief that Jack now speaks fluent French. It hits me like a truck, the words spilling out of him with ease and sending an unexpected shiver through me. I shake it off, trying to concentrate. Jessica must have forgotten to mention this when she sent me the tour schedule. Luckily the organisers speak English to me when I greet them, so I don't have to rescuscitate my GCSE French, which mostly consists of asking for directions and ordering food. As soon as the event starts they switch languages, Jack slipping smoothly into French as if he's a native speaker. As I sit watching him a strange feeling passes over me: I'm impressed. In my time I've watched some authors show up to events acting like the audience are lucky to be there. Jack is performing *for* the people in this room, not *to* them. He's treating them with respect, showing his gratitude for their presence. It's … cool. Captivating, even – I find myself unable to look away. The way his jaw flexes as he's considering a question, how his posture changes when he's speaking French: more relaxed, somehow. The gestures he makes with his hands as he leans forwards to address each member of the audience. He's so attentive, so – I trail off, alarmed by the direction my thoughts are taking. *Get it together, Andie. He speaks French. So do a lot of other people – everyone else in this room, in fact.*

The talk finishes, and I spend the few minutes while Jack thanks the event organisers reading my emails, not wanting to force them to switch into English with my presence.

'Andie?' a voice says. *Fuck.* Jack is in front of me, and I almost jump out of my skin at the sight. *What is wrong with me?*

'Yes?' I say, shock still rippling through me.

'Didn't you say the car would be here at one?'

I check my watch. It's 1:05 p.m. *Shit.* I scramble up out of my seat, rush over to thank the event organisers, and practically drag Jack out of the shop to the waiting car.

We make our way across town to a television studio, and I spend the car journey recovering from the last hour. Now I've double-checked the schedule, I can see that the interviews Jack is doing are all with French-language media rather than English, so I'm going to have a lot of time to get used to this new talent of his. By the time we're through the studio, and he's greeted everyone we've met with his immaculate accent, it almost sounds normal. Again, everyone switches to English for my benefit, and I manage to get Jack to the correct producer on time, who takes him away to make-up, saying they'll send him straight through to the green room from there and I can take a seat nearby to watch the interview.

I locate one a few metres away and find myself sitting next to a junior producer, who greets me initially in French, but then learns I'm English and is delighted. She introduces herself as Elodie, and says she has been trying to improve her English. After a few minutes of slightly stilted conversation, she's called away on urgent business and I'm alone again. I use the time to check my emails – I send a weekly update to Jessica, letting her know that the Berlin section went smoothly, and respond to an angry email from an author who is offended that I didn't send them a proof of Jack's book, which would've been impossible, considering I started working at the company after proofs had already been sent out. I get the sense from the cantankerous tone of the email, though, that this is the sort of person who might not listen to that kind of reason. I promise to send them a finished copy, and that they'll get first priority for his next novel.

By the time Jack emerges, Elodie has returned – she leans over excitedly to tell me that Jack is one of her favourite writers, and that she's read the French translations of all of his non-fiction since discovering him on TikTok. *Ah*, I think. She's one of the younger members of his audience whose interest perhaps had a less-than-literary origin. I've seen the videos she's talking about, and they're certainly not advertising Jack's writing. But in this case, it's nice to see that it has actually translated into a love of his books.

The interview starts and I zone out slightly, only catching the occasional word here and there: *livre* and *histoire* being the main two I understand. But a few minutes in, Elodie glances at me excitedly.

'What?' I ask, confused.

'Do you not hear what he is talking about?' she asks.

I shake my head, momentarily embarrassed by my lack of language skills. 'I am afraid I barely speak any French.' Jack is smiling, speaking effu-sively about something. His book, perhaps. Or writing, generally – he always seems to light up when interviewers ask him about his process.

'They asked him how the tour was going—' she says. *Oh.* I think. *I mean, I guess it's going OK so far, but I don't understand why*—'and he is talking about you.'

'Oh,' I say, losing all sense of language through shock. *What could he possibly be*—

'He is saying you are the – uh – the spine of this trip. I am sorry, my English is not so good. His last trip was bad. But this one is good. Because of you.'

Her broken English gives the words more weight, and they hit me square in the chest. I hadn't real-ised Jack's opinion would mean so much to me. But hearing it so unexpectedly and sincerely, with no agenda – no idea I'd have someone here to translate for me – is strangely overwhelming.

A few hours later, Jack and I run into each other by the main entrance of the hotel. I have the evening off, and have made up my mind to make the most of Paris while we're here. Having spent the better part of an hour googling things to do in Paris in the evening and thoroughly overwhelming myself, I eventually ended up just getting dressed and leaving the hotel room. I don't really have a plan, beyond wandering around the city, but even if I get a bit lost it will be fun to get a sense of it. It appears Jack has had the same idea — either that, or he's out on some evening plans I don't know about.

'Fancy seeing you here,' he says. He smiles and holds the door open for me, and I walk through it. 'Big plans this evening?' he asks, once we're out on the street.

I shake my head as we fall into step alongside one another. I wonder idly if he's about to head in the same direction as me — if I should turn off somewhere, so we don't end up awkwardly walking alongside each other for too long. 'I'd like to see the city a bit,' I say. 'First time here.'

'Oh, nice,' he says. 'The first time in Paris is always special.' We continue wandering down the street without much sense of direction. But I find, after a few seconds, that I actually don't mind having company for a minute — it's not like I have any idea where I'm going, anyway.

'Any idea where you're going to go?' he says, as if he's read my mind.

I shake my head, again, a little embarrassed now. 'I'd planned to just wander around. But maybe that's a bad idea?'

'There are no bad ideas in Paris,' he says. 'But—' he pauses, rubbing the back of his neck. 'If you like, I could show you a few places?'

I almost stop in my tracks, a little shocked by his offer. 'Don't you have plans?' I ask, deferring for a few seconds while I consider it. It's not so far beyond a normal publicist–author relationship to spend personal time with one another on tour.

'No plans,' he replies, shrugging. 'I was going to wander around, too. So you're welcome to join me, if you like. I – uh. I know the city quite well.'

'OK,' I say, before I can think too hard about it. I was feeling a little nervous about heading out on my own, and I don't want to turn down a tour guide – even if it is, you know, Jack. Better to spend the evening with him and actually see some sights than go off on my own and end up down some dark, dingy alleyway.

'Great,' he says, and keeps moving. We walk for a while in a slightly awkward silence. He takes a few turns, and I follow him, marveling at his ease – even in London, I have to pull up Google Maps half the time to figure out where I'm going.

'Where are we going?' I ask, after a few minutes.

'I thought we'd take a walk along the river, first. Does that sound OK?' I nod, and he aims a soft smile at me, then turns to face back in the direction we're walking, away from me. Silence falls again, and I find myself searching for things to say – since the truce, we haven't spent much time together in a non-work context, and I'm not sure how to go about it, suddenly nervous that I'll say the wrong thing. We reach the river and walk along it for a little while, the city lights glittering on the water.

'Where did you learn to speak such good French?' I ask eventually, my tone conversational.

'I used to live here,' he says, his tone easy. 'I studied it for A-level, and picked the rest up while I was here.' We walk for a little longer, then something seems to occur to him – he slows to a halt and looks up at the name of the street we're on, then takes his phone out of his pocket and checks something I can't see. He nods to himself, then looks up at me and smiles. 'Actually, do you mind if we take a detour?'

'Sure,' I say, confused. Jack leads me across a bridge a few hundred metres away, then along several cobbled streets, weaving through them with the practised ease of someone who knows the city well. It occurs to me how little I know about how Jack's life has unfolded in the last five years since university, beyond his career progression and relative fame. He could have lived in Siberia, for all I know.

After a few minutes of walking, we come to a halt outside a bookshop. Bookshop seems too generic a description, actually: it's one of the most bookshop-y bookshops I've ever seen; the sort of place you imagine when people talk about their dream of opening a bookshop one day. It's tucked away in the corner of a street, with fairy lights strung up in front of it, and everything is perfectly shabby without looking too run-down. The outer wall to the right of the entrance doubles as a bookshelf, stuffed with books of all descriptions, surrounded by tables also piled high – you could choose a hundred books to buy before even entering the shop. The shopfront is a deep green, and ramshackle lettering above the front door spells out its name: *Shakespeare and Company*. A small bell of recognition goes off in the back of my mind – this place is famous.

I turn to Jack and find him totally lost in thought. The expression in his eyes is nostalgic but heavy, weighed down by something. I turn away, suddenly conscious that I'm intruding, and pretend to sift through a pile of books on the table in front of me until he resurfaces.

'Sorry,' he says, still looking up at the shop. 'I haven't been back here in a while. I didn't realise it would be so—' He stops himself, and turns towards me. 'Find anything good?'

I shake my head, and he gestures towards the door. 'All the best books are inside, anyway,' he says.

He walks through the shop with the same attitude he had while guiding me through the streets a moment ago – of someone who knows what they're doing, who has opened the door to this shop many times before. I follow him into an angular room which is just as perfectly lived in as its exterior, the wood of the shelved walls dark and well-worn. He leads me up some stairs which are the same green as the shopfront, each step painted with a line from a poem about finding light in loneliness, and through a small, cavernous stone corridor with a sign about being kind to strangers painted above the entrance. Eventually, we reach a quieter corner of the shop, not unlike the fantasy section where he found me in *The Lost Bookshop* in New York. There's a door to my right, which is closed.

'When I told you I lived in Paris, this is where I meant,' he says. He points towards the door, looking at it with a gaze that's somewhere between melancholy and fondness. 'I lived through there, for a while.'

A memory floats to the top of my mind – the reason I've heard of this shop, the reason it's famous. It hosts struggling writers, when they're in need of a bed and time to focus on their book, in exchange for a few shifts in the shop. 'Ah,' I say, another element of Jack slotting into place.

He nods. 'Mind if we sit for a minute?' he asks, and I shrug and nod, sinking into the rickety armchair behind me. He follows, sitting in one with a view to the street below.

'How did you end up here?' I ask, curious, trying not to make any sudden movements for fear the chair will collapse under me.

'When I was writing my first book,' he replies, 'I fell on hard times, sort of. My dad—' he pauses, choosing his words carefully '—uh, he had promised he'd help me while I was writing, then he changed his mind.' A shadow passes across his face, and I get the feeling that what happened was worse than his tone lets on. Flashes of the last few weeks run through my mind: clearly, Jack has a troubled relationship with his father. A wave of something like pity moves through me, suddenly. 'I was living in New York, and wanted to get away for a while.

I had heard they took writers as residents here, so I got in contact with the shop owners through a friend, and moved a few weeks later.'

'I've always wanted to do something like that,' I say, intensely jealous. Who wouldn't dream of living in a bookshop in Paris, of all places?

'Me too,' he says, smiling wistfully. 'Unfortunately, though, it was a bad decision on my part – my French was terrible and rusty, I didn't know anyone in the city, and I had terrible writer's block. And there were fleas, everywhere.' I make a face, and he laughs. 'I'm still so grateful to the shop owners for taking me in, but it was the loneliest I've ever been.'

Something twists in my chest: that feeling is familiar to me. I turn my gaze to the floor at my feet, examining the marks in the wood from thousands of shoes passing through this room, browsing for books. *So this is why he doesn't like being alone in Paris.* In answer to my fairly innocuous question, he's brought me to the epicentre of his loneliness. This feels wrong, sacred somehow. A privilege that should be reserved for a close friend, a girlfriend even. Not me.

'Sorry if it's weird that I brought you here,' he continues, as if he's read my mind. 'There are no events here this week, and I wanted to visit before we leave. This seemed like a good opportunity. Plus – as a fellow fan of that corner of *The Lost Bookshop*, I thought you might like it here, too.'

I flinch at the memory of our meeting in that bookshop. The emotions he brought up then are no longer so pronounced – still there but dulled, a volcano now semi-dormant, its lava surging under a few layers of rock. We are silent for a moment. 'I do,' I say, quietly.

The air is still between us, broken only by the sound of our breath and the muffled noises of the customers downstairs. He looks around the room nostalgically, then moves as if he's about to get up and lead me back downstairs. But before he can, for a reason that's beyond my understanding, I start talking.

'I know what that's like,' I say, my heart pounding in my chest, a heat creeping up the back of my neck and prickling over my ears. I glance over at him. He stops, still in his chair, his eyes on me. My body all of a sudden feels like it's on fire. 'The loneliness, I mean,' I practically choke out, still not sure why I'm suddenly being so open with him. 'When I first moved to New York, I was miserable. I'd moved an ocean away from my mum,' I continue, 'right after my dad—' my breath catches, and I reroute, my stomach twisting in warning '—right after university, for an internship which paid horribly. I had no friends there, either. I used to sit in that chair in *The Lost Bookshop* for hours every weekend, wondering if I'd got everything wrong.'

He smiles at me, a sad smile of shared loneliness. I stand up and pretend to browse the books, moving from shelf to shelf, finding myself compelled to continue. 'I always feel less lonely around books,' I say, the words coming more easily than they should. 'Does that sound insane?'

He laughs, softly, almost to himself. 'No, Andie,' he says. 'It doesn't.'

I keep my eyes firmly on the shelf in front of me, my back turned, but I can feel Jack's gaze on me. It burns just like it did back then, a million years ago in his room in Edinburgh. Like a laser on my skin. I am suddenly aware of my breath, of my feet on the wooden floor. I squeeze my eyes shut, trying to push away the sensation, to come back to reality, but it doesn't work. Jack is everywhere in this room: I can't shut him out. His foot creaks on the floor behind me – he's standing up. I turn abruptly towards him, my logical brain kicking in and overriding the sensations in my body. I have to dispel this, whatever it is.

'Will you help me find a nice edition of Shakespeare?' I ask quickly, keeping my tone even. 'It feels fitting, given the name,' I say, trying for a joke, hoping it'll break up the atmosphere. He doesn't laugh but looks at me for a moment, then shakes his head as if trying to dislodge a thought.

'Sure,' he says, his trademark Jack Carlson smile back on his face, all traces of the moment before gone.

He moves through the shop with expert skill, taking me back through the corridor, down the stairs and into another small, hidden nook in the back left corner of the ground floor. The strange electric charge between us dims but is still present as I follow him from room to room. I try hard to keep my head, focusing on my breath, on the other people milling around us, reading every sign carefully as I pass it – they're all in English, which makes things easier: otherwise this would be a useless exercise. But even if they were in French, I'd be willing to do anything right now to keep my mind off Jack, and whatever just happened in that room. *I am a publicist, and he is my author, and this is just a bookshop,* I chant to myself in my head as he finds the right section and browses the shelves as if it's his own personal library, his hand gently thumbing through the spines. Within moments he locates a beautiful, leather-bound complete edition of Shakespeare, then haggles in French with the young shopkeeper so well that I end up taking it away for the measly sum of fifteen euros. I do not allow myself to aim more than a small smile at him as he hands me the book, my heart still pounding as I all but push past him to get out of there.

As soon as we're back in the fresh air, my heart rate starts to decrease slightly. I take in a few breaths, regaining a sense of my surroundings. Slowly, the feeling fades – Jack is next to me, and he's looking at me, and it feels mostly normal and fine. No strange burning sensation, no energy between us. Just my heart, still stuttering against my chest, but slowing with every moment. Whatever that was, it's now gone, left in the upstairs room of the shop.

'Shall we find some dinner?' he says. I nod, not trusting myself to speak.

Jack offers to show me his favourite spot for food in Paris, and I blanche, expecting some sort of candlelit restaurant – but instead he takes me to a bakery and instructs me to choose some bread, saying he'll be right back. I pick out a baguette and find Jack outside holding some brie and a bottle of wine.

We walk for a while until we reach the river, and he directs me across a bridge to his favourite spot: sitting on the side of the Seine with a view of Notre Dame on the other side, our legs hanging over the edge to the river bank below.

'So,' I start, as he tears off a piece of bread and hands it to me, thinking to keep the conversation as professional as I am able, 'why did you really make the switch to fiction?'

'I heard there was a new publicist starting, and I wanted to terrorise her,' he jokes, but it doesn't quite land. My hand tightens around the bread, and I turn away and busy myself cutting a slice of the brie to my left so he can't see my facial expression.

'Sorry,' he says, after a moment. 'Bad joke. I'm avoiding answering your question.' He sits back, leaning on the palms of his hands, and takes a deep breath, looking out over the water. 'Put simply, my writing career up to this point has been a lie.'

I almost choke on the too-large bite of baguette I've taken. 'Do explain,' I say, once I've managed to swallow.

'Sure it won't bore you?' he asks, and his tone is jovial but there's a hint of seriousness in his expression which inexplicably makes my heart sink. I shake my head, gesturing for him to continue.

'I'll skim across the details but: my parents are divorced. Dad's based in New York, so I didn't see him much as a kid. When I did, history was sort of our thing. I'm not sure if you remember George mentioning at my London launch, but he's a historian.'

'I remember,' I say. A vision of Jack leaving the room at his launch appears in my mind.

'You can maybe see where this is going. Historian father, historian son. Not exactly original, right?' He takes a breath – he's started speaking fast, as if he wants to get the words out as quickly as possible. 'He remarried a while ago, and sort of—' Here he pauses, losing some momentum, and I watch his posture grow a little heavier. '—lost interest in our relationship.' *Oof. Poor Jack.* He keeps his tone light, but there's an undertone to it. A weight, that wasn't there before. 'I've realised recently that writing those books has been my way of reaching out to him, I guess.' He looks at me with a self-deprecating smile, which doesn't quite hide the sadness in his eyes. 'Trying to start a conversation he didn't really want to have.'

Suddenly I don't feel so hungry anymore. I let the baguette fall into my lap, crumbs settling into the folds of my skirt. Jack's expression is still carefully jovial, as if he's about to give an interview, but I know this pain. I can see it, buried deep beneath the surface, beyond anyone else's reach.

'So I started writing fiction – so I could feel like my writing belonged to me, again. Like—' he pauses, searching for the right words.

'Like a conversation with yourself?' I ask, finishing his thought.

He smiles, and this time some of the sadness seeps through. 'Something like that,' he says, and a knot begins to form in my stomach.

We move on to safer topics – like the best and least-toursity spots in Paris and the agenda for the following day – but I can't shake the unease, growing more and more noticeable with every moment we spend together. It lasts through the wine, which we finish gradually, and the baguette, some of which I tear to pieces in my lap.

A few hours later, we make our way back to the hotel. The walk is long, and Jack points out a few tourist spots en route – the Eiffel Tower, which you can see when you look down certain streets. The Louvre, just round the corner from our hotel. And a few of the cafes and restaurants he used to frequent when he lived here.

We reach the hotel and Jack walks me back to my room. There's a moment of slightly awkward silence, then as I'm turning to pull the door open he breaks it.

'That was nice,' he says, his voice low and quiet. A flash of the feeling I had earlier in the bookshop reappears. I push it away, forcing my walls back up.

'It was,' I agree, the knot tightening as a thrill moves up the back of my neck. 'Thank you.'

A fold appears on his brow, like he's thinking about something, but I don't allow myself to consider what it might be.

'See you tomorrow, Andie,' he says, then turns to walk down the corridor, back to his room. I can feel my heartbeat in my throat as I watch him leave.

I keep the smile on my face until he's reached his room, then disappear into mine and close the door. I lean against it, my breathing heavy, suddenly overwhelmed by the realisation that agreeing to spend the evening with Jack was a terrible idea. Not because of the bookshop, or the moment by the river, or the fact that I accidentally learned more about Jack in these last few hours than I ever did at university. But because, against my better judgement, against every fibre of rationality in my body, I enjoyed it. All of it.

14

As soon as I catch my breath, I sit on the bed and call Sara.

'Hi, babe,' she says, and relief floods through me at the sound of her voice.

'What's up, buttercup?' she says, and I almost start crying immediately at the warmth in her tone. I miss her so much. I take a breath, and everything that's happened in the last few days spills out at once. The book club, Nigel, Berlin. This evening, and the mixed feelings it's set off inside me.

'That's … a lot,' she says, when I've finished.

'It is,' I say, feeling some of the heaviness lift. Talking to Sara, as always, is like a soothing bath. I bask in it, tension seeping out of me.

'Are you doing OK?' she asks, and now the tears start to come.

'Sort of,' I say, my throat thick. I'm grateful I don't have to hold it together around her. 'I miss you.'

'Oh A,' she says. 'I wish I could give you a hug.'

'Quit your job and fly to Paris?' I ask, only half joking.

'You'll be back in New York so soon, babe. And you're doing so well, by the sounds of it. You can do this.' I hold her words to my chest, willing myself to take heart from them. She pauses for a second, and I pull the phone away from my face to check I still have a signal. 'Can I give you some advice, though?'

'Please,' I say, emboldened by her words.

'It might be worth thinking about clearing the air with Jack, again,' she continues, and my stomach drops. 'You know – you're talking about all this confusion, all these weird feelings towards him. I think if you had a conversation about what happened, it might help you to sort through them. Then once that's sorted, you'll have some space to really sort through your other feelings – about Nigel, about your dad.'

'I can't do that, S,' I say, trying to keep my tone neutral even as my chest grows tight, panic spreading through me.

'I think you can. You're stronger than you—'

'Please, Sara,' I say, cutting her off, my tone sharp and pleading as the fear builds, lighting up my senses. Some part of me deep down can hear her logic, can see where she's coming from. But I don't want to open the box I've been keeping so tightly closed. 'I just – I can't.'

'OK,' she says quickly, her tone gentle, and the fear starts to abate, some tension releasing in my chest. 'It was just an idea.' My heart rate slows, my breath coming more steadily.

'I know,' I say.

There's a pause for a moment, and I feel that awkwardness again, the sense of something being off between us, the silence slightly strained. She suddenly feels very far away.

'I miss you,' I say, aching to be with her. And I mean it: I feel it in my gut, the pain of being apart – like there's some invisible thread between us that's being stretched to its limits.

'Miss you too, babe,' she says, her voice warm, and I wonder if it's in my mind.

'Listen, S—' I start, trying to keep my voice steady through the tangle of fear that's reappeared, contracting in my chest. I want to communicate all this to her, somehow. But before I can say anything else, I hear the sound of the door opening behind her, of James's voice. I tense up, anticipating the goodbye before it comes.

'I have to go, A,' she says, her words landing like a lead weight in my stomach. 'I'll speak to you really soon, OK?'

'OK,' I say, trying to keep back the tears that are suddenly threatening. But my voice sounds hollow.

I open my contacts and – on impulse – scroll down to my mum's name. I wish I could talk to her, right now – could tell her what's going on. I hover over it for a few seconds with my thumb, willing myself to press it. But in this moment, I can't bring myself to call her. I miss her like hell, but I don't know where to even begin. So much has gone unsaid between us, and the miles feel too numerous to close in this moment. I check the time – it's 10 p.m. in the UK, anyway: she'll be in bed by now, with her phone on do not disturb. Since I showed her that feature, she uses it every night.

I text her instead: *Miss you xxx* then throw my phone on the bed and flop backwards next to it, pressing my palms to my eyes. The loneliness that I've been staving off for the last few days hovers around me, ready to close in. The distance between me and the people I love most feels greater than ever, right now. As if I'm adrift, moving further and further away from them. At sea, alone, and powerless to stop it. I miss my mum, but she's moving on with her life and I don't know how to talk to her about it without falling apart. I miss Sara, but I can feel her pulling away from me. *I miss my dad*, I think, the thought surprising me, and the tears fall faster, blurring my vision, a knife twisting between my ribs.

I take a few deep breaths, and as my mind begins to clear an unexpected image floats to the top of it: the chess-playing café down the street. The memory it evoked of my dad is like a balm to the fire in my chest. In the next moment, almost as if my limbs are acting without thought from me, I find myself getting up and making my way out of the hotel room, down the stairs and through reception, then heading down the alleyway towards the café.

The chairs are all there, still: the café staff are slowly winding down, but there are a few people still playing in the soft street light. I sit at the nearest unoccupied table and stare down at the board. The image is still there, still clear: I can feel the carpet under my knees, see him kneeling opposite.

'Pawns first,' he says, his voice ringing out in my mind.

I reach to move the pawn in front of the queen, and my fingers are the same fingers that touched the pieces with him all those years ago. I make his move for him: the same, opposing pawn. Next, the queen. I close my hand around the piece.

'The queen can do anything she wants,' he says, and he winks at me, my hand moving with his in diagonal motion across the board. I focus in on the tone of his voice, so familiar and yet so far gone it's like an ache in my chest, and let his instructions guide me until pieces are scattered across the whole board. But after a few more moments, my memory falters. I pause, letting my hand fall, unwilling to put the pieces back just yet. I want to stay here, where the game with my father is still happening.

I drop my hand to my side and sit back, my gaze turning to the other people playing: old men, mostly, and a younger couple in the corner, visibly on either a first or second date. Two boys, messing around, about ten years old. I wonder if their fathers taught them to play. My breath comes slow and steady, and the cool night air brushes across my skin. I sit, unmoving in the street light, until the last table has been cleared. Eventually, the café owner makes her way over to my table, gives me an apologetic look and says she is locking up. I nod, hesitant to leave the safety of this memory. But the world is calling – the world without my dad. I can't stay here forever, no matter how much I want to.

I carefully pick up each piece to put the board back as it was when I sat down, my hand lingering over the queen on what would have been my father's side of the board. *I miss you,* I think, willing it to reach him. Then I take my hand off the piece, give her a final smile, pick up my bag and make my way slowly back to the hotel.

15

The next day passes quickly in a slew of signings and press across the city, and the following morning I wake up bleary-eyed for our flight to Dublin, probably looking like I've been dragged through a hedge backwards. I meet Jack out the front of the hotel with my bags. He, as always, is looking irritatingly good for the ungodly hour.

'Morning,' he says, his cheery tone like nails down a blackboard to my tired brain. *Ugh. Morning people.*

'Morning,' I echo back, my tone much less enthusiastic.

He smiles at me, a genuine smile, then he looks down at his phone. I close my eyes. It feels strange to think of London, where standing even two metres away from him like this made me want to scream. Where before he unleashed a storm of violent feelings in me, now I feel almost … calm.

But before I can dwell too much on that thought, the car arrives to take us to the airport. I turn my gaze out the window, watching Paris pass us by. It's beautiful at this time of day – the soft morning light grazes empty streets, and Notre Dame sits silent and majestic, free of milling tourists. In my short time here I haven't found Paris to be a particularly peaceful place, but in this moment that's just what it is: a city asleep, its elegance shining quietly, all the more lovely for being unobserved. I'm going to miss it, I realise – but leaving means we're moving on to the last leg of the tour. One more location. Then I'm back to Sara, and New York, and my plants. I can show up at Sara's big glass flat and hug her, and we can work out all this stuff with my mum, and I won't have to miss her anymore.

We navigate through the airport and board the plane easily – we're two of about five passengers. It seems early morning flights to Ireland aren't all that popular. Just as I reach my seat, my phone lights up with a call from my mum. I take a deep breath and answer without thinking.

'Hi, Mum,' I say, my voice cracking.

'Andie!' she says, her tone full of joy that I've answered. 'How are you doing, love?'

'I'm OK,' I say, another half-lie – they're becoming more and more common with my mum. But I don't need to get into that now. 'We're about to leave for Dublin. I'm on the plane, actually. I might not be able to talk for long—' I start, but she cuts me off.

'Don't worry, love. I am just calling because there's something important I need to tell you, something that Nigel and I have been discussing—' the name sends a ripple of panic up my spine, my senses alive for the pain that will follow. But it doesn't come immediately.

'Yes?' I say, relieved by its absence, but still tense, expectant. 'I hope you had a nice lunch, by the way,' I add, in an attempt to sound normal, to diffuse the emotions that are currently raging through me.

'Oh, thank you, darling – it was lovely. Now, I wanted to tell you—'

A voice chimes from my right, cutting my mum off. 'Excuse me,' the air hostess says, hands on her hips. I pull my phone away from my ear momentarily, my mum's voice still ringing out of it. 'All phones on airplane mode, please. And seatbelts on, ready for take off.'

'I'm so sorry, Mum,' I say, putting my phone back to my ear and talking over her. She's saying something about the summer, a garden. 'I have to go.'

'Oh—' she says, sounding disappointed. 'OK, love. But you got all that, right? And you're okay with it?'

'Yes, of course,' I say. My dad always said he wanted to do more with our garden, but he was hardly obsessed with it. If Nigel wants to plant some rose bushes, it's not my business.

The air hostess raises her eyebrows at me. 'Love you, Mum,' I say, talking over her again. 'I'm so sorry, but I really have to go now. Bye.'

'Bye, love—' she starts, but I hang up.

Love you, sorry. Air hostess being grumpy! Xxx I text her.

No worries, love. So pleased you're OK with it all. I'll tell Nigel! Xxx

I frown slightly at her text – it seems a bit of an odd response, for some gardening. But I suppose stranger things have happened, and given my display on the Heath she wasn't wrong to be concerned I might overreact. I lock my phone and put it in airplane mode then put my headphones in. Jack does the same, and we settle into our seats in comfortable silence. I fall asleep about half an hour in and wake up to see rolling green fields outside the plane window. I can almost smell the fresh, clean Irish air. I turn to find Jack asleep too, and gently nudge him with my elbow. He wakes up looking a little disoriented, then smiles the same wide, genuine smile he aimed at me earlier. I look away, rifling through my bag to check my passport is there.

'We're here,' I say, my voice informative and nonchalant, and turn back to gazing at the Irish countryside as our plane pitches lower and lower towards it.

The plane lands, rattling onto the tarmac, and a few moments later we're clambering out of our seats and rooting around for our bags. Mine is in an awkward corner of the overhead cabin – it must have slid to one side while we were landing. I reach over and manage to grasp it by the handle, dragging it towards me, but it's heavy and I lose balance as it tips out, hurtling towards me. Before it hits me, Jack's hand shoots past me and steadies it, his fingers clasping over mine on the handle. They stay that way for a moment, and I catch his eye, my hand horribly and completely aware of his touch. For a split second I see a look in his eyes that I recognise, that takes me suddenly and inescapably back to a bar in Edinburgh, five and a half years ago. Then he springs away and turns to grab his case, deliberately avoiding my gaze. *So he's thinking about that, too.* A blush spreads across my face, my cheeks blazing. I focus intently on the handle of my suitcase, sliding it up carefully, avoiding his gaze as he's avoiding mine, willing my thoughts away from that night, that dark bar, his hand grazing mine.

The announcement blares that the doors to the plane are opening, breaking me out of my extremely dangerous reverie. I take a breath of the cool air as it rushes through the cabin, breathe it out slowly and make my way swiftly towards the door.

I don't look at Jack again as we go through the airport, and he seems to have developed a sudden and burning interest in airport signage, so we make it most of the way to the car without having to make eye contact again.

I slip into my seat, willing the journey to be swift and short so I can have some time in my room to decompress and get my brain the hell away from any thoughts about Jack that aren't totally and completely detached and professional. The streets of Dublin pass us by, a blur of old buildings and new, Georgian shopfronts adjacent to high-rise buildings, ramshackle lanes giving way to wider city streets. I catch sight of a few people wearing what look to be rugby shirts. There must be a game on.

We're in the car for a while, and I look up from scrolling through my emails to find the streets are no longer ones I recognise from the trips I took with my dad when I was little – this hotel must be on the outskirts. I really should've paid more attention to our hotels from a geographical perspective, rather than just memorising their addresses. But we keep driving and a few moments later the streets have given way to a road that looks suspiciously rural and winding. I pull out my work phone and scroll through my emails, looking for the hotel booking confirmation. A few ping through at once, suddenly loading now I'm connected to an Irish data network. All from Jessica, all in increasing states of panic. I read through them, digesting the information. Our hotel booking was cancelled last minute: flooding, apparently. She found out a few hours ago and has been trying to get through to me but we were still on the plane. Everywhere in Dublin is booked up for the Six Nations – which explains the rugby fans I spotted. The closest place she could find with availability is in a village half an hour outside Dublin. She gave the driver the new address before we landed, so that's where we're heading now.

As I'm about to explain the situation to Jack, my phone chimes with a final email: the new hotel booking. I open it and stare at it for a few seconds, my brain not quite registering what's happening. This can't be right. Jessica must have made two bookings, and only sent one. 'There's only one room,' I say to myself, horror slowly spreading through me.

'Sorry?' Jack says, his brow furrowed in confusion.

'One sec,' I say, scanning the email again. *Fuck*. It's there, clear as day – two guests, twin suite. I look up at Jack. 'Sorry, it's just – our booking was cancelled, and my boss has found us a new hotel outside Dublin. But there must be something wrong with the new booking. It says there's only one room.'

'May I?' Jack asks, and I hand the phone over. He looks over it for a moment, and raises his eyebrows. 'It's a twin room, apparently,' he says, looking up at me. 'So we won't have to share a bed, at least.'

I squeeze my eyes shut, hard. 'Excellent news, thanks Jack,' I say, in a faux-enthusiastic tone, then sigh. At this point, reality is sinking in – Jessica must have either made the booking in a hurry and not noticed the rooms were joined together, or neglected to tell me because she was so tired and stressed. I take a deep breath and kick my brain into gear: there must be a way out of this. Perhaps I can find a camping shop and buy a tent to sleep in?

Jack doesn't respond, so after a few seconds of silence, I open my eyes and look up at him, to see that he's – smiling, his eyes sparkling with amusement. *How the hell is he enjoying this?*

'This isn't funny,' I huff, crossing my arms and turning to look out the window.

'Come on, it's a little funny,' he says, and when I look back at him he raises his eyebrows at me, expectant. I'm still horrified by the prospect of having no time away from him, but to my surprise I find a laugh building in my chest. I repress it, and return my face to its previous horrified expression quickly, before he can register any amusement.

'Shut up, it's not,' I say, and return to staring at the Irish scenery.

But he's not giving in. 'I saw you smile just then,' he says, his voice light and mocking. *Damn. Not quick enough.*

I breathe out. 'Fine,' I say, through gritted teeth. 'It's a little funny. In the way that the story about the man who was pretending to fall into the Grand Canyon to make his daughter laugh and then actually fell into the Grand Canyon and died is funny.'

He laughs. 'Jesus, Andie, that's dark.'

'My point exactly. It's both horrifying and hilarious that I'd rather throw myself out of this car than share a hotel room with you, but I'm going to have to sleep next to you for the next four days.'

I bite my lip, aware that my words came out a little harsher than intended. He is silent for a moment, and I'm momentarily worried I've gone too far, but then he breathes out a slow whistle.

'I think that might qualify as a violation of the truce.'

'Oh for God's sake. I don't care about the truce right now.'

'I'm just saying, that was not very nice.'

'Jack—'

'—In fact, I think it was definitely hostile.'

I exhale sharply and turn towards him, my retort on my tongue, but find him with such an open and amused expression that it completely disarms me. I stare at him in silence for a fraction of a second, then suddenly the laugh builds until I can repress it no longer – it bursts out of me, and he's laughing too.

In the seconds of silence that follow, as I'm looking at him and catching my breath, everything that's been weighing me down for the last few weeks falls away, the pretence momentarily fading. We really could be just two people, in a car, with no past between us. My breathing slows, and he opens his mouth like he's about to say something. But then, suddenly, we're shunted forwards, the car coming to an abrupt halt. The jolt of the brakes brings me to my senses, and I look away, the moment gone, my attention very firmly back to the present and our less-than-ideal sleeping situation. We gather our various bags and exit onto the gravel driveway leading up to the hotel.

It is magnificent: stone turrets rise up into the sky above us, giving way to a cliff which falls into the sea, waves lapping against the shore. We're staying in a *castle*. A castle! The new hotel booking gave us something, at least. I drag my suitcase across the driveway, bringing a large clump of gravel with me as I do so, and enter a room with a vast, vaulted ceiling. Wooden beams curve across it, giving it the feel of a medieval entrance hall. It probably *was* a medieval entrance hall, once. But now it's a hotel reception. I take the lead, heading across the room to the desk and asking if they have a spare room. The concierge shakes his head – I'm the third person to ask today, apparently, but they're fully booked. He checks us in and hands me two keys. I give Jack his, and it occurs to me as we're climbing the stairs that we're going to have to talk about ground rules: what if I walk in on him naked? But I immediately regret this line of thinking – it brings up an unwanted image of Jack, his eyes on me, unbuttoning his shirt, which I swiftly shove back into the box it came from. *Jesus. What is wrong with me today?*

Jack presses the key to the door and opens it. My first thought is that it's not as bad as I'd imagined: the front room has a few amenities – a kettle, some teabags, a fridge full of drinks and an ironing board. The view out to the coast is breathtaking. There's a chaise longue in the corner and a small, glorified camp bed by the window. To my right is an opening into the main suite, where a four-poster bed takes up the bulk of the space. *'Twin' is a generous term*, I think. I'm also disappointed to see that there's not a door to close between us, but with some creative use of the imagination this is almost separate rooms. In the grand scheme of unfortunate situations it's still not ideal, but there's a wall, at least. Jack and I glance at each other awkwardly for a fraction of a second. 'I'll take the smaller bed,' I say, before he can do anything noble, and he nods and moves through into the other room.

I put my suitcase next to the bed as the full reality of this situation settles over me: all I want, right now, is a little time to get myself together and strategise for the next four days. But Jack is still here, three metres away, unpacking his bag. His presence draws my attention like a magnet: I hear the slow unzip of his suitcase, the rustling of his clothes, even the sound of his breath. 'I'm going to shower,' I say, grabbing one of the towels and heading towards the bathroom.

He looks up from his unpacking – I can see him, through the entryway to his part of the suite – and nods. 'Enjoy,' he says, and returns his attention to his suitcase.

The hot water reaches parts of me which desperately need soothing, washing comfort over my limbs. I breathe in the steam, grateful for the privacy. *Four more days.* I scan through the reports I've been sending Jessica every few days in my mind: objectively, on a purely professional level, we've been doing OK since the truce. I've been much more on my game, and Jack seems reasonably happy – he no longer jumps like a startled rabbit every time I look in his direction. Overall, the tour has gone smoothly. No cancelled events, no catastrophes – except for the journalist from London, who seems to have gone sour on us after her aborted attempt to corner Jack about his relationship to his father. But even that turned out fine: she's just declined to print a review, which is more of a relief than anything – it definitely would've been coloured by her personal bias. The rest of his press has been excellent, and the TV director did reply to my email in the end and has booked Jack for a show in a few months' time, when he's back in the UK. We even had an email from the grumpy radio host in Berlin, thanking me for my performance with the interview. So far, so relatively good. *Touch wood.*

This evening, we're going to an event in one of the largest bookshops in the city, Hodges Figgis. It's half Irish launch, half celebration of Jack's best-selling status over here – he's been top of their bestseller list since publication. I am absolutely praying that I'm not going to encounter anyone like the charming men I met in London at Jack's launch. I'm not sure I could handle that – not on top of everything else. If someone says something dismissive to me this evening, after I've discovered

I have to share a room with Jack for four days, I'll probably cry.

As I get out of the shower, I realise I have made a fatal mistake – I've forgotten to bring a change of clothes with me. Jack is, quite possibly, about to see me in a towel. *Fuck.* I briefly consider just staying in here for the rest of the evening, but really there's nothing else for it. I open the door and emerge slowly, towel wrapped like a vice, intending to grab some clothes and return to the bathroom as quickly as possible, but to my surprise – and intense relief – I find the room empty.

Even still, I keep my towel firmly wrapped as I make my way over to the bed, unzip my suitcase and choose a simple skirt and blouse combination, rooting around for a pair of tights I haven't yet laddered on this trip.

I'm self-conscious as I change, worried that Jack might come back at any moment – I pull my clothes on quickly, keeping the door in my peripheral vision. When I'm dressed, and I've applied my lipstick, I sneak a glance at my personal phone. I've somehow had it on airplane mode since I got off the plane, so preoccupied by the hotel scenario that I didn't think to check it. A text welcoming me to Ireland and letting me know about phone rates greets me, along with something else – a missed call and a voicemail from my mum. Oh shoot – I had planned to call her back after the plane landed, but was so caught up in the hotel debacle that I forgot. I pause for a second, considering. Even though the message will be run-of-the-mill, probably, an extension of her earlier questions about the garden, this feels too personal to listen to in here, where Jack might walk in and find me. The thought makes me feel vulnerable. I check the time: I have about fifteen minutes until we need to leave for the event this evening, so I might as well head out early and find somewhere to sit outside before the car arrives.

I make my way down to reception and back through the vast wooden entrance. The air is still and cold, the silence broken up only by the sound of waves hitting the cliffs below. I walk around the edge of the stone walls until I find a bench which overlooks the ocean, then take a seat and pull out my phone, clicking the 'call voicemail' button.

I gaze out at the sea as I listen to the automated message – I've always found the ocean soothing, its vastness making everything seem smaller somehow. I click on the right number to listen to my mum's voice, and for a moment it blends with the sound of the waves, its tone as soft, as soothing.

'Andie, love!' her voice comes out of the phone. She asks me if I've landed in Ireland, if the flight was OK. I wait for the mention of Nigel and only flinch momentarily when it comes: she's spoken to him and he's delighted that I've given my blessing, apparently. They've done a lot of the planning already, but would love my input on a few things. The message is short – she gets cut off by something Nigel says in the background, then tells me she'll call me back. *They're really taking this garden stuff seriously*, I think – it's sweet, though, that they want me to be involved. I lock my phone and put it back in my pocket, making a plan to call my mum back in the morning – I don't want another short, abortive phone call. I want to talk to her properly. To give her a chance to tell me about this person in her life, without making an excuse to leave. After all, I've managed to hear about Nigel twice now without falling into a black hole of grief. Maybe I've been overthinking this – maybe I just needed a second to process things. The more I hear about him, the more I get used to the idea of my mum spending time with someone else. And I like the idea of our garden being full of flowers again. I lean back on the bench, closing my eyes and letting the rhythmic crashing of the waves wash over me. As I do, the muffled sounds of someone talking reach me – they must be on the other side of the wall.

'OK, sure,' the voice says. As my ears adjust, I pick up more of the sound and realise the voice is familiar: it's Jack.

'No, really, it's fine,' he says, moving into my peripheral vision. He's far enough that he probably won't notice me, but I can see him: he's pacing along the grass about a hundred metres away. His posture is tense, strained. Whoever is on the other side of the line has given him some bad news, clearly.

'Yep. See you then.' He finishes the call, his tone clipped, and throws his phone to the ground. *Wow, OK. That must have been some really bad news.* I watch as he takes a run-up towards the castle, kicking out at the wall with his right foot. The resulting collision looks incredibly painful, but he doesn't seem to notice.

I've never seen this side of Jack. At Edinburgh, he was always the peacemaker, the calm one. The other sports boys used to get in fights all the time, but never him. Jack broke up the fights, cool as a cucumber, then went back to standing on the sidelines with an easy smile on his face. He was never angry, or violent like the others. *And I know all too well how violent they could be*, I think, suddenly. My stomach twists, my mind flashing without warning to a much younger me standing outside the student union in Edinburgh, shock pulsing through me, my hand pressed to my face. But I don't want to think about that, not now. Not ever again. I pull my thoughts away and turn my gaze back to Jack.

He's moved away from the wall, now, and I watch as he sinks into a nearby bench and puts his head in his hands. The tension in his posture crumples – he looks defeated. The charming veneer is totally gone. This Jack is stripped back, vulnerable.

I go back and forth in my mind, unsure what to do. On the one hand, Jack is clearly upset and should probably be left alone. On the other, I'm not sure how I'm going to spend the whole evening pretending I haven't just seen him playing football with the battlements. In the end, just as I decide I should leave, it's too late: Jack turns to walk towards the car park and spots me. He stares at me for a moment, stunned, then walks slowly towards me.

'Hi,' I say, lamely, once he's in hearing distance. 'I promise I wasn't following you.'

To my surprise, he laughs. In a moment, all traces of his outburst have disappeared: normal, easy-going Jack has returned. He runs a hand through his hair.

'I take it you saw that?' His tone is playful, but there's an undercurrent I can't quite place.

I nod. 'I won't ask,' I say, trying for a smile which indicates I'm not concerned that he just drove his foot into a thousand-year-old stone wall.

His posture relaxes almost imperceptibly. 'I think I broke my toe,' he says, laughing again and indicating his right foot. 'It really fucking hurts.'

'Do you think it falls under my job description to take you to hospital?' I ask, only half joking. The next few days won't be much fun if he has to hobble around the city on a broken toe.

'I've seen worse,' he grimaces, shaking out his foot and putting his full weight on it. Pain briefly crosses his face, but only for a second. 'See? Good as new.'

'Jack—' I start, but he just balances on one leg and aims the full wattage of his charming smile at me. I give up and sit back, looking over the ocean. 'It's really beautiful here,' I say to no one in partic- ular, watching the waves crashing against the rocks below, the soft dusk light fading on the horizon. The vast space before me, the grass under my feet, the castle behind me – all seem to be of another time, another life. I feel a million miles away from New York.

'It is,' he says, and he walks over to the bench and sits down next to me. We watch the swell together for a few moments, a silence settling between us. I become increasingly aware of my proximity to Jack: if I moved a few inches to my right, our legs would touch. 'Thank you,' he says, his voice low. I look up at him, surprised.

'For what?' I ask.

'For not asking.'

I draw a breath and shift in my seat, a warmth moving up the back of my neck. I need to stifle this before it goes any further. 'You underestimate how little I care about your life, Jack,' I say, my tone carefully nonchalant.

In the brief silence that follows, I'm worried I've gone too far again. But he laughs, then stands up. 'Fair enough,' he says, smiling.

I check my watch. 'The car should be here by now,' I say. 'You can go ahead – I'll be there in two seconds.' He nods and starts walking towards the car park.

I gaze out at the sea for a moment longer, wrestling with the half-truth I just told him. It's true that it isn't my business how many walls he kicks. But watching him fall apart on that bench, part of me wanted to reach out, to ask what happened to make him so angry, to make the Jack Carlson persona fall away. I take a deep breath and stand up. *Keep your head in the game, Andie,* I think, as I turn my back on the sprawling coastline and head towards the car. *Just four more days.*

16

The ride in the taxi passes in mostly silence, save Jack pointing out the occasional landmark as we approach the centre of Dublin. I don't tell him it's unnecessary, that I've been here before, a lifetime ago, with my dad: that's not a conversation for this evening. We're dropped off outside a beautiful bookshop, with about five hundred copies of Jack's book making up a spectacular window display. I look over at him to see his reaction, but he seems distracted as we arrive, his mind on something; perhaps the news he received on the phone. His limp is almost imperceptible but I see the way he winces as he transfers weight onto his right foot. I've never understood men punching and kicking things when they're angry: I'd never have the force of will to risk hurting myself like that, however angry I was. Even the thought makes me feel ill.

The shop is full – the event is open ·to the public, so industry people are clustered in groups alongside locals, all holding glasses of warm wine. This is much more my speed than the event in London: friendly, not too official, and with the UK publishing staple of cheap, room temperature alcoholic beverages. I grab a glass of red for myself. Jack grabs a glass of white. For a moment, I hesitate, unsure what to do: there's a man here somewhere called Declan who we were supposed to be meeting at the door, but I can't really see anyone around who looks official. I'm about to pull out my phone and search my emails for further instructions when a joyful voice trills from behind me:

'There's the man of the hour!'

Whoever the voice belongs to claps Jack on the back so jovially that he chokes a little on his wine. We both turn to find a man who is about five feet tall, portly and exuding warmth. He looks delighted to see us, and I brighten as he reaches out his hand to shake mine.

'Declan Sweeney – a pleasure to meet you, miss.'

'Andie,' I say, returning his smile and his hand-shake. At this, if possible, he looks even more delighted.

'You're the famous Andie! Delighted, I'm sure. Thanks for all you've done.'

All I've done is sort out some stock issues with the Irish sales team to ensure there were enough books this evening, and — my main job — getting Jack here on time and in one piece (mostly successful, apart from his almost-broken toe). So in the grand scheme of things, not much. But this is worlds away from the audience I received in London, so I find myself basking in his gratitude. I look up at Jack to see him looking at Declan with an almost familial gaze. He mentions the window display, which results in an effusive spiel about how much this particular book means to the Irish community, and how delighted they are to be publishing it. Jack seems more himself here than I've seen him in a while — he's relaxed, blushing at Declan's praise rather than brushing it off. Declan then takes us over to what he calls his 'secret' fridge in the back of the shop, stocked with a small amount of chilled wine and beer — 'only for the VIPs,' he says — secures us each a cold drink, then asks if he can steal Jack from me for a moment to introduce him round. I nod my assent, and watch as Declan steers Jack towards an excitable group of people on the other side of the room, who look to be the rest of his Irish publishing team. There's a woman at the centre of it who I recognise — she's beautiful, with strawberry blonde hair, and she greets Jack with the familiarity of an old friend. It takes me a moment, but eventually I place her as another successful author: Aoife Smith.

I watch as she touches Jack's arm and throws her head back to laugh at something he's said. Something stirs inside me. Wasn't her last book a bit crap? I'm sure I read that somewhere. In fact, I remember the review: it described her writing as dull and dreary.

But this is none of my business: just a beautiful, successful author flirting with another beautiful, successful author. I mean, a reasonably and objectively good looking successful author. *Ugh.* I tear my gaze from them and scan the room for anyone I've met before, eventually finding a few people from Jack's literary agency who I've seen on Zoom calls before. I head over and introduce myself to them, and pass the next hour in small talk. I'm convinced I've put Aoife to the back of my mind but then the person I'm talking to says 'Keeping an eye on your charge, are you?' and I snap to attention. *Fuck.* I must have been glancing over there without realising. I nod, and take a swig of my wine. The woman who spoke raises her eyebrows. 'Looks like they're having a nice time …'

I follow her gaze and see Aoife whisper something in Jack's ear. He laughs, and for a moment I'm transported back to that bar in Edinburgh, my face close to his like that, him asking if I wanted to go somewhere more private. *Oh God.* Unsafe thoughts, unsafe thoughts. I down the rest of my wine and sneak one more glance in Jack's direction. He's looking right at me. The wine I've just gulped sticks in my throat and I have perhaps the most embarrassing coughing fit ever, resulting in my white blouse being thoroughly stained by red wine. When I look back up, Jack has disappeared. I'm thanking God that he didn't see and wondering where I might find a new blouse at this time of night when he reappears next to me.

'Nice shirt,' he says, a knowing smirk on his face. So he did see. Brilliant.

I smile sweetly back at him, aware that we are surrounded by industry professionals and he is my author, and whisper, 'Bite me.'

He throws up his hands in mock-surrender and says, 'I only came over because I can solve this problem, if you like. But if you don't want my help …' He turns to walk away.

'Jack,' I hiss, and he turns back around. 'What kind of help?'

'Follow me,' he says ominously, and I follow him across the room to the coat rack, where he retrieves his rucksack, then to the back room with Declan's secret fridge. He rummages around for a moment, then pulls out a patterned button up shirt. I frown at him, confused, and he looks at me for a moment as if assessing something.

'You must take this to your grave,' he says, throwing the shirt at me.

'Take what to my grave?' I ask, eyeing up the shirt. It's cool, and not too large – I can make it work. It's certainly better than my current situation.

'I get nervous at events, sometimes, especially big ones like this.' He gestures to his armpits, covered at present by a blazer. 'And I sweat. A lot, actually. I once sweated through my shirt, and it was mortifying. I didn't have a jacket to cover it. Ever since that happened I always bring a spare.'

I'm not sure how to react to this – I'm halfway between endeared to him and disgusted by this information. 'I'd never have guessed you get nervous,' I say, checking the door is firmly locked and gesturing at him to turn around. 'You always seem so confident.'

'It's all a front,' he says, turning to face the wall.

'Interesting,' I say, distracted, fumbling with the buttons of his shirt as I pull it on. 'I've never understood why buttons are the other way around for men. Are you all left-handed, or something?'

'Throw it here,' Jack says, after a few moments of listening to me struggle. 'They're surprisingly stiff on that shirt. I'll do some of them up for you.'

I pull off the shirt and throw it across the room, keen to get this over with so we can get back to the party. It lands half way between us. *Fuck.* 'Have you thrown it yet?' he says, as I lunge for my blouse so I can cover myself while I retrieve it and throw it the rest of the way.

'I didn't throw it far enough,' I say, grappling with my blouse, 'give me a—'

But he's already, reflexively, turned round to look for it. Our eyes meet, and for a fraction of a second it's as if we've rewound five years and we're back in his dorm room, our clothes scattered across the floor between us. But then he looks down, grabs the shirt and mumbles 'Sorry', before quickly turning back to the wall. I catch my breath as he buttons up the shirt, and by the time he throws it back to me I've come to my senses.

'Aoife seems to like you,' I say, keen to divert the subject literally anywhere else, but also – despite myself – driven by curiosity about what exactly is going on between them.

He laughs. 'Ah, yes. Aoife. She's good fun.'

My cheeks burn. If he picked up on the loaded nature of my comment, which he must have, he hasn't denied that anything is going on. In fact, I think 'good fun' is pretty well known slang for 'we've fucked.' I have a sudden, inexplicable urge to peel off my own skin.

'It's a shame you won't have a hotel room to bring her back to, then,' I say, and immediately regret it: the silence which follows is heavy and awkward.

'Is that what it looks like to you?' he says. His tone is odd, his voice quiet.

I can't help myself. 'Can you blame me?' I say, some of my Edinburgh pain seeping out without warning. He mutters something under his breath which sounds like a swear word, and I want to ask what he said, but I don't. Instead, I watch as he slowly turns around and looks at the shirt I've now successfully pulled over my head.

'Looks good on you,' he says, his expression carefully controlled. A thousand things come into my mind that I could say in this moment, but I push them all away. 'Shall we go back out?' he says, and I keep my eyes averted from his and say 'Sure', then follow him through the door and watch him return to Aoife.

I sigh and go to turn away, to find the people I was with earlier. But something stops me and I watch them for a moment more. Jack's posture is different this time – more closed. He's put a little more distance between them. When she puts her hand on his arm, he shifts to point something out on the wall, so her touch falls away. The signs are subtle, but they're all there: clearly my words have affected him. As I'm watching, Jack's gaze flickers around the room and suddenly lands on me. *Fuck.* That's the second time he's caught me being a creep this evening. *What is wrong with me?* I feel a blush cross my cheeks, give him a tight-lipped smile and turn away, crossing the room in search of another drink. This evening is already really, really out of hand: I've exposed myself to Jack, insulted him and voluntarily alluded to the fact that we've slept together. I might as well lean in while I'm here.

Happily, after a few moments of wandering I bump into Declan, who pours me a glass of his 'special wine' – an expensive red, which he keeps hidden with the rest of the nicer drinks. Just as delightful as he was when I met him earlier, he asks me about my career and listens with interest. At the end of my description of the last five years – moving to New York, working my way up from intern to here – he kindly says that if I ever want a job in Ireland I should get in touch. After this evening, I'm not sure *I* would hire me as a publicist, but nevertheless a few glasses later, we are getting along like a house on fire. So well, in fact, that I haven't noticed that most of the shop has emptied while we've been talking. Jack's soft tap on my shoulder alerts me to the party drawing to a close. He tells me the car has arrived on schedule with minimal eye contact, then heads off to wait for me by the door. Three weeks ago this was my goal – to annoy him enough that he would leave me alone – but this evening I don't feel good about it.

I say my goodbyes to Declan, grab my coat and the wine-splattered blouse I've balled up inside it, and head over to the door, which Jack wordlessly holds open for me. Guilt curdles in my stomach. I could apologise, but that would involve revisiting what I said, and I'm not sure either of us wants that. So instead, I get silently into the car, praying that the journey back to the hotel will go by quickly so I can get into bed and sleep off this whole evening.

He spends the first ten minutes of the car ride with his back to me, looking out of the window. The wine is swirling in my brain and my eyes feel heavy. I lean back in my seat and let them flutter shut. For a few moments, I let myself drift off – then, suddenly, the car pitches with a horrible scraping sound, and we grind to a halt. My stomach drops. That didn't sound good, and we're still a few miles from the hotel. Jack looks at me, concerned, apparently now acknowledging my existence. My breath catches for a second and I'm flooded with strange relief at his gaze. Then the driver swears and gets out of the car to assess the damage, breaking me out of it. I push open the car door and stumble onto the road in my heels.

It's bad. I don't know much about cars, but I know that having most of your back wheel jammed in a pothole, the tire creased and coming away from the wheel, means you're probably not going anywhere anytime soon. I pull out my phone, ready to call a taxi, or for roadside assistance, and the dreaded 'No Signal' appears in the top corner. I look across at Jack – he's frowning at his phone, too.

'Any luck?' he says, breaking the silence that has stretched between us since we left the party, and I shake my head. He goes to talk to the driver, who appears to be having the same issue. Brilliant. We are in the opening of a *Criminal Minds* episode, about to be horrifically murdered.

I take a few deep breaths and force myself to think straight, cursing myself for tempting fate in the shower earlier by celebrating the lack of catastrophes so far. 'That village we passed a few minutes ago,' I say, eventually, the image of a few lit-up houses coming to mind. 'It's probably only a short walk. Let's go there and find a landline.'

It's as good a plan as I can think of in these circumstances, except for the fact that I'm wearing heels, but that can't be helped. Jack and our driver, Jonathon, take the lead down the deserted country track. They remain a few paces ahead of me, making small talk, Jack back to carefully ignoring me as I drag my feet through the gravel. We walk for what feels like five hours, but is probably about twenty minutes, until we reach a small, quaint village.

In the darkness, the warm lights from peoples' windows are a welcome sign of civilisation. I look around briefly and spot a pub a few hundred metres away with a few people clustered outside it. Jack has spotted the same thing – I follow him towards it, crossing the village green, trying not to lose my shoes in the grass.

Inside, the pub is warm and lively, with oak-panelled walls and exposed stone, and a beaten-up piano in the corner. Most of the village appear to be here this evening, watching recaps of the rugby matches from today. The mood is jolly: it seems Ireland had a successful day. I make for the bar, passing a few men wearing Ireland scarves and swaying on their feet, and find a bartender with unruly red hair and an open, kind face who looks to be in her mid-fifties.

'What can I do for you, love?' she says, with a warm smile. I take a breath and explain our car situation, asking to use her phone.

'Of course you can, dear,' she says, gesturing to a landline at the end of the bar. I move towards it, then realise I don't know who I'm supposed to be calling. A taxi first, probably. Then some kind of vehicle recovery service. I glance back at Jack, hovering by the door, and quickly turn away.

'Do you have the number for a local taxi company or mechanic?' I ask, and she laughs.

'Well,' she says, pointing across the room at an extremely drunk man sitting in the corner, nursing two pints at once. 'There's Dave, your local taxi man.' As I'm watching, Dave attempts to stand up, loses balance, and thumps back into his chair. *Excellent.* 'And our mechanic Simon is in the Seychelles, if you can believe. Lucky bastard.' *Even more excellent.*

'What about Uber?' I ask, desperately. 'Do you have WiFi I can use?'

The look she gives me is one of gentle pity.

'You'd be hard pushed to find an Uber this far out of Dublin, love. And I'm afraid our WiFi's been down since Tuesday. Bad signal round these parts.'

Fuck. I thank her and start to turn away, thinking about what I'm going to say to Jack and Jonathon. Perhaps I'll convince them to resort to plan B – banging on peoples' doors and begging them to drive us back to the hotel. But just as I'm about to leave, she calls from behind me: 'Tell you what – my son is Simon's apprentice. He's got some tools in his truck. I'll have him take a look at the car, and if he can't fix it he can give you a lift to Malahay.'

I glance at Jack again, who's shifting his weight off his injured foot. I would rather not sit with him in a pub, alone, at this point of the evening, but unless

I want to offer my own services as a mechanic it looks like this might be our only option.

'Thank you, that would be great,' I say, careful to sound as grateful and cheery as possible. She ventures briefly upstairs and returns with a boy in his late teens who looks like he hasn't left his room in a few weeks. Jack makes his way over to the bar to find out what's happening – I fill him in, and we watch the bartender's son introduce himself to Jack's driver. The two disappear through the door into the darkness outside, and I don't envy them. Or perhaps I do. Because Jack is currently standing next to me, avoiding eye contact, and it's clear that neither of us want to speak first.

'Drink?' he says, finally, still not looking at me. There's a weird charge between us, like in the bookshop in Paris, but far less comfortable. I nod. He orders – a pint for himself and a glass of red wine for me – and we find a corner of the pub which is quiet enough and far enough from the television that we're not at risk of being accosted by any drunk locals.

We sit down opposite each other, our knees almost touching under the cramped table.

'So,' I try, searching for safe ground. 'That was a nice event.'

'It was,' he agrees. He's still closed off, his tone carefully neutral. It's jarring – even when I've really attacked him, his easy charm has never failed. Sitting opposite me now, his manner is almost cold. I shift in my seat and silence settles between us again.

'Declan seems lovely,' I try, after a few moments, and this gets a warmer response – Jack perks up at the mention of him, and his expression thaws slightly.

'He is. I love working with him.' He takes a sip of his pint, and as he leans back in his seat, regarding me, I imagine him weighing up his options – sitting opposite me in silence, perhaps all night, or at least humouring my attempt at conversation. 'He's actually the reason I set the book in Ireland,' he says, finally.

'Really?' I lean forward, grateful he seems to have chosen the latter.

He nods. 'He's been my publisher in Ireland for years. When I told him I was thinking of writing a novel, he suggested I set it here. My grand-father was Irish, and I still have family here, so he convinced me to lean into those roots. I felt like a bit of a fraud at first, being only about a quarter Irish, but the way the market here has embraced it has been amazing.'

'That window display was very cool,' I say, an image of hundreds of Jack's books piled up flashing into my mind. I wonder what it must feel like, to witness so many copies of something you've poured yourself into, piled up for the world to see. 'Clearly, they love your book.'

'Have you read it?' he asks. The question catches me off guard.

'I have,' I say. 'Part of the job.'

'Did you like it?'

'Classified,' I say.

'Come on, Andie. Give me something, at least.'

I shake my head slowly and sip my wine, hoping he'll drop the subject. But I can see by his facial expression that dropping it is the last thing on his mind.

'Another drink?' I ask, getting up and gesturing towards the bar.

'Sure. A beer, please.' I breathe out, relieved that my ploy has worked.

But as I turn my back on him, he says, just loud enough for me to hear, 'I'm not going to drop this, you know.' *Fuck.*

I make my way through the crowds of locals to the bar and order another round of drinks, searching for ideas to put Jack off this subject. I'm racking my brain for a solution when I see a sign advertising two shots for £5. It's not the most professional of moves, but this hasn't been the most professional of evenings. This may well distract him enough to drop the subject. I lean over the bar and order two shots along with our round.

Jack's eyebrows nearly hit his hairline when I return to the table and place the shot in front of him.

'To toast your Irish success!' I say, smiling cheerily and holding up my shot glass, indicating for him to do the same. He doesn't move. My hand hovers in mid-air, lamely.

'I have a better idea,' he says, leaning forwards. I stop smiling and put my shot glass back on the table. Whatever this is, I'm already sure I'm not going to like it. 'I was thinking,' he continues, 'that it's not fair for me to press you on this subject.'

Well, thank God for that. I sit back in my seat, relieved, and go to take a sip of my wine. But he's not done.

'Not without a quid pro quo.'

'Jack, what are you on about?' I ask, wine poised halfway to my mouth.

'I suggest a trade,' he says, gesturing to the shot glasses. 'One shot, one question you think the other person won't want to answer.'

I exhale sharply. 'That sounds incredibly stupid.' And reckless. And dangerous. But as I open my mouth again to tell him 'No', Aoife pops into my mind. The back of my neck burns.

He shrugs. 'Your alternative is to for me to pester you about my book until they come back from fixing the car.'

I sip my wine slowly, meeting his gaze, deliberating. There's no question it would be an interminably stupid move to take Jack up on this offer. And yet...

'Could be hours,' he adds, checking his watch for added effect. 'I don't tire easily.'

'OK, fine,' I say, finally, blocking out the rational half of my brain and lifting the shot glass again before I can regret my decision. He smiles, content with his victory, and lifts his. We knock them back at the same time. The alcohol burns the back of my throat, but I hold my smile as if I've just taken a sip of water.

'Right,' he says, leaning forwards with interest. 'Did you like my book?'

'Yes,' I reply, ignoring the shiver that moves through me as I do. I feel surprisingly vulnerable, admitting this to him.

'Which parts in particular?' he asks, leaning in.

'Whoops,' I say. 'One question only.'

He smiles. 'Touché.'

'My turn,' I say, and I blurt the question before I can stop myself. 'What did you mean, when you said Aoife was "good fun"?'

He blanches, and I can see from the look on his face that, of all the questions I could have asked, he didn't expect that one. 'Uh,' he says, rubbing the back of his head, 'nothing, really. We've had a few drinks, after events. She can put away pints like you wouldn't believe.' He looks at his own pint, his expression clouding slightly. 'She – she has approached me, before. But that's not – I wasn't interested.' He looks more flustered than he should, and I'm not sure why. I'm even less sure why I'm relieved by his answer.

'Another round?' I ask, to hide my own embarrassment. He nods, and I head to the bar and return a few minutes later with two more shots. He grabs his shot. I lift mine, and we drink them together again. This time, my throat is a little more numb than the last. I pick up my wine glass and prepare myself for the inevitable question of which sections of his book I enjoyed the most.

'Why do you care what I think of Aoife?' he says, with the shaky bravado of someone who has just spent the last five minutes building themselves up to the question. I almost drop my wine. *Jesus*. I steady the glass and take a sip, delaying.

'I don't know,' I say, finally, my ears burning, staring at a scratch on the table. He regards me for a moment in silence. After a few painful seconds he seems to accept that I'm telling the truth and gestures to me. It's my turn. *Well. Two can play at this game, Carlson.*

'Why do you care what I think of your book?'

He purses his lips, caught. I lean back in satisfaction and sip my wine. Jack seems to be wrestling with himself. I watch for a few moments, undeterred, until eventually he answers, his voice quiet. 'I don't know.'

We sit for a few moments, the silence between us growing gradually less comfortable. This might be considered a stalemate, and it's painfully awkward. I pick up the coaster in front of me and spin it on its edge.

'It was my dad I was talking to, earlier, at the hotel,' Jack says quietly, breaking the silence, his eyes fixed on his pint. I look up, surprised, my gaze flicking to his injured foot. The coaster I've been twirling drops onto the table.

'It was stupid,' he continues, still not looking at me. 'A dinner we'd arranged, for when I'm back in New York, that he was cancelling. It shouldn't make me so angry, because it happens all the time, but for some reason it still does.'

A memory flashes into my mind, now – Jack, in The Lost Bookshop in New York, telling me he used to spend hours there when he was visiting his dad. How old was he at the time? How long did his dad leave him in the bookstore, alone? I refocus on Jack, before my own dad – warm and ever-present and forever gone – intrudes on this chain of thought.

'Remember how I told you my career so far has been an attempt to get his attention? Well, here's the most pathetic part: he has never read a single one of my books,' he continues, as if he's talking to himself, sipping his beer and swallowing with vigour. 'Not even when I've sent him copies. It's why I got so flustered when the journalist asked about it. It's not because of nepotism that he doesn't review them. It's because he doesn't care.'

This admission hits me somewhere deep, filling me with inexplicable sadness. 'Jack, I'm so sorry—' I start, but he cuts me off.

'It's OK. Really. He would just find things wrong with them, anyway.' His tone is carefully flippant, but I can see the muscles in his hand move as he clenches his glass. 'Anyway, after my third book went ignored by him, I made the decision not to care what anyone thought about my books but myself,' he says, folding his coaster in half, forcing a crease across the centre as if channelling his frustration into the inflexible cardboard. 'It's been a good policy so far,' he says. Then he looks up, meeting my gaze, and something in his eyes makes my breath catch in my throat. 'But for some reason, it doesn't apply to you.'

Our eyes lock, and we sit for a second, unmoving, as if we're fixed in place. Where the silence between us was awkward before, now it's tense, taut – a string pulled across the table that could snap at any moment. Just as the cogs in my brain start turning, to work out what I'm supposed to say next, a raucous sound reaches us from the other side of the bar.

My head turns automatically towards it, breaking our eye contact and the strange charge between us. I can't see what's happening from here, but as my ears gradually adjust I realise it's music: someone is playing the beaten up piano, and everyone else in the pub, if the deafening noise is anything to go by, is singing along. Jack catches my eye and inclines his head towards the noise in silent question, raising his eyebrows. I hesitate for a moment, then nod and stand up.

We make our way through the crowds of locals and reach the musician – a tall, thin man with a shock of black hair. He is poised, fingers over the keys, a silence descending on the pub around us. The crowd waits in anticipation, a thrill passing through them. As the music starts up again, the room comes alive: everyone clapping, singing, stamping their feet. Jack and I join them, the strange air between us caught up in the crowd, the noise, the music. We're jostled into each other a few times, and I pull away quickly, careful not to have contact with him for too long.

As the pianist launches into another song, a feeling slowly creeps over me, dulling out the events of the last few hours, the last few weeks. I find my thoughts growing quieter, my focus pulling towards my surroundings: the music, the people, the solid oak floor under my feet. Then Jack is there, and he's looking at me, and for a second – just a second – the room seems to slow down. He reaches up, gently, to move a piece of hair from my face, and my body comes alive with feeling.

'Andie,' he says, and for a moment everything falls away, like it did in the car earlier. Like we've just met, and we're strangers in a bar, and I could reach across and kiss him if I wanted to. I am intensely aware of our proximity – all it would take is one step forwards to close the distance between us. The look in his eyes from the plane, from the party earlier, flashes through my mind, sending a shock across my skin. And I consider it – closing the distance. Allowing myself to stay here, for just a moment longer, in a place where there's no pain between us. Following the desire that's burning through me the longer he looks at me. But then there's a sound behind us – the door to the pub opening, a rush of cold air hitting the back of my neck. I turn to see Jonathon standing in the doorway.

His arrival and the cold air brings me to my senses, knocking me back into the present. The landlady's son crosses the room to his mum, now standing near me in the crowd, and tells her he fixed the car. Turns out it just needed the tyre changing, and he had a spare one in his truck. Jonathon waits by the door, gesturing for us to follow him. I look up at Jack, his eyes still locked on me, and the noise around me is suddenly far too loud, the pub far too crowded.

'Thank you so much for your help,' I say, to the woman and her son. Then I turn to Jack, avoiding eye contact. 'Let's go,' I say, and I walk towards the door without looking back.

Once we're in the car, an unbearable silence falls between us. For the first few minutes of the journey, I keep my gaze fixed on the road, determined not to break it. Though I can see Jack in my peripheral, fidgeting, his posture tense, I refuse to look at him. I just need to get back to the hotel and find somewhere to clear my head – the bar, perhaps. I'll sleep there, if it means I can get away from Jack for a while.

'Andie—' he starts after a few seconds, and I'm about to interrupt him, but he cuts himself off before I can, seemingly out of words.

'Please, Jack,' I say gently, taking the opportunity to shut this down before it starts. 'I'm tired. I just want to get back to the hotel,' I say, without looking at him. He doesn't speak again, but I can hear his breath, feel his agitation as he clenches and unclenches his hands in his lap. I focus on my own breath, deploying the same gentle yoga technique my dad taught me. I can feel my heartbeat in my throat, but it works, keeping my mind firmly blank until mercifully the car slows, pulling into the gravel driveway of our hotel. I wrench the door open almost before it has stopped moving.

'I'm going to the bar,' I say quickly, turning back to the car, still avoiding his gaze. 'Don't wait up.'

He nods, and I think I catch a flash of frustration pass across his face. But then it's gone, and I shut the car door and practically sprint into the hotel.

17

I wake up the following morning and sit bolt upright in bed, listening for signs of Jack. But the hotel room is empty. I breathe a deep sigh of relief, glad that I can defer seeing him for a bit longer. It was difficult enough to avoid him last night, without having to repeat the experience this morning. I ended up staying in the bar until 1 a.m. to be sure he was asleep when I returned to the room. I'm completely exhausted.

I roll over, pick my phone up off the bedside table and see about fifteen notifications lighting up the screen: all from my mum. I sit upright, my chest constricting, braced despite my more rational instincts for some horrible news – she's in hospital, she's had an accident, something is terribly wrong. Since my dad's death, something as small as a few missed calls in a row can set off this dread – bone-deep and always only a moment away – that I'll lose her, too.

There are three missed calls and, after them, some texts, small excerpts appearing as notifications on my home screen. As I start to digest their tone, my heartbeat slows slightly. 'So sorry, love – I realise I forgot to ask you about the date,'; 'Hope it's OK with you'; 'The e-vite had to go out today – can you get time off?'. An e-vite? Strange. But relief starts to move through me, even as my confusion deepens. At least she's OK. It strikes me momentarily that maybe I misunderstood her earlier calls – perhaps she and Nigel are throwing a summer garden party?

But then I tap into my inbox and find the email, and suddenly it all falls into place – I have misunderstood my mum's calls, much more seriously than I thought. *Oh God.* A very different kind of dread twists in my gut. The subject line stares me in the face, the bold text startling: 'Join us to celebrate our union.' I scroll through the body – a date, a time, a location. And at the bottom: Nigel and Deborah.

Suddenly, the events of last night seem trivial, a million miles away. I thought I'd have time – to meet Nigel properly. To have a relationship with him, perhaps. To become the supportive daughter my mum deserves. But this: a wedding, a new life. Not just someone she's spending time with, but someone who is going to be around forever. It's so sudden, so permanent, and it's caught me completely off guard. The broken part of me that surfaced on the Heath, that I've being doing my best to repress ever since, breaks free in this second of all restraints, overwhelming everything else with a thought that sends dread rippling through me: my mum will no longer be married to my dad. I will still be his daughter, but she will no longer be his wife. The last solid ground I had been standing on – that even despite Nigel's presence, we were somehow still tied to my dad, still a family – has been suddenly ripped out from under me. My dad, my wonderful dad – his face comes into my mind now, sending hot tears trickling down my face, a force squeezing my throat until it feels like I can't breathe. I'd been holding that space for him, still – and I realise now that some small part of me had naively assumed that my mum would always do the same.

I sit for a few moments in silence, staring at my phone, trying desperately to slow my breathing, to suppress deep, raw ache that's pulsing in my chest. *I miss you*, I think. *I love you*. And then: *I'm sorry*. But I can't dwell on this further. It will tear me apart.

I take a deep breath and force myself to look up, at my surroundings, away from the news that's suddenly tilted my world on its axis. My gaze passes across the room: the light coming through the curtains, Jack's bed, the sheets still strewn across it. It lands on my suitcase, tucked in the corner by the door, my clothes for today carefully folded inside it. As I focus in on the gentle floral pattern of my shirt, the corduroy skirt I picked out with Sara just before the trip, the ache in my chest dulls slightly, the panic growing less immediate. The outfit is something solid, a tether. The day stretches before me, suddenly comforting in its scheduled certainty: there is still this trip, still Jack, whatever might or might not have happened between us last night. For now, I can be professional Andie. I will get up and I will take Jack to his panel this morning. And I will deal with this later.

When I arrive at breakfast, Jack is sitting at a table in the corner, reading a book. I swallow, my throat suddenly dry, and make my way across the room. I say a silent prayer that he will make this easy for me, that he will pretend nothing happened between us last night and we can just get on with the day as planned – I'm not sure I can deal with much more turbulence today. I reach his table and he looks up from his book. For a second, his expression is so open that it startles me. But then he puts the book down, and gestures for me to sit, and his usual charming and ever-so-slightly distant demeanour returns.

'So,' he begins, taking a breath. I brace myself, but he just picks up the cafetière in front of him and looks at me questioningly. 'Coffee?'

I nod and he pours a cup, slowly, then passes it across the table. I thank him, and take a sip. It's lukewarm, bitter on my tongue. There is a short pause.

'Look, Andie—'

'Jack—'

We speak at the same time, our words tumbling over each other and dissipating into an awkward silence. He ventures into it first.

'I think we need to talk about last night,' he says, his voice mostly smooth but with a nervous undertone. I flinch internally. *Fuck.* I stall, avoiding his gaze, and retrieve the milk from the other side of the table, slowly stirring some into my cup. He watches, undeterred, waiting for my response.

'I'm not sure there's anything to talk about,' I say, finally. I catch a flash of hurt in his eyes, but it disappears almost immediately, giving way – to my surprise – to frustration.

'Come on, Andie. You know that's bullshit.'

I'm momentarily silenced by this – it's the sharpest tone he's used since, well, since I've known him.

'Please,' I say once I've recovered myself, some of my emotional exhaustion seeping into my tone. 'I just – I had some … some news, this morning.'

He takes in my tone, my expression, the tears threatening to pool in my eyes.

'What news?' he asks, softening slightly. 'Is everything OK?'

I shake my head. 'Fine,' I say. 'I just – I don't want to talk about last night. I want us to get on with things, like normal.'

'I don't think there's such thing as "normal" with us,' he says. He lets go of the spoon he's been using to stir his tea and sighs, exasperated. 'Aren't you tired of pretending everything is fine all the time?'

'It's better this way—' I start, but he interrupts me.

'Please don't give me that, Andie. It's not. You know it isn't. I've done everything I can to respect your terms, to make this trip OK for you. But—' he hesitates, then breathes out, slumping backwards into his chair '— I felt something last night, and I think you did, too.'

I'd known it wouldn't be easy, but I hadn't expected this. I lean forward and press my palms into my face, shutting out this room, this conversation, everything. Frustration builds inside me, then melts suddenly into a deep overwhelming exhaustion. And then, without realising it, I'm crying – everything bubbling up and coming to the surface at once, releasing in great sobs that rattle through my whole body. I had it in me to hold it together this morning, to keep pretending everything was fine – with Jack, with my mum. But Jack has pulled down those defences, and I don't have the energy to put them back up. Maybe he's right. Maybe I've had enough of pretending. I can't deny that in this moment it feels good, to let some of this out.

I hear movement across the table – a chair being pulled across the carpet, and then he's there, sitting next to me. After a few seconds, his palm settles gently and tentatively on my arm, as if he's ready for me to flinch away. I don't, and it rests there, its warmth seeping into my skin, until I've cried myself out. As the overwhelm begins to fade, replaced with a tentative calm, I remove my hands from my face, turning to him. And for a moment, he's looking right at me – Andie with her defences down, vulnerable Andie, who I never let anyone but Sara see. I hold his gaze for a moment but it suddenly feels overwhelming, being so vulnerable in front of him. I look away, reaching across the table for a napkin to wipe my face with.

'I'm sorry,' I say, shame flooding through me. He shakes his head.

'*I'm* sorry, Andie,' he says. 'You said you'd had bad news. I shouldn't have pushed you. I just – I just wanted us to be honest with each other for once.'

I close my eyes, the email from my mum flashing into my mind, again. Perhaps I can be honest about something, at least.

'My mum's getting married,' I say, the lump in my throat suddenly reappearing.

His brow furrows, confusion spreading across his face. 'Isn't that good news?' he asks, and my heart drops.

I shake my head, and swallow, the lump huge now. 'My dad—' I take a breath, my chest tight. '— he died, five years ago. The news – it's brought up some, um,' the tears start flowing again, and I wipe them away, sniffing, 'some feelings.' I laugh then, self-deprecating, because 'feelings' seems like an understatement.

Jack doesn't laugh, his expression fixed – I can see him doing the mental maths and my stomach drops at the memory. Five years ago, Jack broke my trust and set off a chain of events that completely unbalanced the world I'd built for myself at university. Then my dad passed away two months later, after a short and brutal battle with cancer, and what was left of my world was wiped out by a nuclear explosion. After everything that happened with Jack, I barely had time to collect myself before I got that awful phone call from my mum, and then I moved back home, my days spent in and out of hospital, my thoughts on nothing but spending all the time he had left at his side. I was like a zombie. *You still are*, a voice says, and I flinch internally, but I know on some level it's true. I put all my feelings in a box far at the back of my mind, determined not to show my dad anything other than my smiling face when I visited him, determined that the last memories I had of him, that he had of me, would be happy ones. I never really figured out how to reopen that box without causing destruction, and now it's too late. Sara was right. I have been running away. But I don't know how to stop.

Jack breathes out slowly. 'Oh, Andie, I'm so sorry,' he says, and I know that sorry contains more than an apology for my loss. I flinch at the reminder – that's the last thing I need to be thinking about right now – but whether it's because I'm vulnerable right now, or because he's caught me off guard, the apology unexpectedly reaches some small, hurt part inside me, soothing me momentarily. We are silent for a few moments.

'So, today,' he says, clearing his throat. I breathe out, relieved that he's changed the subject, but also strangely disappointed. 'If you don't want to do the event, that's fine – I can go ahead and tell them you're sick.'

But I shake my head – I don't want to go back up to my hotel room, to desperately read and re-read my mum's email and spiral further into a hole I might not emerge from. I need distraction. And though just two hours ago Jack was the last person I wanted to see, I now find myself strangely calm in his presence, my brain mercifully quiet. It's paradoxical, that the one person capable of disturbing my mental peace more than anyone else also seems to be capable of restoring it. The thought arrives unexpectedly, but I reflect on it for a moment and realise it's true. It was true in London, where my anger at him was a rope out of the ocean, pulling me away from thoughts of my dad. Or Berlin, where him just buying me a sandwich for the plane helped lift me out of the devastation I felt after leaving my mum on the Heath. Paris and the unexpected evening we spent together. At every turn, whenever the past has begun to drag me into its depths, Jack has arrived just when I've needed him. I'm not sure what to make of this sudden and startling epiphany, so I put it momentarily out of my mind.

'I'll be fine,' I say, reaching for a napkin and using it to blow my nose.

He looks at his watch and makes a face. 'Well, then we'd better go. We're already cutting it fine.'

I follow him out to the car, rooting around in my handbag for a make-up wipe to clean myself up. I don't find one, so I end up using the non-snot-covered side of the napkin in my hand to wipe mascara off my face while Jonathon drives us into Dublin. By the time we arrive at the event I'm almost looking presentable.

I've been so wrapped up in the events of this morning that I've completely forgotten this event's location, so I'm pleasantly surprised when we pull up at Trinity College. The campus is gorgeous: all sandstone and symmetrical architecture, grass and trees, with a beautiful bell tower at its centre. The surroundings calm me, comforting in their beauty, their suggestion of my own impermanence.

Jack and I arrive a few minutes before the event is due to start, to the immense relief of the academic in a scuffed tweed jacket who greets us. As he rushes us through imposing corridors, his steps soft on the old stone floors, he tells us that he's had quite a few last-minute cancellations to this literature festival, resulting in university staff having to fill in for bestselling authors. We're told this all came much to the dismay of the event attendees of the day before, who had arrived expecting to hear about the process of writing a crime novel and instead ended up receiving a lecture on the ethics of murder from a moral philosophy professor. I introduce myself and apologise for the delay, which he waves off as he leads me to a seat to the right of the stage. Jack takes his place at the main table, and it's a moment before I realise that the person he's sitting next to is Aoife, the beautiful author from last night. My throat dries up as I remember: the wine, the shots, my ill-advised blurted question. That for a moment, before Jonathon arrived and brought me to my senses, all I had wanted to do was press Jack against the wall of that pub and – but I can't think about that right now.

I sit for a few moments, trying to restore my mental balance, but thoughts of Jack and the events of last night keep rushing through my mind, confusing me beyond belief. My emotions towards him are changeable by the minute: I find myself seeking him out, even as I want to pull away. I don't trust him at all, but he's the only person I want to be around. It's a tangle, a mess. One I can't figure out.

I miss the next few panel questions and resurface when the chair is in the middle of asking Jack a question about how he stays grounded and creatively focused.

'I have a policy – while I'm writing, I try not to care what anyone thinks about my book except myself.' I inhale sharply. 'And my editor, obviously,' he adds, to laughter from the audience. My heart is hammering against my chest as he delivers the next line, almost as if speaking to himself. 'But the policy isn't foolproof.'

His eyes find mine, and for a moment all I hear is my pulse pounding in my ears. Then the panel chair moves on to Aoife and Jack looks away, politely turning to listen to her answer.

'Andie?' Jack says after the panel ends, waving a hand in front of my face – by his expression I deduce he's been standing next to my chair for a moment, and this probably isn't the first time he's called my name.

I blink. 'Yes?' I say, coming back to the present.

'Fancy a walk? I'd like some fresh air,' he asks.

Before I can overthink it, I nod. 'I know just the place.'

Phoenix Park is busy enough for a Thursday afternoon in summer, but still sprawling and beautiful. The air is peaceful, still – a haven in the city, only broken by the occasional sound of a child laughing or a dog barking in the distance. People say about this park that it's where Dublin goes to breathe. I can see what they mean.

'This place is beautiful,' he says, breaking the silence.

I nod. 'It's my favourite spot in Dublin,' I say. And then, without really thinking, 'I came here with my dad, once.'

The last part sort of slips out without me realising – a memory spoken aloud. I panic briefly, worried I've shared too much. But when I look at Jack for his response, his expression is unchanged.

'What was he like?' he asks, eventually.

I hesitate, waiting for the emotions to overwhelm me, for the warning signs to emerge. But

I can't find them: the overwhelming sensation is peace. Calm, even. The grass is soft under my feet as we keep walking, and I can almost see my dad walking ahead of me, like he did all those years ago.

'He was a real park person,' I say after a few seconds. 'Anywhere we were in the world, any city, he'd seek out the local parks. It was our thing, sort of.' The information spills out suddenly, as if it has been straining against the dam I've placed against it. Waiting for someone to ask. Waiting for me to answer. 'He used to bring me here as a kid, and we'd spend hours just walking around. Talking. Even when I was really small, and most of what I talked about was trees and birds and grass. He never seemed to mind.'

'That sounds really wonderful, Andie,' Jack says, his tone gentle and encouraging. My heart is beating fast, the first sign that I should pull back. Usually, at this point, I'd change the subject, move on to something else. But even as a small flicker of fear moves through me, a slow warmth overtakes it, an overwhelming sense that I should keep going, keep talking. More memories pressing against the dam, begging to be let out. And so, as we continue along the path towards the tree line, I do. I tell him about how my dad would not only find a park, but find multiple friends within the park, striking up conversations with strangers. I tell him about his love for dogs – how he'd always say 'I met a lovely dog today' rather than 'saw', as if the dog were a person. I tell him about the yoga, about how he'd sometimes run impromptu outdoor classes on Hampstead Heath and get told off for not having a permit, but never fined because he gave free classes to the community enforcement officers. How people would sometimes roll down the hill, because they could never find a flat patch big enough. Jack laughs at this, and at the sound a crack in my heart bursts wide open – I hadn't realised how long it's been since I've spoken about my dad properly. It hits me in a rush: before I realise what's happening, tears fill my eyes. Jack catches sight of them before I can wipe them away, and slows to a halt, putting his hand tentatively on my arm.

'I'm really sorry for your loss, Andie,' he says. It's different to earlier, in the hotel – there I felt tight, claustrophobic. There his apology was laden with other things. This, despite the subject, feels light.

'Thank you,' I say, exhaling a breath that moves some of the weight off my chest. *I miss you*, I think, directing it to my dad. And for the first time in a very long time, it doesn't feel like it's going to rip me in half.

As silence settles between us, Jack's hand drops to his side and he looks away at the park, giving me a moment to compose myself. I find myself searching for something more to say, to thank him. He has no idea what he's just given me, and I'm still making sense of it, too, but it feels momentous, somehow. It's the first time in a long time that I've been able to speak about my dad without falling apart.

'I really liked your book,' I say, looking down at my feet. He doesn't reply, and for a moment I'm worried I've said something I shouldn't.

When I slowly raise my gaze to meet his, after a few seconds of silence, there's an expression on his face that I can't quite read.

'Really?' he says, eventually, as if the breath has been knocked out of him. His eyes are fixed on mine, his gaze deep and warm. My breath catches in my throat as I nod.

'I thought it was wonderful,' I say, not taking my eyes from his.

Then, slowly, he takes a step towards me. I stand stock still, as if the world has suddenly come to a halt. A warmth moves up my spine, and I have the thought that I should step back, that I should move away, like I did last night. But, this time, I don't.

He reaches up, slowly, and gently tucks a lock of hair behind my ear. I find myself moving towards him, blind to all feeling except the sensation of his thumb grazing my cheek as he lowers his hand.

I'm not sure who makes the first move – whether it's me, taking a step towards him, or him pulling me in, but it doesn't matter. Before I can really register what's happening, we're kissing, entwined, our hands in each other's hair, the awareness of my surroundings slowly falling away. Alarm bells are going off somewhere in the back of in my brain, telling me to stop, to think about this, to consider what I'm doing. But I ignore them, erasing all feeling until my awareness sharpens into only his lips on mine, his hand cupping the back of my neck, his other hand gripping my waist, my body pressed up against his. The wind in my hair, his fingers brushing my skin, sending shivers up my spine. It's intoxicating, terrifying. Wonderful. And then it's over, and Jack is catching his breath, still looking at me, and my head is spinning.

'Wow,' I say, breathing out slowly. 'That was—'

'Probably a violation of the truce?' he jokes, catching me off guard. I laugh, ignoring the twinge

in my stomach at the reminder of our professional relationship – another reason on the list of
a hundred reasons why we should absolutely not
have done that. But right now, I don't want to think
about any of them. I'm all fire, all desire for him.

'You know,' I say, the words spilling out of my
mouth before I can think too much about them,
'I think I left something important in the hotel
room.'

His eyebrows lift almost unnoticeably, and he
keeps his gaze fixed on mine.

'Shall I book an Uber to the hotel and we can go
back and, uh, look for it?' he asks, his eyes tracing
the outlines of my face. I nod, not trusting myself
to speak. He reaches for his phone and takes his
gaze off me momentarily to look at the screen. I
wait for reality to crash in, for the spell to break.
But it doesn't.

Not in the car, buckled in for the most excruciating journey of my life, our fingers lightly
brushing together on the middle seat as we both
keep our gazes fixed on the road. Not on the stairs
of the hotel, where it takes everything I have not
to grab his coat and push him against the banister.
Not when he fumbles with the key and I take it
out of his hand, unlocking the door and stumbling

into the hotel room. Or when we're inside, and he pushes me against the wall and runs his hand down the side of my face, his gaze tracing the shape of my body and burning through my clothes.

Every part of me knows that what I'm doing is stupid and self-destructive. That this is someone I'm supposed to hate, supposed to never want to see again. But that's not how I feel about him in this moment. Right now it feels too good, too right, to stop – everything I've been avoiding for the last few weeks is fading into the background, replaced by pure sensation, pure desire. A tension builds between us, only increasing as the distance closes again and again. I kiss him again, fiercely, undoing the buttons of his shirt as I do so.

'Look at you, suddenly an expert at men's buttons,' he says, as his shirt falls to the floor and he pulls mine over my head, unhooking my bra. A thrill runs through my body as I remember how he looked at me yesterday at the launch party, in my bra – how he's looking at me now, not with possession like other men have, raking their eyes over me like I'm something they've won, but with pure wonder, pure desire – as if I'm the only person he's ever wanted. His hands are on my waist now and his thumbs dig into my hips as

I arch towards him, pulling him in so I can kiss him again.

I move backwards until I hit the bed, drawing him towards me. Every cell in my body wants him, comes alive as he kisses my shoulder, the edge of my hip. His hands move over my body like he's seeing everything for the first time – gently cupping my breasts, dragging the elastic of my underwear until it slides down my legs. I barely have time to catch my breath before his mouth is on me, and he's kissing me in places I haven't been kissed in a while, and it feels so good I never want it to stop. But I'm desperate for more, for him, and there's only two days left of the tour, and we're here right now and it feels perfect. So I pull him towards me, kissing him again, feeling how much he wants me. I guide him towards me and we crash into each other, his hand grasping the back of my neck as he plunges into me. When he's inside me I let out a breath of equal parts relief and plea- sure. I am all feeling, completely in the moment. His hands move across my skin, leaving a trail of heat in their wake. I close my eyes, tracing my hand down his arm, his abs. I move with him as if my body remembers exactly the last time we did this, the thrill I felt that he wanted *me*, the thrill that now pulses through me even stronger than before. He moves his hand down, caressing me, increasing his pace as he does so, his thumb moving in circles, touching me in exactly the right place to send shivers up my spine. It feels amazing, unbelievably so – I close my eyes and lose all awareness of my surroundings as I start to come apart at the seams, losing myself in him, in this moment that I hope will never end. He thrusts into me harder and my hand grips the sheets tighter, a cry escaping my mouth as the tension that's been building between us finally finds an outlet. I close my eyes as it comes to a head, his hipbones grazing mine, his mouth pressed to my neck. Waves of pleasure wash over me as he comes apart, too, sinking into me, moaning 'fuck' softly and shivering with pleasure as he buries his face in the pillow behind me.

Oh god, I think, as I come back to my senses. It is, without a doubt, some of the best sex I've ever had.

'You have—' he says, his eyes now locked on mine, still catching his breath, '— no idea how long I've wanted to do that.'

I stare at the ceiling until my pulse starts to slow, trying to hold on to this feeling as long as I can before the thoughts I've been keeping at bay begin to press at the edges of my mind. Jack and I just had sex. And it was great. *Shit.* I take a breath and sit up.

'That definitely wasn't in the truce,' I say, reaching for humour to stave off the inevitable.

He leans over and kisses me again, running his hand along the back of my neck.

'Maybe we need a new truce,' he says, and somewhere in the back of my mind it begins to occur to me how stupid this was. Thankfully, before the thought can fully form, he starts kissing me again, long and hard, and suddenly my mind is mercifully blank once more, and I don't care about anything except being with him, right here, right now.

A while later, we emerge, breathless, sheets tangled around us. I am silent for a moment, suppressing the urge to roll over and kiss him again so I don't have to process the weight of what just happened – a weight which is increasing with each moment we're no longer entwined, threatening to fall on me like a ton of bricks.

'I like you, Andie,' he says, the words tumbling out of him as if he's not quite in control of his own voice. *Shit. This wasn't what I expected.* But he keeps going. 'I know we have things we need to talk about, but I don't want you to think I'm messing you around.' *Oh god.* We've gone from kissing to sex to now – something else? I don't know what to feel, how to respond – the blissful oblivion I felt moments ago, the deep sense that what we were doing was right, that all I wanted was him, is fading slowly into panic which grows with every second: the slow realisation that I have just done something very, very wrong.

'I don't know, Jack—' I say, sitting up. 'I—' *Fuck. What did we just do?* 'I need a minute.'

He nods, his expression indecipherable, and opens his mouth to respond, but before he can the sound of his phone ringing cuts through the silence. I let out a breath, glad that this conversation has been interrupted. But then mine starts ringing, too: we look at each other for a moment, confused, then move across the room to each of our devices.

'Hello?' I say, nodding as Jack motions to me, pulling on some trousers and a T-shirt, that he's going to take his call in the corridor.

'Andie!' Jessica's voice trills through the phone. I become suddenly, embarrassingly aware of my own nakedness, wrapping the sheets closer around me as if she can somehow tell from New York what I've just done.

'Hi!' I say, putting on my best I-definitely-did-not-just-sleep-with-your-star-author voice. Now Jack is out of the room, the reality I've been keeping at arm's length since I kissed him in the park starts crashing down. Hard.

'I have some excellent news,' she says.

'Oh?' I say, doing my best to stay in the moment, despite the fire that's just started in my mind.

'You're going to Edinburgh.'

What? Her words throw petrol over the fire, sending it into an inferno. My heart drops into my stomach. *This can't be happening. Not now. Not when I've just—*

'Um – sorry, could you repeat that please?' I choke out, panic gripping my chest like a vice.

'You're going to Edinburgh!' she says, again, more excited this time. As if her words have not just smashed my world into a million pieces. 'I just got off the phone with the head of programming at Edinburgh Book Festival, and they've had a cancellation.' I pull the sheets tighter around me, a shield against this. The panic rises in pitch, ringing in my ears. 'Jack will be filling in for a major event, as a priority author. We've managed to rearrange some of the press and bookshop visits from tomorrow, so you can go: Jack will do the interviews over Zoom, instead, and visit the bookshops when he's back in the UK doing some more press next month. Isn't this great?'

I close my eyes. I am about to be back in Edinburgh, the scene of the crime. The reason why I've hated Jack all this time, why I should still hate him. And he is going to be there with me. Of all the tricks the universe has played on me in the last few weeks of my life, this is by far the worst. I have no words for this feeling: it's a black hole, consuming me completely. 'So great!' I manage to lie, nausea swirling inside me as the horror of my current situation is followed swiftly by a realisation of exactly how stupid I've been. Jessica's words have just dumped a pail of ice cold water over my head, the haze that I've been living in for the last two weeks sharpening into a horrifying reality of my own creation. The hatred and anger that first took root in Edinburgh five years ago, that I've buried deeper and deeper as the tour has gone on, rises to the surface all at once, sharpening my senses and sending bile up my throat. What the fuck have I done? I just slept with *Jack Carlson*. Who shattered my trust, and shattered me in the process. I've spent the last five years piecing myself back into a semblance of the person I was before he betrayed me, before my dad. And now I am about to go to Edinburgh, where it all began – everything around me crumbling into dust, leaving me a shadow of the whole, big-hearted Andie who arrived at that university. The box I've been keeping carefully closed rips open, releasing a world of pain that breaks down all my defences and tears through me, stealing my breath, almost drowning out Jessica's words as she talks about the changes to our travel arrangements. I manage to get through the rest of the call, somehow, grabbing a pen to write down the details and giving her as concise answers as I can until she eventually hangs up the phone and I am free from this nightmare of a conversation. Except I'm not free: tomorrow, I will be living it. Even in my wildest dreams I couldn't have imagined this. I was so nearly home free: just two more days here, then back to New York and my normal life. Instead, there's this. Whoever the hell is up there, weaving the tapestry of my life, can get absolutely fucked.

The door quietly opens, and Jack enters the room slowly and carefully. I deduce from his facial expression and his hair, wild and messy like he's been running his hands through it, that he's just had the same conversation with his agent. He's looking at me with roughly the same expression that you'd give an untamed lion – half-cautious, half-waiting to see if I'll pounce and tear him to pieces.

'Andie—' he starts, but I put up my hand and shake my head. Resolve has formed inside me, firm and cold, extinguishing any warmth towards him.

'This—' I gesture to the bed, ignoring the lump that's forming in my throat. '—whatever this was, was a mistake.' I watch my words hit him like I've stabbed him in the chest, but I ignore it and continue. 'It can't happen again, Jack. We can't—' My voice starts to crack, the pain and anger welling up all over again, but I shove it back down and fix a closed expression on my face. 'We can't do that again. It was stupid, unprofessional. We need to go back to the terms of the truce for the next week, do our jobs and then go our separate ways. That's why we're here, after all.'

To my surprise, Jack seems to recover his composure quickly. Resolve burns on his face.

'No,' he says, simply, his voice unwavering. The lump in my throat grows bigger. *What does he mean no?*

'You can't just say—' I start, but he cuts me off, walking towards me. He stops a few paces from the bed, his gaze fixed on me. I suddenly realise how vulnerable I feel: me naked, him clothed, me with all the emotional baggage, him with none. It takes me right back to that first night in the bookshop in New York, and it hurts more than I could have imagined.

'I don't want to go back to the truce. Fuck the truce. Fuck pretending there aren't a million unsaid things between us. I like you, Andie, and I think you feel the same way, but if you don't want to admit that to yourself, that's fine. Either way, I'm not doing this anymore. I'm going to Edinburgh, and I can't stop you from joining me for the sake of your career, but I mean it when I say I want you to stay as far away from me as you possibly can. I'll tell your boss that you were the best publicist ever. But I'm not doing this, not anymore. If you're not willing to talk about what happened, after all this, to let me explain, then beyond the strictest limitations of our jobs, I'd like you to leave me alone.' He pauses, hurt contorting his face as he runs his hand through his hair. 'It's too painful, being so close to you every day, pretending there isn't this history between us, buried underneath everything we say or do. I'm done.'

Anger flares up inside me. 'Do you think you're the victim here? Have you forgotten—'

This time, Jack holds up his hand. His eyes are soft and sad, his voice deep and grounded. 'I won't ever forget what happened, Andie. I regret it with every inch of me. More than you'll ever know, or apparently allow me to tell you. But I'm a person, too. And I have feelings. I can't keep ignoring them for your sake. It's not fair. Especially considering—' He cuts himself off, shaking his head as if he's changed his mind about what he's about to say. I close my eyes for a moment, trying desperately to ignore the writhing pain in my chest and think of a response. But nothing comes, and I hear the sound of the door opening, then gently closing. When I open my eyes again, Jack is gone.

18

As soon as the door shuts behind him, I deflate, the weight of everything pressing against my chest, making it difficult to breathe. I take a deep, shuddering breath and call Sara. It rings a few times, but she doesn't answer.

I send a text: *SOS. Can we talk?* And receive a response a few moments later: *Sorry, A. With J.* My stomach sinks, and a sense of dread moves through me, my throat growing suddenly thick. SOS has always been a drop-anything-and-answer-right-now text, a code Sara and I have relied on in the last nine years of our friendship. She always joked that if she ever didn't answer, it would be because she was missing a limb.

Later? I text, the panic that has been simmering through me now reaching a peak – how am I supposed to figure this all out without her? Her reply comes through fast, again. *I'll let you know.*

Something about the formal tone, the lack of ceremony or personality to her texts, sets off a million alarm bells in my head – this doesn't sound like Sara at all. My gut twists. There is clearly something more going on. With James, as I've suspected on the last few calls. Maybe the fights got worse after I left. Maybe something is horribly wrong. A deep, visceral sadness hits me suddenly that whatever's been going on, she hasn't felt able to tell me about it.

All ok? I text, chewing my bottom lip, worry moving through me.

All fine. Just busy. Love you x

This last text flashes up on the screen and I stare at it for a few seconds, worry giving way to shock as her tone sets off the same deep instinct in me that has been building every time we've spoken for the last two weeks – she's lying, I can feel it. Something is definitely, seriously wrong. And I don't know how to reach her in this moment. My chest grows tight, panic building inside me. I think of how she avoided my question about James the last time I spoke to her, her noncommittal text saying he was 'fine'. I can no longer feel the thread that's been pulled taut between us since I've been on this trip – as if we're not just further away than we've ever been, but totally separate. In this second, the distance between us feels totally crushing.

Ok, I text back, tears streaming down my face. *Love you, too. Always here if you need. X*

I watch the read receipt change from delivered to seen and wait a beat, hoping she'll change her mind and text me, asking for a call, asking if she can talk to me about something. Reaching out and needing me, again, like I need her so desperately in this moment. Leaning on each other, like we used to at university, like we've always been able to since. But nothing comes, and her status on Whatsapp moves from active to last active three minutes ago. The lump in my throat grows so large I can barely breathe. But I have to accept the truth, settling over me suddenly and turning me cold: whatever Sara is going through, whatever I might be going through in this moment, we can't help each other, right now. And at any rate, she doesn't want my help. Which means I'm also going to have to deal with this without her sage advice, her understanding of the right path. The compass she's become in my life, that I hadn't realised I was so reliant on until exactly this moment, when it wasn't there, anymore.

I take a long, slow breath that sticks in my chest, then click the lock button and watch the screen fade to black. Whatever is about to happen, I'm on my own.

The next morning, I pack in a daze. The room is visibly empty of Jack's belongings: after Sara's texts yesterday, I went for a walk to clear my head. When I came back everything except my suitcase was gone. I have no idea where he slept last night. Apart from the professional consideration that I've managed to lose my author on tour, I can't find it in myself to care.

Jack is waiting, emotionless, in the hotel lobby. He nods briefly to acknowledge my arrival, and gestures to the door. We walk outside to find the car waiting for us, and spend an uncomfortable journey silently staring out of separate windows. Jonathon doesn't seem to notice any tension and provides a low-level hum of monologue, telling us how much he's enjoyed being our driver for this trip, and how the story of the tyre and the pothole is already his go-to pub anecdote. I flinch at the memory of that evening, just two nights ago though it feels like two years, and glance towards Jack. His expression is still carefully calm, but his Adam's apple bobs, his throat giving away his tension. He's thinking about it, too. With a rush, a different memory floods my brain: of yesterday, of how it felt to press my body against his, to kiss him. A shiver moves up my spine, but I shove the feeling and the memory away, turning my gaze back to the passing streets of Dublin.

We move through the airport in silence: baggage control, passport control. At the check-in desk, Jack quietly and firmly requests a seat change, and he is moved to a seat at the back of the plane, as far as possible from where I'm sitting. *Good*, I think, but the nausea in the pit of my stomach isn't entirely convinced. I have a sudden, stupid urge to reach out to him as he moves past me to continue up the aisle, to tell him to stay, but I don't know why I would even want that. *What the fuck is wrong with you, Andie?*

I find my seat, and Jack's seat next to me remains empty: evidence of his anger. I feel viscerally uncomfortable, like I want to climb out of my skin again. I haven't felt this way since London: a huge storm cloud hovering over me, darkening everything in my path. It's unbearable.

When we've taken off, I take some herbal remedy to try and help me sleep through this flight. I don't want to be alone with my thoughts.

It works, and an hour and a half later I'm awoken to the juddering sound of wheels hitting tarmac — we've arrived. *Oh, fuck.*

Every cell of my body is on fire as I exit the plane, waiting awkwardly for Jack alongside the gangway. He spots me, but walks right past without acknowledgement. I weave through the airport behind him, quickening my pace to catch up — he's really punishing me now, and I hate it. The power balance has reversed, and it's searingly uncomfortable.

While we're waiting for the car, I pull out my personal phone to distract myself, momentarily, and immediately regret it: a few texts from my mum have come through, asking if I saw her email, if that's all OK with me. I type out a quick reply, on autopilot, careful to keep up the façade that I already knew — I don't need to hurt her by explaining my shock:

Congratulations again! So sorry I haven't texted you yet. I had a bit of a tour crisis. On my way to resolving it now. That date should be fine. So thrilled for you, Mum xxx

The lump that's been steadily growing in my throat now feels so large I almost choke on it as I put my phone back in my pocket. I take a long, shaky breath, willing myself to keep it together in front of Jack – right now, I have to focus on getting to the hotel without throwing up. Our driver collects us and I practically leap into the front seat, desperate not to sit next to Jack. It's not set up for someone to sit there, so I have to awkwardly remove his jacket from the seat before I sit down, and slide the seat back to fit. I try to take subtle deep breaths as the car weaves through the streets of the city I used to know so well, keeping my gaze fixed on the dashboard as we drive past the campus, the library. When we pass the student union I squeeze my eyes shut, terrified of even catching a glimpse of the asphalt outside, where it all went so horribly wrong. I open them and involuntarily catch sight of Jack in the rearview mirror, looking right at me, his expression soft and concerned, but when I catch his eye he immediately looks away, his face restored to stony indifference.

We have the first day here off, so once we arrive at the hotel – another beautiful place, but at this point I could not care less what it looks like – I go straight up to my room and switch into work-mode to get through it, closing the curtains and scrolling through my inbox, which has become more and more unwieldy in the last two weeks. There are a few excited emails from Jessica confirming the schedule for tomorrow, which I file away until I have the strength to look at them, focussing my energy instead on upcoming campaigns, due to kick off when I return. I just have to get through the next few days, then Jack's campaign will mostly be over, and I'll be working with other authors. Ones I haven't slept with, who don't serve as a reminder of the most painful time in my life. The thought is just about enough to get me through the afternoon, and by 8 p.m. I've cleared most of my inbox. I shut my laptop, feeling ever so slightly lighter than I did when I arrived. It's not hope, exactly – but it's something. A tether out of this darkness I've found myself in. And it gets me to the bathroom for a long, hot shower, and then back into bed. I take what's probably more than the recommended dose of my herbal sleep remedy and rest my head on the pillow, trying to still my thoughts. Tomorrow, I'll have to leave the protection of this dark, safe hotel room. And it's going to be awful. But for now, at least, I can pretend these four walls are all there is. I close my eyes and fall into a fitful sleep.

19

Leaving the hotel the following morning is even more excruciating than expected. Edinburgh is alive with activity: people file through the streets, dipping in and out of bookshops and festival tents. The mood is of excitement, joy. I could not be further from them all.

Jack moves through the crowds as if I'm not there, weaving through the bookshops we've arranged to visit before the big event at 4.30 p.m. I follow him in a fugue state and perform my perfunctory duties, then stay at the back like a ghost, making my presence as unobtrusive as possible. It's 4 p.m. before I realise that he hasn't spoken a word to me all day.

In a break between shops, Jack strides off, muttering about going to find a coffee and meeting me at the event, and my phone flashes with an incoming call: Sara. *Thank God.* I light up at the sight of it, sitting up straighter and pressing it to my ear.

'Hey, stranger,' she says, and I almost cry with relief. Her voice is tired, cracking. I want to ask her how she's doing, what's really going on, but I feel my own problems spilling out of me before I can – I'm desperate for her, for someone, to tell me what to do.

'S, I fucked up,' I say, tears starting to fall as I speak.

'What happened?' she asks, and I can hear her shifting in her seat, her attention totally on me. A weight lifts off my chest, even as it constricts with everything I'm about to say. I take a deep breath and recount the events of the last twenty-four hours: sleeping with Jack, my mum's wedding e-vite, the fact that I'm somehow currently living my worst nightmare, back in Edinburgh with the last person I'd ever want to be here with.

'You *slept* with him?' she says when I'm done, all tiredness leaving her voice. Despite myself, I feel a flash of hurt at the fact that out of everything I've just said, that's what she picked up on. 'What the ever-living fuck, Andie?'

I swallow the hurt and laugh. 'Yeah. Pretty stupid, right?'

'I wasn't going to say that,' she says, some of the shock fading from her tone as she processes the information. 'But yes. Very stupid.' I said it first, but something about Sara echoing my words stings.

I laugh again, though my chest feels hollow, and press on, sure that she'll know what to do, how to help me through this. 'I don't know what to do,' I say. 'With my mum. Or this. I feel like I'm messing everything up. There's still a few days here, and the truce—'

Her voice cuts through mine, her tone suddenly and unexpectedly exasperated. 'Not that truce again, A. Can't you see that's how you've ended up in this situation?' There it is again: the tone, the judgement. My stomach drops. I don't know where it's coming from, but it's not normal for Sara. Usually she's a gentle hand; my constant source of support. My Sara. The one who, once upon a time, would have dropped everything to help me figure this all out.

'Ouch, S,' I say, my throat suddenly thick. 'Bit harsh.'

She takes a breath. 'Sorry,' she says, and I breathe out, relieved and hopeful that she's reverting to her usual form. 'I just—' she pauses again, then sighs and continues, her tone still clipped. Dread seeps through me, and I have sudden déjà vu, the same feeling I had with the texts yesterday – that something is very, very wrong. 'Obviously you can't help the Edinburgh part. But honestly, this whole situation could have been avoided.'

Shame spreads through me, heating my face. My hand clenches tighter round the phone, and I'm overwhelmed with a sudden, panicked urge to justify myself. Like a child, being told off. 'I was just trying to—'

She cuts me off again, her tone a little gentler this time, but still firm, still endowed with the sense that she's right about this. And she probably is. But I don't want her to be right – I want her to be my friend. 'You were trying to do what you always do, Andie. What you're still doing.' I hold my breath, braced for the blow that comes. 'You're running away.' The blow hits harder than I thought it would. I close my eyes, willing the tears not to come. I know that she's right. Because she's always right. And if she'd called me back in Berlin or answered my SOS last night, I might've taken this all in, might've listened. But now, standing in the city where it all went wrong, trying desperately to avoid the memories it brings up, her words only open a deep wound.

'S, please,' I say, making an attempt to get the conversation back in control. 'I just need support right now.'

She sighs, sounding weighted down, and my stomach drops. 'I'm sorry, A, but I don't think I can give you that right now. You're spiraling, and you're hurting yourself. If you'd just listened to me—' Another sigh, and this time I can hear the exhaustion in her voice. I press the phone to my face, intent on her next words. 'You need to talk to Jack, to clear this all up, or it's just going to hurt you further. And I can't just stand by and watch that happen. If you want a best friend who is going to cheer you on while you self-destruct, you need to find a new one.'

A hole gapes inside me, the fear blowing it wide open – I can't lose Sara, too. I squeeze my eyes closed to the streets around me, momentarily speechless.

'I didn't mean—' she starts when I don't respond, apparently realising the impact of her words. But it's too late – they burn through me, igniting my worst fear.

'I know,' I say, but I'm lying, my walls going back up to protect me. 'Listen, I'll call you later,

OK?' I choke out, trying desperately to keep a lid on the hurt that seeps through me, overwhelming me, and hang up, my hand trembling, before she can reply.

I put the phone back in my pocket, almost shaking with the effort, my breath still coming in gasps. Loneliness rips through me. It hits me in the next second that I haven't even managed to call my mum back, yet, I've been so wrapped up in my own problems. And yet the thought of her moving on in such a permanent way still brings me to my knees: I don't know what I'd say, how I'd be able to keep it together when everything is going so horribly wrong. Sara, drifting further and further away from me. Perhaps forever. And me, on a street in Edinburgh, surrounded by memories I never thought I'd have to relive again.

I take a long, shaky breath and attempt to shut out my surroundings, pressing my hands to my temples and willing the horrible thoughts spiralling in my brain to shut the fuck up. They don't, converging into fear, blinding fear that runs like electricity through my veins. The fear I've been keeping one step ahead of for years now: that if I let myself go back to that time again, it will shatter me. And this time, I might not be able to put myself back together.

But here, in this city, I can't get away. It presses in, shutting out everything else. The car park, Jack. Those months afterwards: the call from my mum, the visits to the hospital. The memories merge, a vast tangle of pain and sadness, collapsing into a black hole I'm not sure I can emerge from this time. It's all too much, all at once. Without warning, the image of my dad's face in those final days drifts into the forefront of my mind, bringing with it a wave of grief so immense it paralyses me. And this time I can't push it away. In this moment – totally alone, in the city where everything started falling apart – I need him, even just his memory, even if it hurts. He comes into my mind's eye: larger than life, slowly wasting away. A bear hug of a man. My best friend. Gone, just like that. It hurts so much, still, even to think of it – forever: the word so final, a cliff edge with nowhere to land. My breath catches in my throat, the wave increasing with each second. But even as I hold it there, waiting for it to tear me apart, as I always knew it would, his words come to me, echoing Sara all those weeks ago. Sara, who's always right. Who

I should have been listening to, this whole time: *The only way out is through.*

For a moment, I hesitate, then my feet start to move as if of their own accord – as if they know where I need to go. What I need to do.

I move down the street and take a left, my step firm, the roads familiar. I don't need to think about where I'm going – it's like an invisible force is pulling me to where I need to go, leading me. It's only when I arrive, my feet crunching on familiar gravel, that I allow myself to look up. The student union is busy. Somehow I'd envisioned that the car park would be empty, like it was that night. But it's not: it's full of students, milling around, going about their days. They pass me without really noticing my presence: perhaps they think I'm a postgrad. Either way, it doesn't matter. Invisiblilty is good considering what I am about to do.

I walk over to the bench in the corner, by the bar, three feet from the spot, and sink down into it. I dig my nails into my knees and close my eyes, letting the memories come.

20

Edinburgh, five years ago. Andie.

It's freezing outside and my jacket isn't warm enough. My clothes never seem to be warm enough for Scottish weather: every winter, I almost get hypothermia, and even in the summer I always seem to be shivering.

I pull my jacket tighter and adjust my scarf. I'm on a mission today: I don't have time to worry about my clothes, or go back and get a warmer jacket. I have a job to do. For Sara. I promised Sara I would do this for her, and I can't go back on that.

I open the door to the student library and find him sitting in the café, bent over a book. We've been coming across each other in lectures in the English course we're both taking for the better part of a year, and sure, I've noticed he's attractive. But it occurs to me now for the first time how beautiful he is, when he's not aware he's being watched;

my gaze passes over his perfect cheekbones, his dark, curly hair. His deep blue eyes, which look up from the page and find mine. A knot forms in my stomach. Nerves, but something else, too: the way he's looking at me feels like it's piercing my soul somehow. I break eye contact. *You're just here for information, Andie. You can flirt later.*

I sit opposite him and he smiles nervously.

'Thanks so much for meeting me,' I say, reaching to pull a notebook and pen out of my bag. He nods.

'Of course, happy to. Though I have to say I found your message very cryptic. The cute girl I sit next to in English lectures emails me, telling me she needs help with something she can't explain now, and asks me to meet her here? Colour me intrigued.'

I smile, my lips tight, doing the best to ignore the 'cute' comment even as my stomach swoops. 'It was cryptic for a reason.' I reach down and pull a piece of paper from my bag – an NDA template I found on the internet. It probably isn't legally binding, but it's good enough for my purposes. I need to scare him into never mentioning this conversation to anyone. He takes it from me and looks at it, his eyebrows lifting.

'Andie, what is this about? I thought you just needed notes from our last lecture or something. Now you're pulling legal documents on me?' He turns it over, examining it. 'Is this even a real NDA?'

'Look, Jack. I can't tell you more until you sign it, except that you'd be helping me, and someone I care about, a lot. No hard feelings if you want to walk away. But if you're in, I need to know sooner rather than later. And I need you to sign that document,' I say, tapping my foot involuntarily under the table. I don't want to pressurise him, but I'm impatient: I want to get this done. He gives me a long look, then sighs and signs the document. I relax as he hands it back to me: step one, complete.

'Thanks, Jack. Sorry for all the mystery. I just want to be really careful.'

He nods. 'Now I'm extremely intrigued. What's going on?'

I take a deep breath. *You rehearsed this. It's going to be OK.* 'You're on the swim team, right?' I ask, levelling my gaze even as my heart starts pounding at the thought of what I'm about to ask of him.

He looks just as confused as ever, but nods.

I steel myself. 'I'm about to ask you to do something big, which could get you in a lot of trouble with your teammates. All the NDA means is that you can't talk about this conversation with anyone, not that you have to do what I ask.'

His expression is more serious now, and he's leaning towards me. *Good. This is serious.*

'I need you to spy on them for me. For an article I'm writing for the university newspaper.'

At this the serious expression disappears and he sits back, laughing. 'Jesus, Andie, you really had me going there. The way you were talking it sounded like you wanted me to drown one of them. What kind of spying are we talking about? Tell me it's not a tell-all on our locker room conversations. Because, I can give you an exclusive now: all the ones I'm involved in are incredibly boring.'

I don't join him in his laughter. My stomach twists. None of this feels funny, because it's not. A great wrong has been done to someone I care about, and I need to fix it.

'Are you familiar with the website slutsofedinburgh.com?'

This wipes any joy from his face immediately. His expression darkens. 'That cesspit of a website where low-life morons post paragraphs rating girls' sexual performance? Unfortunately, yes. I am familiar. It's fucking disgusting.' He looks at me, worry crossing his features. 'You weren't—'

I cut in, interrupting him. 'Last week, my friend Sara was posted on there. Pictures of her sleeping that were taken without her consent, and a rating of a one night stand she had with one of your team members. I know it was him, because she told me, even though they conveniently never include the names of the men involved.'

He shifts in his chair, his posture stiffening. 'Jesus fucking Christ. Who was it, Andie? I'll—'

I raise my hand. 'I don't want or need you to beat anyone up, Jack. I just need you to do a bit of digging and find out who runs the website, who might be involved in it. I want to publish an anonymous exposé in the university newspaper, with the names of every single fucker who has had any hand in it, then have the whole fucking thing taken down. They deserve a taste of their own public shaming.'

Anger ripples through me as I almost spit out those last two words. I've never seen Sara like this. She's exhausted, ashamed, hardly leaving her room, worried about attending lectures in case people judge her. How fucking *dare* they break her spirit like this. I will make them pay.

'I know we don't know each other all that well, and this is a big ask,' I say, forcing the anger aside and focusing my attention back on Jack. 'No hard feelings if you don't want to be involved.'

I wait a few moments while he contemplates the prospect, pretending to examine the NDA while my heart pounds in my chest. I've already put myself at so much risk, told him so much. After about thirty seconds, the crease in his brow unfolds and resolve crosses his features. My shoulders relax, some of the tension leaving my body. *Thank God.* I came up with the idea for the article last night, after leaving Sara despondent in her room, and spent hours lying awake, trying to figure out how to get the necessary information. Jack's face popped into my mind at about 2 a.m., and this plan slowly formed around it. I've had little contact with anyone in other sports teams, and certainly not enough to find any of them trustworthy. To be honest, I don't know Jack that well, either. I'm going mostly on instinct, based on the small talk we've exchanged outside lectures and the fights I've observed him breaking up on nights out. Still, it was a risk.

'I'm in,' he says, reaching across the table to shake my hand. 'Meet me back here, same time next week. I'll hopefully have something for you by then.'

I smile, even as another flash of anger surges at the thought of discovering who was responsible for all this. I'm grateful, and glad that I was right about him. And, I have to admit, more than a little turned on by how furious he was about the website. Nothing gets me going more than a feminist. I pick up my bag. 'Thanks, Jack,' I say, turning to go. 'I appreciate it.'

As if he's read my thoughts, Jack calls to me as I walk away. 'Hey, Andie?' I turn back to face him, half way to the café doors. 'Once we're done with all this, can I buy you a drink?'

Despite myself, I feel a blush creeping up my neck. I nod, giving myself a moment for my thoughts to unscramble before I speak, but not wanting him to think I'm going to say no. 'I'd like that,' I say, and I turn back towards the doors. I could swear I can still feel his eyes on my back as I leave, but when I turn around to check, there's someone in the way. By the time they've passed, his head is back down, his gaze fixed on his book. I tear my eyes away, worried he'll notice, then push the library door open and step back out into the cold air. I take a deep breath, my lungs prickling with the cold. *A spy and a date. Not bad, for a Tuesday afternoon.*

When we meet again, a week later, the weight in my stomach feels like a lead block. I remind myself of Sara's face, lighter than I'd seen it in days, when I told her Jack had agreed to my plan. He's sitting at the same table, reading a different book with a dragon on the cover, just as breathtakingly beautiful as he was a week ago. He looks up and his eyes find mine, and I can see in them that he has something. He puts his bookmark in his book, folds it closed and smiles at me.

'Hey, stranger,' I say, as I sit down, mentally focused on making sure my hands don't tremble. *They're just some sports boys, not serial killers*, I remind myself, but it doesn't entirely work. I've seen how they fight each other outside the union when they're drunk. They're all huge, and strong, and vaguely threatening in a way that's difficult to put your finger on but very obvious when you're surrounded by crowds of them in a club, and I'm about to take them on head-on. Well, sort of. My name won't be printed, and I've been corresponding with the newspaper editor via an anonymous email address, but I'm putting a huge amount of trust in Jack not to reveal the article was written by me, thus exposing me to the unchecked, drunken rage of the largest and scariest section of the student body. I hope my gut instinct about him is right.

'I have some names,' he says, leaning in and sliding a piece of paper across the table. I reach to take it, and my finger grazes his, and it's like my hand is on fire. I clear my throat and slide the list of the people who run the website towards me, studying it. There are a few names that are no surprise: Dan, the moronic head of the rugby team, who has about three brain cells – he's definitely not the mastermind behind this, but it checks out that he's involved: he has a charming habit of spitting at women who reject him when he's drunk; Connor, who tried to grope my friend Amy a year ago at our annual summer student party, then called her a slag when she stamped on his foot. But then there's an outlier: Robbie. The captain of the swim team, the golden boy with a different girlfriend every week, who should be leaving a trail of broken hearts in his wake but never seems to suffer the consequences. Everybody likes him, even those he's dated and cast aside for someone new. He's led Edinburgh to national victory in division 1 university competitions three times. His grades are perfect, his swimming is perfect, his dad donated a new wing to the library we're sitting in. But despite my initial surprise that he's on this list, a chill runs through me as I read his name. Something about him has always bothered me, rendering me immune to the charms that everyone else seems so susceptible to: the few times I've seen him around, or caught his eye, there's been a deep twist in my gut, a warning sign. If there is someone running this show, I'd put my money on him: the person no one would ever suspect, shielded by his dad's deep pockets and his own excellent reputation. Jack's sheet confirms my suspicion. His name is circled in red.

I breathe out, a slow, rattling breath, dread pooling in my stomach the longer I stare at his name. If I was scared before, I'm terrified now. Jack reaches across the table and puts his hand on mine.

'Have you thought about going to the university, instead?' he asks. 'I could go with you, if you like.'

I smile sadly at his kind offer, his trust in an institution that I know deep in my bones will care more about Robbie's sporting ability than any of the poor women he's shaming on that website. They'll brush it all under the rug, give him a glorified slap on the wrist and make sure nothing touches his impeccable record. No, it has to be this way. I have to do this. I give myself an internal shake, sit up straight in my seat and try to radiate confidence.

'Thanks so much for your help, Jack,' I say, standing up to go. 'I'll take it from here.'

Just as I'm about to walk off, my heart pounding, Jack says 'Wait, Andie,' and puts his hand on my arm. A thousand nerve endings spring to life at his touch.

'Thursday?' he says, pulling out his phone and handing it to me.

My brain is so full of what I'm about to do that I can't think straight. I blink at him, not understanding what he's talking about. He smiles. 'Our drink,' he says, and understanding dawns on me.

'Of course,' I say, though getting a drink with him is suddenly the furthest thing from my mind. I look down at his phone.

'Put your number in it?' he says, his voice gentle. 'I mean – only if you want – I just thought it might be easier than talking over email…'

He trails off as I nod and wordlessly type my number into his phone, his face flushed slightly pink. I hand it back to him and force a smile so he doesn't think my hesitance is because of him, when it's really because I'm fucking terrified of what might happen once this is done.

'See you then,' I say, and I turn to walk away. This time, I keep my eyes fixed on where I'm going.

I work until midnight, anger moving through me, speeding my hands across the keys of my laptop. The words come easily, sentences forming like water flowing down a stream. I keep Sara at the forefront of my mind: I am doing this for her. For every woman on that stupid website. For myself, for all the times I've felt uncomfortable in a night-club, their eyes moving over me like I'm a piece of meat.

I start with a powerful opening, laying out stud-ies I've painstakingly researched and collated of the misogynistic culture rearing its head in univer-sity sports teams across the country, citing similar cases to this one at other universities. They're not always websites: social media accounts, forums, WhatsApp groups, Facebook groups. You name it, they'll find a way to shame you in it. I then weave in a few personal accounts from women featured on the website, which proves the hard-est section to write. Once Sara's name went up, a few other victims reached out to her, and some have provided devastating testimony about how ashamed this website made them feel, how small. Sara decided not to contribute, even anony-mously – it was all still too raw for her. I totally understood: she's felt so exposed for the last few weeks. She deserves to feel safe for a while. Despite this, as I write a strange loneliness comes over me, a sadness that she of all people isn't standing with me. But right now, my feelings aren't important: the most important thing is getting it out there, making sure that Sara is OK, that she and the other women feel justice has been served. And besides, it doesn't make any difference: all my sources' names will be as anonymous as my own, anyway.

At 11:59 p.m. I finish, putting the final touches on the pièce de résistance: the names I have of the main boys involved, ten of them, citing the anonymous source from an unnamed male sports team who provided me with this information. It's comprehensive: their name, what they study, what sports team they play for. A hit list, if you will. I smile to myself, imagining future women using this as a 'who not to date' guide, imagining these men never getting laid again. It's not as satisfying as having them kicked out of the university, but it's pretty good.

When I'm done, I'm exhausted, totally hollowed out. I send the article to the newspaper and a text to Sara saying *It's done xx* and drag myself to bed, falling asleep almost immediately.

Three days later, the article goes out, and all hell breaks loose. The whole university is buzzing with gossip: who wrote it, and how did they get the information? And — I'm not sure why I didn't expect this, but somehow I hadn't thought things through this far — there's just as much speculation about the anonymous source as there is about the person who wrote the article. Who's the snake in all this, who broke the most sacred rule of guy code and landed everyone in trouble? And then — amongst the sports teams, and those associated with them — the anger, the insistence that they've done nothing wrong. It wasn't a big deal anyway, right? Just a load of fuss over nothing. A big joke. Don't know what everyone's crying about.

I move through it, my face so hot I feel sure people must see the responsibility written all over it: I might as well have written 'IT WAS ME' in sharpie on my forehead for how conspicuous I feel. Underneath my fear for myself, though, there's a deeper fear for Jack. He's the one at real risk here, the 'snake'. I hadn't really seen it at the time, probably because I didn't want to, but he put a lot more on the line than I did.

But though I'm more terrified now than before, though I had hoped I would feel better after the article went out and I do not, I know that I did the right thing. I know because Sara is back, shiny and happy and buoyant. She's left her bed, and showered, and she's attending lectures again. It was worth it, for that. For her. My best friend, my person. I'd do anything for her.

I sit through my lectures in a daze, barely registering any of the information because I'm on such high alert, trying to catch snippets of people talking about what happened, their judgements for or against the article (so far, the split is roughly 50% those fuckers deserved it and 50% that was an unnecessary piece of public shaming, and the author should be ashamed of herself – because of course it was a woman, who else would be whining about this?). When I get to my renaissance poetry lecture, though, my heart starts beating faster. Jack is also taking this course, as one of his core modules alongside his history degree. It's where we met, where I first spotted him. Where I decided that if anyone was the person to help me with this, it was him. Will he be there, or is he lying low? Has he realised the position I've put him in? Has he heard what people are saying about him and decided he hates me?

I don't have to wait long for an answer: he's sitting at his usual desk, doodling idly in his note-book as if it's a normal day. There are two takeaway coffee cups in front of him, and a packet of salt and vinegar crisps. I eye them in surprise, and he looks up at me, his face lighting up when he spots me. For the first time since this morning, when the article was published, my thoughts slow down and I start to relax. Jack's here, and he understands, and I'm not alone in this.

I walk towards the desk, feeling lighter than I have in days, and he pulls out my chair for me. I sit, moving the crisps out of the way briefly so I can put down my books. He notices, and smiles. 'Thought you might want some sustenance,' he says, quietly so only I can hear. 'Big day and all.'

Though his words should put me back on high alert, worried someone might hear them and put two and two together, I'm so touched by his gesture I almost cry.

'Thank you,' I say, as I take a few sips of strong coffee. 'These are my favourite. How did you know?' I whisper, gesturing to the crisps. He shrugs and taps the side of his nose. I think back to the last few months of lectures; the number of times I've had a packet of this exact brand of crisps in my bag, on the desk. I hadn't realised he'd been paying so much attention. A rush of affection for him appears at the thought.

The coffee hits my veins, giving me a welcome hit. *This is probably going to be fine*, I think. Sara is happy, and Jack seems fine, and my name isn't anywhere anyone could find it. This will all die down in a few days, and I'll be able to go back to my normal life knowing justice has been properly served and I've done right by my friend. But something deep in my gut is telling me this isn't over yet.

When is it coming down? he writes on a note to me, half way through the lecture. He's referring to the website, to the second part of my plan: having the computer science student I've befriended take it down. I look around, still on high alert, then write back *Tomorrow*.

He nods and smiles conspiratorially, and yet again a rush of calm moves through me.

As we're packing up after class and I head towards the door, prepared to go back to my room, Jack appears at my side.

'So, where would you like to go?' he asks, sling-ing his backpack over his shoulder. I blink at him, uncomprehending.

'Don't tell me you've forgotten again,' he laughs. 'Our drink, Andie?'

'Oh,' I say. 'Sorry. A little distracted today.'

'It's OK,' he says. 'If I weren't so aware of my own devastating good looks, I might take it person-ally.' He gestures out the door like some old-timey gentleman, and despite myself I burst out laughing. I like this boy. I've not liked a boy in a long while. It feels good, a delightful contrast to the worry I've been carrying around for the last few days. Perhaps I can take the weight of the world off my shoulders for one evening and have some fun.

Three hours and several drinks later, Jack and I are making out. Hard. I'm not sure who kissed who first, but somehow on our way to the bar for another round I end up pushed up against the cold stone wall of the student bar, kissing his face off. And I can't lie, I'm enjoying it. A lot.

'Do you want to go back to mine?' he says as we come up for air, his voice low and deep in my ear. A chill runs up my spine, the good kind. Rooted in place, I nod.

Jack's room is small and surprisingly neat. A row of books lines his top shelf: Dickens, Atwood, Austen. And then a few I don't recognise, but which look like fantasy books: they have dragons curling along the spines. He notices my gaze and looks embarrassed.

'I, uh, have a bit of a thing for dragon books,' he says. I smile.

'Come on, Carlson, I thought your embarrassment threshold was higher than that.'

He smiles and visibly relaxes, then reaches up to brush my hair out of my face. His touch feels amazing: I've never felt so alive to the sensation of someone else's skin on mine.

'Do you think I did the right thing?' I ask, feeling unexpectedly vulnerable in this moment. Jack is, in some ways, the only one who understands how I'm feeling right now. He's put himself on the line too. He's also the target of the university witch hunt. We're in this together, and even through my guilt I can't deny I am secretly pleased about it. It feels good not to be alone.

He is quiet for a moment, then smiles at me, his face lighting up with warmth. 'Andie,' he says, tracing a hand down the side of my face. 'I know you did the right thing.'

And then he kisses me again, and all thoughts of today, of the article, totally disappear. All I feel is the sensation of his hand on my waist, his lips on mine. I drink him in, deepening the kiss and undoing the buttons of his shirt. *Jack Carlson, the unexpected silver lining.*

The next morning, I wake to find Jack has already gone. There's a note on the pillow next to me that reads *Early swim practice, sorry. Drinks again this week?* I rush to pull my clothes on, smiling to myself as I leave his room in halls – I have an early lecture to catch, and it's on the topic I'm researching for my dissertation, so I can't miss it. I rush across campus, not caring that I'm wearing my clothes from the night before, the thrill of it still rushing through my mind. I enter the lecture hall, which is already full, surprisingly so for a Friday morning, and settle into my seat, pulling out my laptop and furiously typing notes as the lecturer begins. This professor lectures at 1.5 speed, so blink and you could miss the idea that the entire hour-long lecture hinges on.

I'm so focused on my typing, I initially don't notice the whispering. But as the lecture goes on, it grows louder, and when I look up from my laptop

I find the people in the next row not-so-con-spicuously looking over their shoulder, trying to catch a glimpse of me. I'd been in such a rush this morning, and so distracted by Jack, that I'd totally forgotten about the events of yesterday, but now, as more and more people turn to look at me, barely disguising it at this point because most of the other people in the lecture theatre are doing it anyway, they hit me like a freight train. They know it was me. Somehow, they know. And that means I am well and truly fucked.

I text Sara: *SOS*. Her reply comes swiftly. *My room. Now. Damage control.*

I get up and pack away my things, leaving the lecture hall as quickly and quietly as I can, ignoring the glare of Mrs 1.5-speed as I pass her.

I try to steady my breath as I make my way across campus, suddenly and irrationally afraid that Robbie might jump out from behind any univer-sity building. *It will be OK. It will be OK. It will be OK.* I repeat to myself, a mantra circling round and round again in my mind as I rush to Sara's room.

When I enter, I find her in bed, her laptop out, plushies around her. I lean over to look at the screen. It's on a post to slutsofedinburgh.com which went up at 8:30 a.m. today, outing me as the article's author. A picture of my face, absurdly pulled from my LinkedIn profile, stares back at me, along with some choice words like 'super slut' and 'bitch'. If it weren't for the nausea swirling in my stomach, I would be rolling my eyes. I slump onto the bed and Sara hands me a plushie: her favourite penguin, Percy. I squeeze him to me.

'This is bad,' I say.

She shuts her laptop, and looks at me.

'It's going to be OK,' she says, and somehow, coming from her rather than me, it feels like it has more of a shot at being true. Her gaze meets mine, and the solidity of her friendship shines through. Sara is my safe place to land. As long as she is by my side, we will find a way to get through this. Besides, that stupid fucking website is not long for this world: my computer science friend Angela is going to take it down today.

'Here's what we're going to do,' Sara says, getting up out of bed and heading to her wardrobe. She begins rifling through her dresses, pulling a few out and discarding them on her floor. She keeps rifling until she finds the one she's looking for: a tight, blue, glittery number. Her favourite dress, her lucky dress. The one she wears when she's looking to get laid, or needs good grades, or just wants to have an especially good day. She throws it at me, and it lands in my lap.

'Tonight, you are going to put that on, and we are going to go out, and get drunk, and act like everything is fine, because it is.'

'But—' I protest, her blasé energy freaking me out.

'Fuck 'em, Andie,' she says, placing a hand on her hip. 'They didn't deserve my wallowing and they certainly don't deserve you hiding indoors until this blows over. Fuck that, fuck what they did, fuck what they might say. Fuck 'em.'

I look down at the dress, still not sure I'm onboard with whatever this epiphany Sara's had is. I run my hand across its fabric and find my thoughts dialling back to Jack last night, how he pulled my dress over my head in one movement, how he looked at my body like it was the first time he'd ever seen anyone naked, how he couldn't look away – fascinated by every curve, every crevice. A suspicion creeps into my mind that I desperately don't want to be true. It can't have been him, can it? He couldn't be that cold, to tell me I'd done the right thing, have sex with me then sell me out. Maybe someone at the newspaper found out it was me, somehow, and leaked my name? I thought I'd covered my tracks, but I suppose they could have traced my IP address if they really wanted to know. It could also have been Angela, I suppose – but my gut tells me it wasn't, considering how delighted she was that I asked for her help taking the website down. Confusion rattles through my brain, and I emerge from it to the warmth of Sara's hand on my shoulder.

'Andie, say it with me,' she says, her eyes fixed firmly on mine. Her steady, unwavering, trustworthy gaze. I sit up straighter, emboldened by her presence. 'Fuck them,' I say with her, my voice small and timid.

'Louder,' she says. 'Like you mean it.'

'Fuck them,' I almost shout, all the rage that's been building through the last week tumbling out of me. A resolve dawns on me as I say the words, and slowly but surely I start to believe them. Sara's right: they don't deserve to take today from me, or any day, for that fact. I have done the right thing, I have taken away some of their power. And I still have that – the knowledge that I was in the right. In fact, their anger, their retaliation is evidence that my plan worked, that I've rattled them: I put myself on the line, and it has paid off. I can handle a post outing me – their words are just that: words. It's not like I've ever cared what many people beyond Sara think of me, anyway. For the first time in the two weeks since the post went up about Sara, I feel like I can breathe again. And that's a feeling they can't take away from me.

A few hours later, Sara and I walk arm in arm towards the student union. I'm pretty much shaking with nerves, but I've had a couple of drinks already to take the edge off. I approach the bar and my phone pings. I've had it on silent all day, shut in the drawer of Sara's bedroom, unable to bring myself to look at it in case anyone was texting me about the article. Now as I pull it out of my pocket and unlock it, the screen lights up with notifications. Several missed calls, and a text from Jack: *Can we talk? It's urgent.* I frown at the screen, my stomach twisting. I'm not sure how I feel about this whole situation yet. I don't know if I can trust him. My heart is telling me that it couldn't have been him, that he was being truthful when he told me he thought I was doing the right thing. But there's something, some small, scared doubt in the back of my mind saying that I don't know him that well. I put my phone back in my pocket and decide that, at least for this evening, I won't think about it any further. Tonight is for celebrating, for showing them they haven't won.

For the next few hours I drift around the bar, the drunken haze growing stronger the more I consume. Many of them aren't bought by me: though I'm still getting the occasional death stare from a member of the rugby team, or one of their girlfriends, more often people are grabbing me as I pass them and pulling me into hugs, telling me they or their friend or their now-girlfriend was featured on that stupid website, and that I've done the entire university a favour. It's buoying me up, this feeling: the small flame inside me, it grows stronger with every person that thanks me. Sara is glued to my side the entire time, her skin a comforting presence against mine, a grounding force. I begin, little by little, to allow myself to feel proud.

As I'm twirling on the dance floor, feeling lighter than I've felt in a long time, Sara stops dead beside me. When I look at her, smiling, to ask her what's wrong, I find her staring at her phone with a horrified expression on her face. The smile drops off mine, and my stomach feels as if it's falling from a great height. Whatever she's looking at, I know it's going to burst this new, wonderful bubble I've found myself in. As much as I don't want to read it, my eyes are drawn to the screen: she's on the website again, slutsofedinburgh.com.

I relax slightly – she's probably just reading more comments on the post they put up about me this morning. But I'm drunk, and I don't care, because it won't be up for much longer. Angela emailed me earlier to say that the code is slightly more complex than she anticipated, but that the website will definitely be gone by midnight tonight. It will all disappear: the post outing me as the article's author, the post about Sara, all the horrible posts that came before it. I feel lighter even at the prospect. But then I focus on the screen properly, and see that she's not looking at the post from this morning, or the one about her. My name is there again, at the top of the page. But this time it's next to a review of my sexual performance.

All of the noise around me dies down to the hum of my blood pounding in my ears as I read the post, refusing to believe it's there even as my brain processes the information. Every cell in my body wants to believe that Jack can't have written this, that he can't be responsible. But then I see something that makes my heart lurch. It's a small detail, a reference to a freckle on the back of my neck that gives me extra points, apparently.

The memory of him touching that freckle gently, telling me how much he liked it, flashes through my mind.

I feel like I'm going to throw up. Ignoring Sara's concerned questions and the crowd around me, I stumble to the back of the bar, heading for the doors. As I'm about push them open, I catch someone's eye across the room: piercing, blue, looking right at me. Full of remorse and regret. Jack.

I tear my gaze away and stumble out into the car park, taking deep breaths of cold air. I don't have a jacket, but this time I don't feel the cold at all. I should've known I was alone in this, that he never would've actually helped me, let alone wanted me for anything more than just one night. I should know by now that the sports boys all only want one thing. I should never have trusted him. I make my way to the shadows, find a cold, damp bench to sit on and lean forwards, pressing my weight into my hands against my knees, my breath coming in gulps now. I've never had a panic attack, but if I had, I imagine this is what it would feel like. Adrenaline surges through me, and it feels like my heart is about to burst out of my chest, it's beating so hard.

I hear footsteps behind me, and my first thought is that it's Sara, but the tread is too heavy, too careful to be Sara's drunken gait, especially in her heels. It must be Jack. I whip around, ready to tell him exactly where to go, and find myself face to face with Robbie. A chill runs down my spine. The golden boy does not look so golden right now: the hard, impenetrable edge I've seen glimpses of in his eyes is now all over him. The way he's looking at me makes my blood run cold: he's furious, his steel gaze fixed on me, unmoving, with a quiet anger burning beneath it. I open my mouth to say something, or scream, or tell him to fuck off – whatever my plan was, it doesn't matter. As he reaches out to grip my arm, firm and threatening, my voice dies in my throat. He leans in, his breath on my face.

'You're vile, you know that?' he whispers, his words laced with venom, his voice level and low. I am paralysed by fear, my senses centred around the grip his hand has on my arm. It suddenly hits me how stupid I've been: I should have stayed closer to the union, in the light, closer to the other people out here. 'Just a stupid little whore who thinks she can ruin my life.' He leans in further, and I can feel his breath on my cheek. I want to flinch away, but I can't make myself move. 'I've got news for you, Andie. The university don't give a shit about the website. They know how much I'm worth. How much more I'm worth than you. If you were trying to get me sent down, your little plan has failed.'

'That wasn't my—' my voice falters as his grip tightens.

'You, on the other hand – you could very easily be dealt with. My father practically owns this university.'

My breath catches in my throat.

'Fix the damage you've done, or you can say goodbye to your degree, or to any chance of ever getting into another university. My father knows someone on practically every board. You'll be well and truly fucked.'

He looks at me for a long moment in stony silence, assessing my levels of fear, whether he's done enough.

'I suggest you retract that article, leave our website alone, and fade back into the background where you belong.'

A stone sinks in my stomach at his words.

'I can't,' I start, but he takes another step forwards. I feel frozen in place.

'You can't?' he says, a trace of amusement in his tone. 'Can't is an interesting word. I find many people can find the will to do things if you just give them a little … nudge.'

At this point, without warning, he pushes me, the palms of his hands hitting my shoulders with full force. I stumble backwards, shocked: it's all I can do to stay standing.

'I—' I start, but I find myself out of words. I am all fear – seeping like a cold stream through my veins and erasing all rational thought – that he'll hurt me, now. That he'll make good on his threat to have me kicked out of university, which at first sounded ridiculous but which now, in this moment, his unflinching eyes boring into mine, gives me pause. I've seen his dad before, at university conferences. Stony and terrifying, and the university seems to be at his beck and call. I'm not sure whether Robbie is bluffing or not. But I'm equally sure I don't want to find out.

My heart sinks as I realise the reality of the situation I'm in. I am filled with dread about breaking my promise to Sara, losing everything I've worked on for these last two weeks, but I also can't lose my degree, my chance at making my dad proud. He was so happy when I told him I got into Edinburgh, his alma mater. I picture his face: smiling, pulling out the cupboard champagne he was keeping for a special occasion.

'OK,' I say, nodding, even as something breaks apart irreparably inside me. Every fibre of my being is telling me this is all wrong, so wrong, that this is exactly the opposite of the justice I was trying to deliver. But I can't risk losing everything. If I'd realised how much was really on the line, I don't know if I'd have done it in the first place. Shame floods through me at the thought that I'm putting myself above what's right. But the survival instinct is too strong. I can feel myself retreating inwards, curling away from the parts of me that care about anything other than getting out of this situation.

Satisfied that he's made his point, he releases his grip. He turns away, and for a moment I think it's over, that he's going to leave me alone, but he's just checking no one is watching before what he does next. He lifts his hand, and before I can even register what's happening, I feel it hit the side of my face. The pain is delayed a moment, then lands all at once, mingled with shock which pierces me to my core. Somehow, even when he was threatening me, even when he shoved me, some part of my brain was still relying on my gender for my safety. I didn't think he'd actually hit a woman, but of course that was naive of me. I put my hand up to my face, red raw and stinging where his palm connected, and close my eyes, waiting for whatever's coming next. But nothing comes. I open my eyes, a tear rolling down the side of my face, to find him spitting at my feet.

'Poor, helpless, pathetic Andie,' he says, leaning closer again. I flinch, bile moving up my throat, fighting every instinct to run. I will not run. I will not give him that satisfaction. And then it comes: the moment I've been anticipating since the start of this interaction. Pure, deep hatred enters his expression, everything else falling away. In this moment, I am suddenly and horribly aware of the physical difference between us. If he wanted to hurt me, really hurt me, he could. And no one would know. 'You stupid whore,' he spits, his voice low. 'If you even so much as look at me the wrong way, I will make really fucking sure you learn never to open that stupid mouth of yours again.' He leans in, his eyes boring into mine, and I feel his breath on my face. My hand shakes involuntarily, the fear building now. 'I will fuck *you* up, not just your university career. Do you understand me?'

There's a strange relief at his words – the certainty I wanted, a confirmation of the danger I'm in, of the calibre of the person I'm dealing with. It's comforting, for a moment. Then, immediately, fear spikes, freezing me in place. I find I no longer know how to move. His threat is real: I know it, as much as I feel the sting on my face. And, in this moment, I'm terrified. I manage a slow, shaky nod and he spits at my feet again, then turns and walks away. I stand, numb and frozen in place, for God knows how long. *You're OK,* I try to tell myself, but the voice is overwhelmed by the fear that drowns everything else out. I was terrified this would happen, terrified that by crossing them I'd end up hurt. I ignored my instincts, sure that they were unwarranted. Relying on a stupid, naive view of the world – a sense that if I did the right thing everything would work out OK. I can see now just how stupid that was. Shame starts to pool in my stomach – for putting myself in this situation in the first place. For not staying invisible, safe, where I belonged. For thinking I could fix something that's clearly so ingrained the likes of me weren't going to do anything about it. And now I'm hurt, and terrified, and I have nothing to show for it. And I have to tell Sara – *Oh God.* After what feels like forever, I look up to find Jack walking towards me. Pain rips through me. *No. Not now, not him.*

'Andie, are you OK?' he says, his voice panicked. 'I just saw Robbie—'

'I'm fine, Jack,' I say, my voice robotic. I just need to say enough that he'll leave me alone and I can get inside, and find Sara, and go back to my room. 'I don't want to talk to you right now, OK? I need to find Sara.'

'But—'

'Please, Jack. I don't want to hear it.'

'If you'll just let me explain—'

'Leave me the fuck alone.' The words burst out of me, all of the feelings I've been suppressing for the last few weeks laced into them. 'Clearly, I misjudged you. You're just as bad as the rest of them.'

He stops, frozen in place, words deserting him as he processes the weight of my accusations.

'Is that really what you think of me, Andie?'

No, says some small voice, deep down. The part that remembers how gently he touched my face before he kissed me. The conviction in his voice when he told me I was doing the right thing. Somewhere inside me, I know there must be an explanation for this, but that part of me is drowned out by a vast, overwhelming anger that's spreading through my body. I don't want to hear how or why it happened. I just want somewhere to put this feeling before it consumes me completely. 'Yes, it is.' I say, my tone final, and I watch his face crumple. Something twists inside me, then hardens into a firm resolve. This feels right, like I'm putting up a wall between us, between myself and the rest of the world. Somewhere I'll be safe. I close my eyes to block out his pained expression, willing my voice to stay firm, and deliver the last words I'll ever say to him. 'I never want to see you again.'

When I open my eyes a few moments later, he is gone.

21

Edinburgh, five years later. Andie.

It doesn't hurt as much as I thought it would. Despite all my expectations, the pain I've been avoiding for so long feels suddenly small in comparison to the obliteration of my dad's death. As if two events were tangled, tied together in a great knot in my chest, and now a piece of rope has loosened enough to pull them apart. A dull ache compared to a great cavern.

My shoulders relax, my heartbeat beginning to slow. I'm still on the bench, in the car park: I can hear the noise around me, the chatter, the footsteps, some of which are moving in my direction. I open my eyes, and he is there.

This time I don't react, I don't try to push him away. I just look at him, more open to his presence than I have been this whole trip. It makes absolute sense that he's here now – he's the last piece of this.

'I was worried when you didn't show up at the event,' he says, sitting gently down next to me. His movements are slow and soft; he doesn't want to startle me. 'As soon as it ended, I went out to find you. For some reason, this was the first place I thought to look.'

'I think,' I say, slowly, the words coming from somewhere deep inside me, somewhere that's not quite so afraid now. Somewhere that knows this is the right thing to do. That's resolved, finally, to take Sara's advice. To face this, whatever might happen. 'I think I'm ready to talk about what happened.'

'Are you sure?' he says, turning to me now, a frown crossing his features. 'Don't humour me just because I'm angry.'

'I'm sure,' I say, and something on my face convinces him, because he takes a breath. And then he tells me.

22

Edinburgh, five years ago. Jack.

Jesus Christ. Did that actually just happen? It did. I didn't dream it. I just slept with Andie.

My mind swirls as I rush across campus to the pool, kicking myself for drinking so much alcohol the night before. I'm going to be five minutes late, which means extra laps, and I already feel like I'm going to throw up. But I'm not worried about any of that right now, because I just slept with Andie. And, if I haven't misread the signals, I think she might want to see me again. I resist punching the air — it's early, but there are still students milling around — but elation is the only way to describe how I'm feeling. Since she sat next to me in the lecture hall at the beginning of this year, her red hair falling over her face as she pulled her books out of her bag, and made a joke about how little she cared about dusty old Chaucer, I've been absolutely hooked. I barely remember any of the material that's been covered, I've been so distracted trying to build up the courage to talk to her beyond that first exchange. Before her cryptic email a couple of weeks ago, all I'd managed was a few comments about the weather, a joke about my hair being wet from swim team practice, not greasy (not my finest hour, I'll admit – but she did laugh) and asking her to borrow a pen.

I rush into the changing rooms, unable to wipe the smile off my face, only to find the place surprisingly empty. I know I'm late, but I can't be the only one. Niall, at least, is always late. I've actually never seen the room this empty: it's almost creepy. But I don't have time to dwell, or I'll have to do so many make-up laps that I'll definitely throw up. I rush over to my locker and start rifling through my bag, when I feel a hand on my shoulder. I flinch, startled, and shake it off, turning to confront whoever decided it would be funny to scare the hell out of me. My words die on my tongue. Robbie is standing in front of me, looking at me with mild curiosity. My stomach falls. *He can't know. I only spoke to Niall. He's my friend, he'd never do that to me.* But something about his facial expression sets me on edge.

'Carlson,' he says. I stand up straight, drawing up to my full height.

'Why aren't you at practice, mate?' I ask, trying to keep my expression neutral, my tone casual.

'Cancelled, today,' he says. 'A few of the guys were so upset by that article bullshit that they went heavy last night. I gave them the morning off.'

I frown, ignoring his bait and pulling out my phone to find the email that he must have sent round, but there's nothing.

'When were you going to tell me?' I ask, keeping my voice even.

'I've told you now, haven't I?' he says, smiling to himself. He picks up my goggles, which have fallen out of my bag, and examines them.

'These are looking pretty rough. Had them for a while?' he asks, holding them between his thumb and forefinger. I nod, slowly, not sure where he's going with this. A deep, gut instinct is telling me something is wrong. Very wrong. 'Of course,' he says, a look of barely disguised disgust passing over his face. 'Scholarship boy can't afford new goggles, can he now?'

'Look, mate——' I start, but before I know it he's slammed me against the locker.

'I know it was you, Carlson. You and that slut, Andie. Not that I give a shit who you sleep with, but it's pretty obvious. You start hanging out with her right before this stuff blows up, then suddenly there's an article out. I know you're too stupid to write it, so it must be someone with a vendetta. And would you look at that, the last post before the article came out is about her little friend Sara.'

He tightens his grip on my shirt, leaning in. 'I saw you in the library together, clearly up to something. And I saw you again last night. What did she do, promise you sex if you helped her out?'

I clench my jaw. *Fuck this guy.* 'I have no idea what you're talking about,' I say, fixing my gaze on the lockers ahead of me.

'Really? Because Niall seemed pretty keen to tell me all about your involvement. Especially when I threatened to kick him off the team. Another scholarship boy, bless him. Mummy couldn't afford his accommodation fees.'

His hand clenches around my T-shirt, and he leans in. 'You're playing with fire, Carlson. I could make your life really miserable, if I wanted to.'

I lean back, searching for a response, but find I have none. To my surprise, he studies my face for a moment, then relaxes his grip and lets go, moving a step backwards.

'You're not going to admit it, are you?' he asks, fascination moving across his features as he looks me up and down.

'I don't know what you're talking about,' I repeat, my hands curling into fists. If he tries to jump me again, this time I'm ready.

'OK,' he says, raising his hands. 'Prove it.'

My forehead creases again as I try to decipher his meaning. 'What do you mean, prove it?' I ask, my tone still neutral even as a sense of dread moves through me.

'Write a post about her,' he says. *Not that. Anything but that.*

'I didn't sleep with her—' I start, trying to throw him off the scent, to stave off the panic that's starting to rise.

'Doesn't matter,' he says, shrugging. 'Write a post about her anyway,' he continues. 'Lie. Make it up. I don't care. If you don't, I'll know you did it. And I can think of much worse consequences than a post on the internet. Like, say, having your scholarship rescinded …' His tone is casual, but there's an undertone I don't like. 'Or having both you and that bitch kicked out of this university.'

Shit. His words have the intended effect, stopping me in my tracks for a moment. But, a second later, I frown, processing their severity – it's a bit much, even for Robbie. The scholarship threat could be serious, and I'll have to get my head around that: my scholarship is dependent on participation in the first team. He chooses the team with the coach, and I've been slipping closer to the bottom half in the last season. It's a stretch, still, that Robbie could be so persuasive, since I have a good relationship with our coach. But it would potentially only take one conversation to have me placed on reserve, at risk of losing it entirely, and meaning my mum would have to somehow figure out fees for the rest of this year. The thought sends a lump into my throat. But having us kicked out? I know his dad is on the board, and is generally a pretty scary guy, but could he really have that kind of power? Despite all this, the panic I've been staving off since he tapped me on the shoulder starts to rise in pitch. I close my eyes, trying to organise my thoughts and assess the actual risk of this situation, unwilling to allow myself to be pushed into something by an empty threat. When I open them again, he's moved a step closer. 'If you think I'm joking, just look at what happened to Sam.'

I blink. Sam was a member of our swim team last year – a first year, on a scholarship. He and I got along well – I was a mentor of sorts. Towards the end of the year, he disappeared: quit the team, dropped out of university. I've tried reaching out since, but he hasn't replied. Horror moves through me, chilling my veins, at what I realise Robbie is suggesting.

'That was you?' I ask, and he shrugs.

'Little fucker got a bit too mouthy one night, started talking about how he thought he'd make a better captain than me. I taught him a lesson. Next thing I know he's gone to the university about it.' He pauses for effect, casually lifting the string of my swimming bag and letting it fall. 'Obviously it went straight to my father. It was ... gently suggested to him that since he had such violent tendencies and had started a fight with me, it might benefit him to drop out, rather than be kicked out, as he might then have at least a chance of getting a degree elsewhere.'

'Jesus Christ, Robbie,' I say. I knew he was shady, but I had no idea.

'People don't fuck with me and get away with it,' he says, bragging now with the sociopathic confidence of someone who has ruined someone's life and is happy about it. *Poor Sam.*

I process this information, trying not to show too much emotion in case it gives anything away. It's clear from what he's just said, if it's true, that going to the university about this will be no help. As I'm thinking, the exchange I had with Andie yesterday rises to the top of my mind – when did she tell me the website was going to be taken down, again? I try to focus, to visualise the piece of paper. *Tomorrow*, she wrote. I check my wrist. It's 7 a.m., and the website is due to come down today, I just don't know when. So I have a choice: I can assume Robbie is bluffing and potentially risk my university career and Andie's, or I can do this, and risk the post being up for a few hours, but at least buy us some time to work out a contingency plan. Maybe, if I can get to her in time, her friend can pull the website down before the post even goes up. If not – my stomach sinks. Even if it's only up for a few hours, it will be awful for her. She'll be disgusted and devastated, and it might ruin my chances with her forever. But I don't see that I have much of a choice.

I take a deep breath, my mum's face at the forefront of my mind, her relief when we got the letter about my scholarship. Slowly, a resolve forms inside me. The prospect of writing this post goes against every value I hold, but the risk is too high. This is by no means over – I know Robbie well enough to know it won't be that easy – but at the very least it will get me out of this changing room, to find Andie and explain.

'OK,' I say. 'I'll do it.'

He nods, then gestures to my bag. 'Your laptop in there?' I grunt by way of affirmation. He spreads his hands, as if inviting me to get it out. I slowly extract it from my bag, every part of me rebelling against what I'm about to do. I open it and navigate to the website's submissions page, repulsion moving through me, and open up the Google form. I type as quickly as I can.

Performance: 10/10

Looks: 10/10

Body: 10/10

I type 10 for every rating, trying not to read them too closely, to pretend I'm writing about some other person, some fictional girl who's not Andie.

Events leading to the score: We went for drinks at the university bar, then back to my room.

Special mentions:

Here I pause, a wave of disgust moving through me, bile in my throat. This is the worst section.

Other posts I've read use this box to objectify, denigrate or offend. I can't write about Andie like that, can't post it on the internet, to be recorded in the ether perhaps forever, even after the website comes down.

Robbie leans over my shoulder. 'What's the hold up, Carlson?' he says, his eyes moving over the screen until they land on the last section, then a smile spreads across his face. 'My favourite part. But clearly, you need some guidance.' He leans closer, and for a moment I panic, terrified he's going to take over. But then he continues, his tone jovial and conspiratorial. The bile rises further up my throat. 'There needs to be some identifying feature. I want her to know you've written this. Otherwise we don't have a deal.'

I pause, hands hovering over the keys, desperate not to do this.

Robbie sighs behind me. 'Jesus, Carlson, stop being such a wuss. Look, fine – if you like, I can handle this part. You give me the details, and I'll get a little creative maybe—' he says, and I shake my head, dread flooding through me about what he might write.

I feel sick at the prospect, but if I'm going to do it, the least I can do here is write it by own hand, not hiding behind someone else's. I can own it, I can apologise. I can explain. As I rub my palms across my eyes, trying to build up to writing something, anything, that won't make this an unforgivable betrayal, an image of last night comes to me, unbidden: the freckle on her left shoulder blade. So small, beautiful, so perfectly Andie. I take a deep breath and open my eyes. That was for us, for no one else. But then I glance at Robbie, and see the firm resolve in his eyes, the subtle threat.

I let out the breath slowly and type the words that take the post from a series of meaningless numbers to something much, much worse. *Focus, Jack.* I keep my eyes trained on the keyboard, afraid if I look at the screen my resolve will falter. I place my attention firmly on the next steps: getting out of this changing room, getting to her.

I finish typing, then glance at the top of the screen, at the words 'slutsofedinburgh.com', and a sense of finality sinks in. After everything Andie has fought for, this will be her worst nightmare. Fuck this guy. Fuck all of this. I flinch as I remember referring to the guys who post on here as 'low-lives' when we first met in the library – that feels ironic now. Robbie's eyes are on the screen, examining my work. It's sparse, compared to the usual posts, but I can't bring myself to write more. The more I write, the more real it will become. He frowns, reading, and I hold my breath, hoping I've done enough. He gives me a curt nod, and I click submit on the form.

23

I sit for a moment, processing Jack's story, letting it sink into me as the students continue to mill around us. The great weight that has been sitting on my chest since I found out he'd be my author lifts somewhat, only to be replaced by a different one. I hadn't realised until this moment that buried under all the anger, all the pain, had been an almost undetectable kernel of hope – that there would be an explanation for what happened, that my instincts about him hadn't been as horribly wrong as it had seemed at the time. For my own sake. But even as it ignites again, a deep sadness moves through me.

I let out a breath, the realisation dawning on me that the huge crime I've been holding over him, punishing him for all this time, wasn't really a crime after all. When all was said and done, it was Robbie's game. Jack and I were just pawns, each doing what we had to to protect ourselves.

And it's more than that: now the threads have untangled themselves, I can see the event for what it was. Jack hurt me, yes. He betrayed me. Both of those things are still true, even despite the new context. But even without what he's just told me, I've been blaming the wrong person. The truth is, it's been much easier to put all of this on Jack, to hold him responsible. Because he was the one I trusted. Because, despite myself, I cared about him. But mostly because I didn't want to face up to the truth of what happened: that Robbie's actions took away my sense of safety in the world. My notion that if I just did everything right, then things would work out OK. That I would be safe. And, just as I was reeling and trying to put that confidence back together, my dad died and it shattered completely.

And there, underneath it all, untangled now, is the kicker – the real event I've been avoiding this whole time. The reason Jack's presence was so terrifying to me, because he represented more than just a painful reminder of what happened in Edinburgh, but a portal back to that time in my life. The months afterwards. The nights in the hospital. The prayers, every day, that something would happen to change the situation, that someone would discover a miracle cure. It's the same reason

I have such a problem with my mum moving on, the reason the mere mention of Nigel's name has sent a pain rippling through me. The reason I've been running, for the last five years, never looking back for too long in case it destroyed me. My dad's death. And the hard, cold, horrible truth it brings:

I miss him terribly. And he's never coming back.

I clench my hands around the bench, winded by the force of this realisation. It settles around me, shifting the air somehow. There's a relief in admitting it, finally, that washes over me, unlatching something inside me that's been holding on so tightly for so long. Even as it's closely followed by guilt, that I've had everything so wrong, for so long. That I've risked hurting the people around me, exploding outwards rather than facing my own pain. That I somehow made Jack a representation of a myriad of things that weren't his fault, clinging to his betrayal as a source of certainty, a shield against my feelings. It's all I can do not to burst into tears right now, finally giving them release. But I have to finish this, to give Jack the closure he deserves. I lean forwards so my gaze is focussed on the gravel and breathe in the cool air, honing in on the sound of students' voices, remembering myself walking across this car park with Sara on my way to class.

'I heard him bragging the next day in the changing rooms, about how he'd shut you up,' Jack continues, his expression twisting with anger. 'I hit him so hard I was on probation for three months.'

'Oh Jack,' I say, looking up at him, my heart sinking. After hearing why he did what he did, to preserve his place at university, his scholarship – it's heartbreaking to hear that he almost lost it all anyway.

'Don't be,' he says, his tone bitter. 'When I heard him say he threatened you, that he *hit* you, I—' I glance at him, and there's an edge to his expression I haven't seen before. He sees me looking and catches himself, running his hand through his hair. 'Clearly, I was an idiot. I knew he wasn't going to let it go, but I thought I'd bought us time, that I could find you and we could figure it out, together. I could never have imagined – I'm so sorry, Andie,' Jack says, his voice shaking. I look up, and his face is etched with remorse. 'If I could tell you how much I regret—'

'Stop,' I say. 'It's OK.' And I mean it. A few weeks ago, I never could have imagined saying those words to him. But that Andie feels like a totally different person now. New Andie suddenly understands, with a wave of remorse, why it hurt so much more than it would've done had it been anyone but Jack. Why I let him kiss me in the park in Dublin, despite it being the stupidest decision of my life so far. Why I have to leave, now, before I make things any worse.

I place my hand over his. A silence settles between us for a few seconds, and I'm not sure how to break it.

'Andie,' he says eventually, turning to me, and I can see in his eyes that he's about to say things I both want to hear and don't. Because the dull ache of grief is moving through me, for the people we were. Because too much has happened between us. But, mostly, because I can't shake the over-whelming feeling that he deserves better than this. Better than someone who almost messed up this tour because of her own selfish impulses. Who wouldn't hear him out, who assumed the worst of him at every single turn. Who tangled him up in her grief, and who used him as a vehicle for her anger and rage, for so long.

'Please, don't,' I say. He looks confused for a split second, then his face falls.

'I understand if you're still angry,' he says. 'What I did – what I wrote. I could've done something,

313

could've found a way to—' He falters, his expression defeated and sad.

This is almost too much to bear. 'Jack,' I say. 'It's OK. I just—' I swallow, ignoring the lump in my throat. This is harder than I thought it would be. 'I need to go home. This whole trip has been a mistake, one that could've ruined your chances with this book. It deserves better than that. You deserve better.'

'But—'

'Please,' I say, interrupting him. 'If you can do one thing for me on this trip, it will be this: let me go.' He stops, his expression pained, but I see his posture shift, resigned – he's no longer tense, no longer primed to ask me to stay. I stand up, and at the sight of him on the bench, as if frozen in time, my heart drops an inch. But I can't continue this conversation anymore. I have to get out of here, back to New York, where I can't hurt him any further. Even the thought makes me feel lighter than I have in days, purposeful: I know it's the right thing to do. I might be running away, but this time it's for a good reason. This time it's for someone else, not for me.

'Goodbye, Jack,' I say, reaching for his shoulder and pressing my hand lightly to the sleeve of his suit jacket. Then, using everything in me to keep from falling apart, I stand up and walk away.

24

The flight to New York feels a hundred years long. Just two days ago I was so excited for this moment – when I'd be heading back to Sara, to New York. To my life. But now it feels wrong, heavy. The prospect of my empty apartment makes me want to cry.

As the flight progresses, I feel worse. Right now, squashed between two kind elderly women in my economy seat, I feel more alone than I ever have – I miss Sara, I miss my mum, who I still haven't called about her wedding. And – now the truth has risen to the surface, the realisation seems inevitable: I miss Jack. I miss seeing him every morning, I miss watching him talk to booksellers and sign books and give interviews on television and make speeches at events. I even miss telling him to get lost – hating him was the most alive I've felt in a long time. But what's done is done. All I can do is get back to New York and face the consequences. I take a deep breath, pull my sleeping mask over my eyes, and allow myself to sink into the darkness. As the plane grows closer to its destination, my dad's face flickers into my mind, gradually fading as I drift slowly off to sleep.

I head into the office the next day, jet-lagged but ready to face the music.

Jessica reacts normally when I arrive, greeting me with a smile and asking me how the trip was. Slightly startled at her lack of reaction to my early return, I reply with 'fine', and sit down at my desk. As I do, she leans over and asks if I have a few minutes to step into her office. My stomach drops. *Here we go.*

'I received a call from Jack this morning,' she says once we've sat down and she's closed the door, her expression neutral. What little strength I had left drains out of me. Oh God. What did he say to her?

'He explained what happened on the trip,' she says, and as she does she reaches out her arm to touch mine. 'I'm so sorry, Andie.' Her expression is sympathetic. 'We had no indication that he'd be a difficult author to work with. Our non-fiction team only had lovely things to say about him.'

I don't say speak for a few moments, shocked into silence. 'What do you mean?' I say, when I eventually find my voice again.

'You don't have to protect him, Andie,' she says, crossing her arms. 'He told me what happened: that he was so stressed about the book being a success he made your life hell on the trip, and that it got so bad he had a change of heart and told you to go home early.'

My heart twists. He's trying to help me. But this time, I can't let him.

'That's not true,' I say, a new resolve moving through me. I can't let him take the fall for this. I feel tears threatening, but I take a breath and hold them back. 'Jack and I have a personal history,' I say, looking straight at Jessica. 'We knew each other at university, and some — some things happened between us, which I didn't want to disclose, so I lied by omission and didn't say anything. But if anyone was making anyone else's life hell, it was me.' By this point, the tears are dangerously close, but I need to carry on or I won't be able to finish. 'I'm sorry, Jessica. I let you down, and I let the company down, and I jeopardised a really important campaign. I'll—' I pause, taking a short, rattling breath. '—I'll see myself out.'

I get up out of my seat and move to start walking towards the door, but she puts an arm on mine
and stops me. 'Wait, Andie. Sit.' Her voice is sterner
than I've heard it since I started this job, so I obey,
and I sit back down.

'Firstly, I have to disagree with you. I don't know
what happened between you and Jack, but from
my perspective you have done a brilliant job on his
campaign. The coverage you secured was excellent,
and all the feedback I've had is that the trip went
very smoothly. I even had an email from Declan in
Ireland saying how fantastic you were.'

I am just about hearing what she's saying, but my
heart is beating so fast it's difficult to concentrate.

'Secondly, Jack himself told us how excellent you
were, and implied that if we fired you he'd never
write another book for us. Personal history or not,
no author who has had his campaign ruined would
be speaking about you like that. Trust me.'

This hits like another punch to the gut. *Keep it
together, Andie.*

'What I want to know,' Jessica says, 'is do *you*
want to keep working with us?'

I wasn't expecting this, and it floors me. I don't
feel like I deserve to think about that right now.
But Jessica keeps looking at me, expectant, so I take

a breath, trying to shut out the negative thoughts and consider what she's saying.

On the one hand, I know there's some truth to what she's just said: I did put a good campaign together for Jack, and I ran the tour as smoothly as I could with respect to the external circumstances. I suppose, if you step back and remove some of the times I told him to get fucked, I objectively did an OK job. On the other hand, I slept with an author on a book tour, and crossed several other serious professional lines. Regardless of everything that followed, regardless even of the past between us, I can't help but feel that my overall impact on the tour – on Jack – was a negative one. I should have been honest from the start, but now it's too late.

With the risk of running into Jack again, I'm not sure I can countenance staying in this job. And, if I'm truly honest with myself, I'm now not sure that I want to. I need some space to put myself back together, to figure out what it is that I actually want. Because I'm no longer sure that it's this: this job, this life. I'm not sure of anything, anymore.

'I really appreciate your faith in me, Jessica,' I say, and her expression turns hopeful, as if she's expecting me to say I want to stay. I take a deep breath.

'But I think it's better for me, and for the company, if I hand in my notice.'

'Are you absolutely sure?' she says. 'If you feel comfortable disclosing what happened, I'm sure we could work something out. It really may not be as bad as you think.'

'I think this is the right thing to do,' I say, resolve moving through me.

She looks disappointed but nods. 'OK,' she says. 'I can't say I agree with your choice, but I respect your decision,' she says. 'And for what it's worth, I'm very sorry to lose you.'

I take a breath as I leave the room, looking around the office that just a month ago was the culmination of so much hard work. The dream of an Andie who was sure beyond anything that this would fix all her problems, would finally make her feel that she'd arrived at her destination. That she could stop running. But – as I found out in spades – it was never going to be enough. I can see that now. I just wish I'd realised a few weeks ago, and saved Jack from being caught up in it all.

I'm surprised by the calm I feel. My lease is up in a couple of months, and I have enough money to last me until then. After that I'll have to figure things out. But the desperate financial anxiety that has been following me around since Sara moved out is suddenly absent. I know that this is the right thing to do, and that's more important than anything else right now.

I pick up my stuff from my desk – nothing more than a few pens and a photo of me, my mum and my dad. I'm so used to its presence that I barely look at it anymore. But, once I'm in the elevator, I reach in and pull it out of the box. We're on the street where my dad had his yoga studio. I stand in the centre of the frame, looking miserable, while my dad beams beside me and my mum leans against the wall on my right. I was fifteen, and I'd just had my hair cut. My dad kept insisting it was beautiful, though I wasn't convinced: it was too short and choppy. I'd gotten the inspiration from a picture in a magazine, but when I saw it on myself I hated it. I'd been crying all morning. After some gentle coaxing, my dad had persuaded me to leave the house to go down the road for a coffee. On the way home, he grabbed my mum and I and stopped someone on the street to take a photograph of us. I remember protesting, embarrassed about the state of my hair, then eventually relenting when I saw how much he wanted it. It was only after the photo was taken that he turned us both around and told us we were standing outside his new yoga studio.

When I've looked back on that memory since I've felt a huge weight of guilt: I made the morning about me, when he clearly had huge news he wanted to share with us.

The thing no one ever tells you about losing someone you love is how guilty you'll feel about every single moment you spent with them where you could've been more attentive, more loving. Where you would've soaked up more of their presence, if you'd known you'd lose them so soon. But now, when I look at this photo which has served as a symbol of my guilt for so long, I remember the warmth of his arms around us. I remember my mum, who'd been sceptical of his idea to open a studio, wiping away tears of happiness for him. I remember feeling loved. Whole.

Before I am aware of what's happening, I'm crying, the tears I held in in that car park with Jack finally coming loose. It feels right, to hurt. To feel this loss, without pushing it aside.

I'm barely aware of my surroundings as I step out of the elevator. I don't know what I'm doing, and I don't have a job. And there's so much still to fix: with Sara, with my mum. But right now, I'm not thinking about that. I step out onto the street, the heat of the New York air hitting my face, and I feel like I'm seeing the city for the first time. *My dad is gone,* I think to myself, the truth of the words settling around me. And that's a truth I will, perhaps, carry around for the rest of my life, facing it in moments where I least expect it: when I pass a yoga studio, or see a shirt in his favourite shade of blue. When I watch my mum marry someone new, or visit the home I grew up in. When I allow myself to think about him, rather than pushing the thought away, leaning in to the memories of his hand in mine, us buying piles of books in local bookshops, him teaching me how to swim. Us in our family home, laughing with mum. They're all there, waiting, whenever I need them. And thinking about them, thinking about him, will hurt, forever, in increments. Sometimes small twinges, sometimes waves that almost knock me off my feet. But in this moment, the New York pavement underfoot, my breath coming slow and deep, a stillness coming over me as the city moves around me, everyone surging forwards into their lives, it hits me, for the first time, that maybe that's OK.

As soon as I get back to my flat, I pick up my phone and call my mum. She answers after two rings. 'Andie!' she practically sings, and the tears start falling again at the sound of her voice. She deserves better than what she's had for the last few weeks, the last few years.

'I'm so sorry, Mum,' I say, feeling suddenly and all at once how stupid I've been, to be so scared of this.

'For what, sweetheart?'

And then it all spills out: the guilt I've been hold-ing on to for the last four years, increasing with each day we've been apart. That I never moved back after the graduate scheme. That I haven't talked to her properly about Dad since I moved away. That I don't call her enough. That I feel like a failure of a daughter, like I'm constantly letting her down. That all these years I've been making an island of myself, when I should have been holding her closer. And as I'm talking it becomes clearer by the second: the problem was never New York. It was me. I put the distance between us, not my job. Not even living on a different continent. I've been using it as an excuse to avoid my feelings, all this time. Pushing my mum away instead of letting her in. Building a prison of my grief rather than allowing her to share in it. She listens, patient and kind as always, and even her silence makes me want to cry. 'The truth is—' I pause, willing myself to get the words out, to do this properly. 'I've been all tangled up in my feelings about Dad. And I didn't know how to talk about it without falling apart. Every time I come home, every time we talk about him, it hurts so much I can't breathe. And then I met Nigel, and it all came up again, and I—' I pause, trailing off, finding I've run out of words. In the next beat of silence my body comes alive with fear, waiting for her response. Waiting for her to confirm what I've been afraid of this whole time: that I'm a terrible daughter, and I've messed every-thing up irrevocably.

'Oh, sweetheart, it's OK,' she says, gently, her tone a little more serious now, and the tension starts to seep out of me. 'Nigel has been very patient with me, very kind. But Lord knows it hasn't been smooth sailing for me either. It's been wonderful, and sometimes difficult, and sometimes sad.' She takes a breath, and when she speaks again there's resolve in her tone. 'I've found, though, in my years on this earth, that life will surprise you. There is never just one thing at a time. There's room for many things, always. Light and dark, all at once.'

The truth of her words sinks into me as she says them, and I sit with them for a moment, feeling her presence through the phone. I take a breath.

'Now, secondly,' she continues. 'And I need you to really listen to me here. You know, of course you do – in those first six months after your father died, it was all I could do just to keep it together. And you were wonderful, and you helped me so much. But I wanted you to take that job. Nothing made me prouder than seeing you get on that plane. It was so brave, like you were seizing life with both hands, even after everything we've lost. It made me feel more brave, too. So don't you for one second feel sorry for living your life. We've all just been doing our best, in the face of a horrible loss.' She pauses, waiting for her words to sink in. I let out a long breath when she's finished, like her words have released me from the fortress I've shut myself in over the last four years. I feel lighter, like a huge weight has been lifted from me, and I can breathe, again.

'I miss him,' I say, the tears starting, now.

'Oh, love,' she says. 'I miss him, too, every day.'

'Do you remember that day at school in Year 9 where we had to wear pink?' I ask, suddenly alive with a memory that's rushed to the surface, with the desire to share it with her.

She goes quiet for a moment, thinking. 'Yes,' she says, eventually. 'You didn't have anything to wear – you were in your rebellious phase, wearing black all the time – and you were so worried about it, bless you.'

'Do you remember what happened?' I ask.

'Your father—' Her tone is gentle, as if she's treading carefully. I wait, and after a moment of silence, she continues, tentatively. 'He went out to buy you a T-shirt while you were at school, to surprise you, but bless his heart he had no idea which one to get you.'

I smile through my tears in anticipation of what comes next. 'Then what?' I ask.

'Well,' she says, and I can hear that she's choked up, now. 'He bought you fourteen shirts, the silly man, and put them all out on your bed for when you got home.'

I laugh, even as my eyes fill with tears, even as my chest contracts with the pain of loss. A great hole opens in the defences I've been putting up, and the grief flows out, a steady stream, breaking down some of the walls. 'There were so many shirts, Mum,' I say, and then she's laughing, too, and we're both hysterical, the sound of her laughter a comfort as tears pour down my face.

'I love you,' I say, my throat thick.

'I love you too, my Andie,' she says. 'And so does he. He loved you more than anything.'

This is it: the last frontier, the last part of the wall crumbling down entirely with her words, the reassurance I didn't know I needed to hear. And then without even stopping to think about it, I take a deep breath, and tell her everything. What happened in Edinburgh, what's happened since. Everything I've felt in the last five years that I haven't told her about, for fear it would be too much, too difficult, spills out of me like a river, flowing freely from the dam that has now burst completely. She listens, again, patiently, silently, waiting for me to finish.

'Everything's such a mess, I don't know what to do,' I say, tears now streaming down my face at the years of emotion I've just released, the overwhelm that I've finally been honest, finally let her in, and that everything hasn't blown up as I expected it to. I'm still here, and the apartment building is still standing, and my mum is still on the other side of the phone. Like she always has been. Like she always wanted to be.

A wave of grief hits me for the years I've lost to all this pain, the years we could have spent growing closer rather than drifting apart. And in the next second it comes to me. The lost time I want to make up for with her. The wedding and everything that will come with it. 'Mum,' I say, my voice small, nerves suddenly taking hold. 'Can I come and stay for a while? Maybe—' I take a breath, holding the phone closer to my ear, 'Maybe I can help with the wedding planning, and spend some time with Nigel.'

She doesn't respond immediately, and for a split second I'm worried I might have misjudged how welcome I'll be, especially when she has a wedding to plan. I might be more of a burden than a help. But then she sighs, as if these are the words she's been waiting for me to say for the last five years, and says, 'I cannot tell you how special that would be for me. My Andie, back home. When can you come? I'll have to start buying all your favourite foods—'

By the time we get off the phone, I've booked a flight for a few days' time and, despite my protests, she's made a shopping list which is probably about three pages long. Maybe my return home isn't going to be as selfless as I hoped, but maybe that's OK. Maybe, after all this time, I can finally let her look after me, too.

25

Over the next twenty-four hours, I slowly pack up my apartment. I have a plant fostering arrangement with my neighbour, who was watering them while I was away: he is going to look after them until I've figured out what I'm doing, and if that doesn't involve coming back to New York, we'll move to an adoption process. James the ficas was initially unhappy about it, but when he realised he could stay in my neighbour's south-facing window, he changed his mind.

As I'm doing a final once-over of the bedroom, rummaging through the back of my wardrobe to see if I've missed anything, my eye lands on a shoebox, shoved to the back of the top shelf. Despite myself, my chest tightens at the sight of it. Out of sight, out of mind. I placed it here years ago, when Sara and I first moved in. I almost threw it away at the time, but Sara convinced me not to: I'd want the memories some day, she said.

When I was ready for them. Of course, as usual, she's right.

I pull the box down from the shelf and sit cross-legged on the wood floor of my now-empty bedroom. *It's time, babe*, I think, trying to imagine the words that Sara would use, to conjure up her strength and warmth in this room with me. I called her this morning and she didn't answer. I plan to try again later today, and have been doing my best to keep the fear that we're not OK at bay in the meantime, but for now the image of her will have to do. I lift the lid and take a breath to still the tide of emotion that surges through me. The first thing, right at the top, is a picture of me and Sara in our freshers T-shirts, in a hand-crafted frame with glitter and stickers. My first birthday present from Sara. I lift it out of the box. I'm almost unrecognisable in it, my posture is relaxed, my expression carefree: all I had to think about then was whether or not I'd be able to make my next essay deadline, or when my next night out was going to be. I've often wished I could go back to that time. But as I look at myself now, all I see is a child. She was so young, so unaware of what life might throw at her. My world then was small and safe, but it wasn't real.

I take a deep breath and put the photo to one side, then reach into the box again. My hand folds around fabric: the freshers T-shirt I'm wearing in the photo, covered in some dubious stains. Then a few postcards here and there – art from various museums, which I had pinned up in my room because I thought it made me seem cool. Some photographs of me and my parents. A letter from the pen pal I kept throughout my first year, part of an exchange programme with the university. A tangled string of fairy lights.

My heart grows heavy as I realise I'm getting to the bottom of the box – I know what I'm about to find. But I've come this far: I can't stop now. It's crumpled, both from being shoved at the bottom of this box for so long and through me screwing it up it in a fit of rage after that night with Robbie. But I've still kept it, all this time. Like a part of me knew I'd want to read it again one day. I lift it gently out of the box, smoothing it out on the floor in front of me. A copy of the University of Edinburgh student newspaper, dated five years ago. The headline splashed across the front page is typically dramatic: *EXPOSED: The dark side of university sports*. I'd talked them out of putting photographs of the boys involved on the front of the newspaper, convinced it was a step too far, that it would make people too angry. *If only I could have known*. I take a breath and start reading.

Absorbing every word, every sharp-edged sentence, an overwhelming feeling stops me in my tracks: I am *proud*. It's a well-written article. My words are righteous and true, the words of someone who is scared but knows she is doing the right thing. And then, almost immediately, the pride is overwhelmed by sadness. By avoiding my pain, my grief, I've also been avoiding this person: this wonderful, angry person who wanted nothing more than to protect her friend. I've tried to be anything but her, so scared of the hurt she carried. And I didn't need to. She was great. But instead of celebrating her, I became ashamed of her. I tied her up in my grief just as much as Jack, holding her responsible for pain that wasn't ever her fault.

I never truly admitted it to myself at the time, but this article felt like the start of something. Using words to create change, to report on things I cared about. A future began to stretch before me, wide open and exciting. Journalism, perhaps. Or books. But then it all fell apart, and I put that version of myself in a box, tightly shut and hidden away. My job in book publicity, which meant communicating with journalists on a daily basis, was as close as I could get to that buzz that felt safe.

The doorbell rings through the silence, interrupting the flow of my thoughts. I place the article gently on the floor, wander over to the door and press the buzzer. I am expecting to see a delivery driver with the packing tape I ordered from Amazon, but instead I see Sara waiting outside my apartment building.

I buzz her up. Emotions swirl inside me, a thousand possibilities of what she might be here to say. Before I can think about it for too long, I hear her coming up the stairs – her familiar rhythm of two steps at a time, always my favourite sound when we lived together, the sign she was almost home – and all of those feelings are immediately replaced by a vast, overwhelming rush of love.

She's hardly arrived at my door before I fling it open and the full force of how much I've missed her propels me into her. She steadies herself and hugs me back with the same intensity. 'I've missed you, A,' she says into my hair.

'I've missed you, too,' I say, pulling away and gripping her arms. I can't believe she's actually here. 'I'm so glad you're here,' I say, tears falling.

'I'm glad, too,' she says, wiping her eyes. 'Can I come in?'

I gesture into the apartment, which was once hers too, and is now full of boxes just like it was on the day she first moved in. She looks around, taking them in, then whips towards me. 'You're moving?'

'It's a long story,' I say. 'I'll explain in a minute.'

We step over the boxes, tracing a careful path to the sofa where we ate takeout night after night for months. Where she told me about her first awful breakup, her first date with James.

'James and I broke up,' she starts, as soon as we sit down. *Oh, shit.* A part of me had suspected something like this, deep down, every time she pulled away, every time my best friend alarm went off, telling me something was wrong. But hearing it confirmed is still a huge shock: I'd desperately hoped that my suspicions were wrong. I shift in my seat, but just as I'm about to reach for her, she continues. 'It's OK. We're back together now. He quit his job and we're working things out,' I sit back down, listening. 'It got really bad after you left, A. His work just kept pushing him harder and harder, and we were fighting all the time. I didn't know what to do.' She looks exhausted, and sad, and I feel so awful that I haven't been here, haven't been there for her – I just want to reach out and hold her and never stop.

'Oh, S. Why didn't you tell me?' I ask, though it hits me like a gigantic punch in the gut that I already know why. Because I was so caught up in my own stuff that I didn't keep track of what was going on with my best friend. Because I wasn't there for her, like she always has been for me.

'I didn't know how,' she says. 'You were in Dublin, it happened the day you sent that SOS text. You were so far away, and you had so much going on. And—' She pauses, gathering herself. 'That night, A. In the flat. You said—' Tears start falling down her face again, and she reaches up to wipe them away. 'You said you sometimes wished that we'd break up so I would stay with you. I've been so scared ever since that you meant it, that you secretly hate him and resent me for moving away.'

Oh God. At her words, flashes of it come back – the haze, the deep well of loneliness. The words that I convinced myself were a joke, but which came out sharp-edged and true, probably hurting her deeply. Looking at her now, sat across from me on my sofa, the person I love most in the world next to my mum, my stomach drops. How have I been so selfish? Sara has been here for every important moment of my adult life – through my dad's death, through what happened in Edinburgh, through my career struggles, everything. She's my best friend. And instead of being happy for her as she finally built a life for herself that didn't totally revolve around me, I made her feel guilty about it, responsible for my loneliness, dragging my feet about finding a roommate because I was so busy grieving her absence and never thinking about how that might feel for her. Then I went on this trip, and I was so absorbed in my own problems that I didn't question her enough about hers. I should have pushed through her avoidance, should have checked in more often, should have blasted through the walls I could feel her putting up rather than running, scared.

Should have been half the friend to her that she's been to me.

'Sara,' I say, my voice thick, reaching for her hand and squeezing it hard. 'I am so unbelievably sorry.'

She squeezes back. 'So you don't hate him?' she says, sniffing.

'I could never hate someone you love, S,' I say, pulling her into a hug. Sadness settles deep in my chest – that I caused this distance between us, which I've been putting down to her moving on and leaving me behind. How stupid I've been, thinking I was blocked from the rest of the world by some unseen force, but it was a wall I built myself: the first bricks laid between Jack and I in that car park, and then layer after layer between myself and everyone else once my dad died. A protection from the rest of the world, which also kept me from the people I loved. Even Sara, who I'd thought was the only person it didn't apply to. How dense not to see that I was at the heart of it, this whole time. 'I just want you to be happy. Always. You're my best friend.'

She holds me tighter. 'Thanks, A.'

After a few moments I pull away, crying, and see she's crying too. We laugh, brushing tears from our eyes. 'I have something to show you,' I say, and I get up and walk over to the spare room, where I've been going through the box of things from university. I retrieve the photograph of us and hand it to her. She looks up at me, momentarily shocked that I've finally opened the box, but then smiles, slowly tracing the 'B E S T F R I E N D' stickers she had stuck to the top of the frame.

She hands it back to me after a few moments, and it's like no time has passed – we're back in her room in Edinburgh, and I'm sitting next to her plushies, tearing the paper off this gift, feeling an overwhelming warmth for her as I read those words. No one had ever called me their best friend before.

'I'm so proud of you, Andie. It must have been hard, going through all this stuff,' she says. Her voice falters a bit as if she's getting choked up again. 'And – I'm really sorry for pushing you so hard about Jack. I—' She pauses, collecting herself. I lean in, sensing that whatever she says next will be important. 'I've never told you, but I've always felt responsible for what happened in Edinburgh. You were so wonderful to me, and you ended up getting hurt so badly. I just – I wanted you to give yourself a chance to heal, but maybe that was self-ish, more about my own guilt than what was best for you.'

Another punch to the gut. I had no idea she felt this way, that she'd been holding on to this for so long. 'Oh, S, I would burn everything down for you, every single time, no matter the hurt,' I say, letting out a sigh – of sadness that we've never spoken about this properly until now; of relief that it's finally out in the open, finally released. 'And you have no reason to apologise about Jack – you were right. About all of it. Like always. I'm only sorry I didn't listen to you earlier,' I continue, my throat constricting at the thought of Jack, in that car park. His face as I walked away. 'It would have avoided a lot of pain.'

She smiles, her eyes welling up, too, and squeezes my hand, but then her forehead creases as she processes the full extent of my words. 'What have I missed?'

26

The day before I leave for England, I make a final stop in my favourite place in the city. It's a Thursday, mid-morning, so the shop is pretty empty: a few elderly people and students mill around, browsing the bookshelves. As I enter, I'm hit with the memory of the last time I was here. Jack's first event, where I was so furious with him that I was worried I was going to throw a drink over him. I smile sadly at the memory of it. That day seems so far away now.

I am browsing the new fiction shelves when I spot it, sitting front and centre, face out. *Homecoming* by Jack Carlson. My breath catches in my throat. My plan today had been to buy a book, any book, and spend the day reading it in my favourite armchair, upstairs in the fantasy section. If I'm being honest with myself, part of me is doing this to feel close to Jack, one last time. So it's no surprise, really, that the first book that caught my eye was his. I'm reaching for it before I can think twice, and I pay and quickly ascend the stairs, moving fast so I don't have time to have second thoughts.

I have a copy, somewhere in my apartment: a beat-up early print of it, left to me by my predecessor when I started my job. One I read weeks ago, driven by rage and necessity and an abject determination to do a good job, whatever the cost. This feels like a new book by comparison. Written by someone else. A boy I kissed in a park in Dublin, for no other reason than I wanted to. The boy who was driven to help me, no matter the hurt. The good parts of him that I shut myself away from, because it was too painful to face the fact that I liked him, I trusted him, and he hurt me anyway. I needed him to be the villain, so I didn't have to feel that pain. But now I've finally moved through it, it's fallen away, and I'm left with everything else. The way he looked at me, right before he pushed that hair away from my face. His hands, caressing my skin. His deep sense of righteousness, his desire to put things right between us. And a deep sense of what could have been, had I only been willing to take a second look.

The soft afternoon light wanes into dusk as I read, delving into the pages for the second time, languishing in them now. It's everything I want in a novel, just as it was before: beautiful and poignant. The scenes set in Ireland are vivid, transporting. I could be there again, on the streets of Dublin with him, the wind whipping through my hair. But this time, I notice something I hadn't seen the first time. Something I only know now I understand Jack better, and which makes me catch my breath: its pages are suffused with a sadness I'm familiar with; the kind of melancholy you only know when you've lost a parent. In his case, one who's still alive. It's a rare feeling: being deeply understood, like his hand is reaching out and taking mine. I grasp it, grateful for the connection even as it fills me with grief.

As the pace picks up in the second half, I read voraciously, taking in every word, imagining his hands typing them out carefully on his laptop, flexing as he tried to find the right words, the right turn of phrase. I wonder about the emotional journey he went on while writing this book, and whether it's comparable to how I'm feeling now. And as the sky slowly turns a dusky grey, signalling that the shop must be near closing time, I reach the last chapter. My breath catches in my throat as I tear through it, desperate to get to the end before the shop closes. The feeling of turning the final page is like emerging from being underwater, taking a first breath – the world feels new again. Tears roll down my face as I close the book, pooling in my collarbone. For the little boy who used to sit in this chair, alone. For the Jack who only ever wanted to apologise, to make things right.

I sit there for a few more minutes, so absorbed in my thoughts that I don't hear footsteps until he's standing next to me.

'Caught red-handed,' he says, smiling sadly, gesturing to the book in my hand. I wipe my eyes carefully, but this time, unlike that night in this same bookshop which now feels so many moons ago, I don't feel the urge to push him away.

'It's so beautiful, Jack.' I want to say more than I did in the park – that it's grabbed hold of me in a way that no book has for a very long time, that I found so much of myself in its pages it was startling. But, somehow, I don't think I need to say those things.

He sits down on the window ledge next to me, his legs dangling. 'I heard you quit,' he says, simply. There's no judgement in his tone, nor surprise; he sounds idly curious. As with most of my interactions with him in the last few weeks, I feel no expectations from him, no pressure to explain myself.

'Jack, I—' I start, and he puts his hand up to stop me, a mirror of the gesture I used a month ago in this exact spot.

'Let's not pretend this is anything other than it is, Andie,' he says, a smile creeping across his face. He's enjoying the symmetry with that night, enjoying being the one in control this time. 'Two people who clearly have feelings for each other.'

'How do you know I have feelings for you?' I say, before I can stop myself.

'Your handover notes,' he says, his smile growing broader. *What is he talking about?* For a second I'm immeasurably confused, then it comes back to me: I was in such a rush on my last day that when I typed 'j' in the search bar to send my handover notes for my replacement on to Jessica, I must've clicked on Jack's email rather than hers. Meaning he read everything I wrote about him, and the trip. Oh, God.

'*Jack is one of the most special authors I've ever worked with,*' he says, now reading from his phone. '*He's kind and generous with his time, a brilliant public speaker, and he gives off such an openness and charisma that people can't help but be drawn to him. Whoever gets to work on his next campaign is very fortunate; you will hardly have to do anything other than watch people fall in love with him, and his books (which, by the way, are wonderful).* Need I continue?' he says. I shrink into my chair. I could not be more embarrassed than if he had found the pictures of me at five years old, naked in my family paddling pool.

'Delete that, now,' I say, standing up and reaching to grab his phone. He catches my hand in mid-air and holds it, circling my palm with his thumb. I want to pull away, but something stops me.

'I was so horrible to you,' I say instead. 'I don't understand why you don't hate me.'

At this he lets go of my hand – my stomach drops in disappointment, and I have to fight the urge to reinstate physical contact. 'Andie, I don't think you understand that I could never, ever hate you.'

'But—' I start, but he cuts me off.

'You acted like an arsehole at points, sure. But you were in pain. And you're human. And I did fuck things up, back then.' He looks down at his legs, swinging them from the ledge. 'I knew what I was getting into with this tour, Andie. And I'd do it all again in a heartbeat.'

'Why?' I ask, not allowing myself to consider the possibility of his answer aligning with my deepest hopes. But then he looks at me, and I know.

'Isn't it obvious?' he says. He gets down from the ledge and moves over to my chair. My breath catches in my throat. He reaches for my hands and gently pulls me to my feet, his gaze burning into mine. 'The only time you hurt me, truly hurt me, was when you left me on that bench in the car park. That hurt like hell, Andie,' he says, brushing my hair away from my face. His fingertips set off a thousand nerve endings on the surface of my skin. I can hardly think straight. Half-formed thoughts like *I'm leaving for England tomorrow* and *this is a terrible idea* flash through my mind but his hand is running down my arm now, and I find myself drawn towards him, pressing myself against him.

He looks down at me, as if waiting for permission, his hand resting softly on the side of my face, barely brushing my skin. My breath catches in my throat, and I hesitate for a moment, a thrill moving up my spine, then run my hand down his back, feeling it arch under my touch.

For a moment, as his gaze burns into me, worry moves through me – that I've misread this somehow, that he's going to pull away. That this is all a dream.

Then he cups my face and kisses me, and my thoughts stop altogether.

I sink into him, soaking up as much of this moment as I can. I dig my fingertips into his back and he moans softly and kisses me harder, pushing me against the bookshelf behind me. I hear some books fall to the ground, and I should care, but I don't – all I care about is getting as much of Jack as I possibly can, my whole body alive with wanting him. I've never felt this way before, about anyone I've ever slept with. It's even more potent than it was in Edinburgh, in Dublin. When we eventually come up for air, breathless, a few moments later I feel lightheaded, like I don't quite know where I am. He leans against the bookshelf next to us and presses his forehead to mine.

'I'm leaving for England tomorrow,' I say. Though I desperately don't want to ruin the moment, I can't let this go further without telling him. I'm done with deceiving people.

'For how long?' he says, his voice soft. His left hand is still on my hip, and his grip tightens slightly, as if he's worried I'll leave right now.

'Indefinitely,' I say, hoping against hope that this won't break the spell, that he'll stay in the moment with me for as long as possible. He lets out a breath, but doesn't move. When he speaks, it sends shivers down my whole body.

'So we still have tonight,' he says, his voice low and urgent. I nod, hardly daring to make a sound. He leans in and kisses me again, soft and slow, pulling away before I'm ready for him to stop. His eyes still on me, anchoring me to the bookshelf behind me, he takes his phone out of his pocket and calls his driver, then practically carries me down the stairs of the shop into the waiting car.

This time, there's nothing rushed about it. When we get back to his flat he undresses me slowly, his eyes running over my body as if he's memorising every inch of it. As my shirt drops to the ground he leans in and pushes my hair away from the back of my neck. I know what he's looking for before he finds it: the freckle, the cause of all this strife. He pauses for a moment, then traces it gently with his finger, like he did so many years ago. I arch my back as he does, pressing into him, feeling how much he wants me.

He turns me towards him, then reaches behind me and unhooks my bra, his lips tracing a path across my shoulder as he does so. I am on fire with want, with need, but I want to savour this. I might not get another chance. I run my fingertips down the back of his neck and he moans softly into my shoulder, then kisses me deeply. I can feel the edge of need in the way he kisses me: he's savouring this, too, holding himself back so we don't lose ourselves just yet. He cups the back of my neck gently and deepens the kiss, leading me towards the bed as he does so. Where before I was so caught up in the moment I was barely aware of time passing, now I feel every second – every glance, every touch. His eyes locked on mine, pinning me in place. It's as if time has slowed down for this, for us. He runs his hand down my side, setting me on fire again.

'Jack,' I say, desperation entering my voice, trying to communicate just how much I want him. 'Please,' I say. He closes his eyes, as if this overwhelms him, then leans down and kisses my neck, slowly pushing me onto the bed.

If last time was a flash of lightning, the culmination of the growing tension between us, this is a slow, delicious burn. As he touches me, I feel seen in ways I've never allowed myself to be seen before – as if he has stripped back not only my clothes but everything I use to keep myself hidden. My defensive humour, my insults, my sarcasm. My focus on being a success in my career. It's all gone. The Andie he is seeing now is just that: Andie, without any accomplishments to her name, melting into the moment, into him. And in return, as he starts to lose control, I see the real him: not author Jack, but raw and broken Jack. The Jack who kicked the ramparts of the castle, who told me he never wanted me to be a one night stand. The Jack who cared enough to help me, when no one else in the swim team would've even considered it. He tangles his hands in my hair, and it occurs to me that some part of me has seen him in this way all along. It's just been buried under everything else: my hatred, my anger, my pain. My grief. Now, in this moment, falling away, allowing me to see him more clearly than I ever have. The pleasure builds to a peak, overwhelming me momentarily then melting slowly into a beautiful melancholy that spreads through me as I kiss him.

We stay up most of the night, sinking into each other as much as we can, slowly at first, the urgency between us growing as the morning creeps closer. There's so much to say, but also so little – we communicate with our bodies, unwilling to speak, to face the reality of the situation, determined to savour every second of one another. But then the morning light starts to filter through the windows as I come apart for the last time, the sun moving across my eyelids as they close, my hands twisting in the sheets. When I come back to the surface I can see in his eyes that he knows it, too. It's time.

'Don't go,' he says, reading my thoughts. He traces his hand gently down the side of my face, his eyes deep with longing.

'I have to,' I say, my heart breaking as I do. 'I can't trust myself to be close to you right now.'

'What if I said I trust you?'

I stroke his face gently, trying not to dwell on how sad he looks, how sad I feel, too. 'I'd say you're misguided,' I say.

'But—'

'I'm in love with you,' I blurt, cutting across him. This shuts him up. He looks at me, suddenly serious. 'I'm in love with you,' I continue, 'and because of that, I can't be with you right now. I'm still working through so much, still untangling so much pain. It wouldn't be fair, to throw you into the middle of all that.' My chest constricts – I am at my most vulnerable right now, my most exposed, but I have to say it. I have to be honest with him. He deserves that much, at least.

There's a moment of silence, while he processes my declaration. 'Well, that sucks,' he says, eventually. I laugh.

'Not exactly the response I was expecting,' I say.

'You know what I mean,' he says. 'You love me, so you don't want to be with me. That's pretty fucked up logic, Andie. And don't I get a choice in all this? What if I told you I want to be in the middle of it?'

I shake my head, slowly, sadly.

'I can't let you,' I say, and a silence falls between us. I'm in the midst of trying to figure out what to say next when I catch sight of the clock on his bedside table. If I don't leave right now, I'm going to miss my plane. He sees where I'm glancing and his expression darkens slightly.

'You need to go, right?' he says, and I nod. I lean in and kiss him once more, memorising the feel of his lips on mine, then take a breath and force myself to focus on the task at hand. I get out of bed, dressing in a frenzy. With every second that takes me closer to leaving, I feel worse, but I know it's the right thing. It has to be. I can't hurt him again, not now I've finally been able to see how wonderful he is. How deeply I care about him. Maybe one day will be the right time for us – but it's not right now.

When I'm ready to go, I turn to him. 'It's not goodbye,' I say, fighting against every instinct I have to stay. 'Just – see you when I see you.'

'I've always hated that saying,' he says, as I walk towards the door and open it. 'Hey,' he calls, just as I'm about to leave. I turn and catch his eye. 'You know I love you too, right?' he says, his voice low. Yearning spills through every part of me as he says it.

'I know,' I say, staring into his eyes one last time, trying to memorise their exact colour, the flecks of green in the deep, clear blue. Then, before I can lose my nerve and run back to him, I turn away, walk through the door and shut it behind me.

27

Six months later.

My mum looks more beautiful than I've ever seen her. So beautiful, in fact, that I've had to ask the poor make-up artist to touch up my eye make-up several times because I keep crying it off. Her dress is delicate, her hair simple – a few orchids pinned to a low bun, a style that we chose together. It's hard to remember the version of myself that fell apart in that hotel room in Ireland, devastated by the news of her wedding. Today I feel nothing but a vast sense of joy spreading through my chest, growing with every moment.

As I watch her put the final touches on her hair, I wonder whether my dad has been on her mind today, whether she's thinking about the last time she got ready like this. Tears threaten at the thought: she must have been so excited then. Just

as beautiful as she is now, only younger, less familiar with the struggles of being human.

I could ask her: we talk about him almost every
day now.

My first week back in London, we pulled down
the old family photos from the attic where my
mum kept them, and have spent some time over
the last few months organising them into albums
together. We've cried – a lot – and shared memories
I'd forgotten about, conjuring my dad in a vibrant
shared memory. At times it's almost felt like he's
been in the house with us. His jokes, his warmth.
Though I still feel a little terrified sometimes, the
dam has not gone back up: the flow of grief that
started on the call with my mum has continued,
releasing gradually into a deep sadness, which has
edges of light. A sense of honouring the loss, but
also a joy in remembering. Both coexisting, like
my mum said they could.

To my surprise, Nigel has also been a great part of
this process: a warm audience for anecdotes about
my dad, a gentle spectator who has brought cups
of tea and removed himself when we've needed a
moment alone. If before I thought he was taking
away the space that should've been reserved for
my dad in the family, I couldn't have been more

wrong. There are photos of my mum and dad, and Nigel and his wife, all over the house. It's been the perfect place to finally let myself grieve, after all this time.

My favourite photograph, which I've framed, is one of us all on the beach together. Mum and I are building a sandcastle, and Dad's kneeling to watch, looking at us both like we're the best thing that's ever happened to him, like he can't believe how lucky he got. It feels heavy, sometimes, when I look at it, but mostly it's a reminder: that he was here, that he loved us no matter what. That Mum and I can keep building, together.

'You look beautiful, Mum,' I say, deciding to focus on the present for now.

She takes my hand, and squeezes it hard. 'If only I could see you this happy, Andie,' she says, her voice thick.

'I *am* happy,' I say, squeezing back. And I mean it: the last few months have been full-on with all the wedding planning, but despite my lack of future plans I've felt calmer and more purposeful than I have in a long time. I've been getting comfortable with my own company, revisiting places I ran to New York to get away from: the cafe I visited with my dad every Saturday, the bookstore. I've even attended a few classes at his old yoga studio, and met some of his students, who've told me stories about him. The time he showed up to class wearing one of the fourteen pink T-shirts he bought me, because everything else he owned was in the wash. How sometimes he would blast death metal music in the middle of his sessions, to 'keep everyone on their toes, and test their mental peace'. I've been writing them all down: a record of him, of us.

'I know,' she says. 'Just, if I can give you a piece of motherly advice—'

'—Mum, if this is about setting me up with Elizabeth's son again, I've already told you he's gay—'

'—OK, OK, that one was a mistake. Elizabeth said he was single, and his sexual orientation had simply never come up. I swear! But this isn't about that. Listen to me, Andrea. I've gained some wisdom in the sixty years I've been on this earth.'

She's called me Andrea, which she only does when she's serious, so I quiet down and listen.

'Sometimes,' she says, putting her hand on my arm and leaning in so I have to look her in the eye, 'you need to believe that you deserve the things that you want. Otherwise you'll spend your whole life settling.'

'What's this about, Mum?' I ask, though I think I already know.

'All I'm saying, love, is that everyone has flaws. You're impressively aware of yours. But that doesn't mean you don't deserve to love and be loved.'

Ah, so this is about Jack. These are the perils of moving towards a more open relationship with my mum, as I've been trying to do over the last few months. She knows everything, and that means she has opinions about everything. Opinions I don't always agree with.

I can't deny I have been thinking about Jack a lot recently, wondering what he's doing, how he's feeling. Missing him, even. But I'm not sure I'm ready to reach out yet. Besides, based on the cosy pictures I saw of him and Aoife at her latest book launch, I don't think it's a line worth pursuing. Luckily for me, Sara interrupts the conversation before I have to respond.

'Ladies!' Her voice calls down the corridor as she clatters towards us in the very low bridesmaid heels that she absolutely cannot walk in. She pops her head round the door, takes a quick snap of us with her polaroid camera with no warning and before I can protest, then pulls us both into a hug which might also just be her using us to steady herself.

'It's time,' she says as she pulls away, ushering us out of the room and giving my hand a squeeze as she does so.

As we emerge into the sprawling, rose-covered garden of the venue that I helped my mum find, the music starts and the tears start falling again. I catch Nigel's eye at the other end of the aisle and see he's been set off, too. He gives me a warm glance and a self-aware shrug that says 'look at us', laughing as he wipes away the tears. I bask in our shared love for my mum, tears flowing freely now. I'm absolutely sure my make-up is ruined again, but I don't care. I'm happy for my mum, overwhelmingly so – she deserves every second of this celebration.

As I glance into the crowd, for a fraction of a second my breath catches – I could swear I see someone who is the spitting image of Jack. I stumble briefly, my heel catching in the grass. I must be imagining things, I've been seeing him everywhere lately: last I heard, he was in Spain at a writer's retreat. I force myself to continue walking down the aisle, turning my attention back to the music, to my arm looped through my mum's, her skin warm against mine.

I reach the end of the aisle and assuming my position to the left, next to Sara, who takes my hand

and laces her fingers through mine. The ceremony starts, and suddenly Jack could not be further from my mind.

After the service ends, and my mum is swallowed by a crowd of guests, I send Sara and James in search of some champagne and find myself drifting towards the lake on the other side of the garden, in search of a moment alone. This view was what sold this venue for us, in the end. It's vast, peaceful, a seemingly endless stretch of blue surrounded by trees.

I gaze over the water and my thoughts drift to my dad, as they often do these days. He'd be happy for her today, I know that. He was completely unselfish in that way – all he ever wanted, before all else, was for her to be happy.

I miss you, I think, willing the words to reach him. It hurts, still. But I'm learning to lean into it, the dull ache a reminder of the love. To let myself miss him, even in the moments when it feels impossible that he's gone. Even though it still sometimes feels vast and overwhelming, it's not something I want to run from anymore.

As I hold him in my thoughts, my gaze moves upwards, towards a flock of geese rising in smooth synchronicity, flying over the lake. A memory comes, floating into my mind – I am five years old, in Phoenix Park. My dad stands next to me, his arm outstretched to the sky. I gaze up in wonder at the formation of birds he's pointing out, moving gracefully across the landscape. I lift my finger, tracing the V across the sky. He reaches down and holds my hand. I close my eyes, willing the memory to stay a little longer, so I can be in his presence for just a moment more. When I open them again, the flock has formed a perfect V, swooping above me. It's as if I'm five, again – I can almost feel him next to me. I lift my finger and trace it, a tear rolling down my face. If I were a person who looked for signs, this would be one.

'Hi, Dad,' I say, under my breath. Maybe I am becoming that sort of person now.

After a few moments, I turn, preparing myself to return to the party, and walk straight into Jack.

'Jesus fucking Christ,' I say, clutching my chest. 'What the fuck are you doing here?'

He smiles. 'Ah, I've missed you swearing at me.'

'Seriously, that was creepy,' I say, smoothing my dress so I have something to do with my hands, hoping he can't tell how flustered I am, how fast my heart is suddenly beating.

'I'm sorry,' he says. 'I was going to approach you, but it looked like a private moment.'

'I was thinking about my dad,' I say. 'How he'd feel about today.'

'Any thoughts?' he says, tilting his head, the silence welcoming. If I wanted to, I could tell him about the memory.

'I think he'd be sad to miss the party,' I say, deciding against it.

He smiles, acknowledging the invisible line I've drawn, and allows silence to settle again. I wait it out. 'The service was beautiful,' he tries, but I can see from his eyes that this isn't what he wants to talk about.

'Jack,' I say. 'Why are you here?'

At this, his gaze moves over my shoulder. I turn to find my mum, standing outside the marquee, not-at-all-subtly staring at us. *Ah. So that's what the pre-wedding pep talk was about.* I wave, and she waves back then returns to the tent. I'll be having words with her tomorrow.

'I still don't understand,' I say, turning back to Jack. 'You know, with the way we left things. It looked like you and Aoife—'

At this, he rolls his eyes. 'What is this thing about Aoife?' he laughs. 'I made a bet with myself that you'd see those photos and say something. I owe myself ten pounds.'

'All I'm saying is you looked very cosy.'

'Andie,' he says, trying and failing to keep his expression serious. 'I was leaning in to tell her that she was about to have a wardrobe malfunction. I don't know about you, but I'd prefer not to be told out loud in front of Ireland's best and brightest that my dress was about to, uh, stop performing its duties.'

'Oh,' I say. 'Well, now I feel very stupid.'

'Not stupid,' he says, taking a step towards me. 'Just jealous. I find it endearing.'

He's too close now, in the danger zone where I might stop thinking and start kissing him. I take a step backwards, and his face falls momentarily, but he recovers himself.

'The real reason I came was to propose a new truce,' he says, clearing his throat, his tone smooth and nonchalant, but I see through it. 'I've had an opportunity to spend the next few months in London. My publishers over here want me to do some PR, and I'd like a change of scene while I write my next book.' He pauses, as if considering his words carefully, then seems to throw caution to the wind. 'But to be honest, the main appeal is that it brings me several thousand miles closer to you.'

This makes me momentarily unsteady on my feet. *Maybe the bridesmaid heels aren't so stable, after all.*

'The terms of the truce are this: I promise I will put all of my feelings for you to one side, if you agree to hang out with me occasionally. I've thought about it a lot, and I'd rather have you in my life than not at all.' He pauses, rocking on his heels. 'You're the best person I've ever met.'

'Oh,' I say, disappointment flooding through me despite how heart-wrenchingly lovely his last words are.

And then, all at once, just how stupid this all is dawns on me in such a rush it almost knocks me over: I love this man. I *love* him.

And he has flown thousands of miles to ask me to be his friend. What are we *doing*?

'Or,' he says, looking nervous now. I listen with every fibre of my being: all my energy is focused on what he's about to say next. 'Or, I can reject the offer, fly back to New York and leave you alone. If that's what you want.'

If the first option was disappointing, this one is gut-wrenching.

I want him, more than anything. And these last six months, I haven't allowed myself to even consider that I might be able to have what I want. But now he's here, right in front of me. I can keep waiting indefinitely, or I can decide, right now, to trust myself, the way Sara and my mum trust me. The way Jack trusts me.

I've taken so many steps forwards in the last six months. All it would take is one more.

'I don't want you to go back to New York,' I say, a sudden resolve forming inside me. I take a step closer to him, and watch his jaw clench almost unnoticeably as I move within touching distance.

'So, option one, then,' he says, his voice quiet and breathless. By this point, I'm right in front of him. I reach out and take hold of the lapels of his suit jacket.

'Is option one what you want?' I ask, looking up at him for confirmation. I have a hunch but I'm still tense, ready to back off at the first sign that I've got it all wrong. He shakes his head slowly and relief floods through me. It's all I can do not to kiss him then and there, but I need to hear it. I need to be sure. 'No, Andie,' he says, his voice firm. 'I think you know what I want.'

'Good,' I say, pulling him towards me until his face is inches from mine, his breath warm on my cheek. My heart is beating at a hundred miles an hour, but I hardly notice, the gravitational pull towards him is so strong. I run my hand down his back, and I hear his breath catch in his throat. 'Because I don't know about you, but I'm really fucking sick of truces.'

Read on for an exclusive look
at Bianca Gillam's next novel...

off
script

Two actors with history.
Can they rewrite their ending
for a second chance?

Available for pre-order now

I

The call came in at 3 p.m. on a Tuesday.

I had imagined this moment so many times, the daydream sustaining me through a hundred late night bar shifts and a thousand miserable auditions. Through sleepless nights wondering what, exactly, was so wrong with me that I'd decided to pursue an acting career, sacrificing financial and emotional stability and any chance I might have had at a 'normal' life for one filled with anxiety and rejection. Through call after call to say that they'd gone with someone else, my stomach swooping in a downward arc of disappointment that was becoming so familiar I now picked up the phone ready, poised like a carriage at the top of a rollercoaster.

But despite it all, the hope always persisted.

That this time, it would be different.

That this time, it would be me.

I'd imagine where I'd be, what I'd say. How it would feel, to know I finally, *finally* had a chance at making it as an actor.

And when it finally came, I wasn't ready for it.

And I certainly wasn't ready for what happened next.

'What?' I breathed on the phone to my agent, my heart hammering so hard it felt like it might burst out of my chest.

'You heard me right. They want to do a screen test.'

'A screen test?' I repeated, as if I was hearing those words for the first time.

'A screen test, Lara. On Tuesday. Can you get time off work?'

'I...' I hesitated. I'd just taken on a 9–5 because the regular bar shifts I'd been working no longer covered rent for my box room in a shared house on the outskirts of London.

'I'll work it out,' I said.

'Great,' she replied smoothly, a glimmer of excitement under her professional tone.

Natalie was an up-and-coming agent at one of the biggest agencies in London. She had spotted me performing in a small pub theatre a few years ago and had signed me the following week. I'd called my mum and cried down the phone, saying this was it – that it would all be worth it, because I'd finally got my big break.

But a few years had passed and still no real luck, aside from the occasional local theatre production and some advertising work.

'Nat,' I said, beginning to shake. 'Is this actually happening? I'm not lucid dreaming, right?'

'It's happening,' she said, sounding as astounded as me. We were silent for a few seconds, our shared excitement filling the space. A small, bright flame inside me lit, again, spreading warmth through my limbs.

A screen test was big – further than I'd ever been in the process before. This audition had been a complete shot in the dark: a screen adaptation of one of my favourite books, about a female detective investigating a string of murders in 1800s London. As dream roles go, it was pretty much at the top of the list.

There was a less than zero chance I ever thought I'd get it.

And now, I was one of the few front-runners for the role.

I could almost feel the part in my hands.

Perhaps, just perhaps, this would be it, I thought, a spike of joy travelling up my spine. The break I'd been waiting for, for years now, while I tried desperately to keep my eyes focused on the next audition, the next tape, the next shot. *You only have to get lucky once,* my dad had said to me when I'd first started.

For a half-second I allowed myself to imagine a future of financial freedom and creative liberation, my dreams being fulfilled over and over again.

Then she spoke again, and my stomach dropped to the floor.

'It will be with Avi Kumar,'

'Sorry?' I said, shaking myself back to reality. Surely she couldn't have said that name.

She repeated herself, the words hitting me this time. Each one a carefully aimed dart to my chest. *Shit.*

Avi Kumar is one of the world's most famous men, gracing the cover of *GQ* as its Man of the Year last year. Described as 'the Darling of Hollywood', ushering in a new generation of male British actors, he has been cast in everything from Marvel films to rom-coms to period dramas. Recently rumoured to be dating supermodel-turned-actress Sienna Marsh, who has twice been voted the most beautiful woman in the world, making him one half of the industry's newest power couple.

But I didn't know that Avi Kumar.

I knew the funny, dishevelled Avi Kumar I had met when I first moved to London. Who showed me the ropes at the theatre pub where we both worked as struggling actors, and taught me to pull the perfect pint. Who I shared my dreams with… because they were his, too.

Avi, who I trusted possibly more than I had ever trusted anyone else.

Who broke my heart, and almost ruined my career in the process.

'Right,' I practically choked. *Oh God*.

'You'll be great,' Nat said, worry entering her tone. 'I know he's a huge name, Lara, but—'

If only she knew.

'It's fine,' I lied. I had imagined this moment so many times: finally being in a room with Avi. Finally being able to ask him all the questions that had burned in my mind for months afterwards, as I watched his star rise into the stratosphere, his face everywhere I looked.

I just never thought it would be like this.

'I know him … from before he was famous,' I continued, levelling my tone so she couldn't hear the emotions burning through me. 'So was just a little shocked to hear the name, that's all.'

'You know him?' she said, sounding shell-shocked. 'How did I not know this, Lara?' she asked, clearly meaning *we-very-much-could-have-used-this-connection*.

'We haven't spoken in a while,' I said, regretting mentioning it now. I suddenly felt a little faint. 'Since he got famous, actually.'

'Ah,' she replied, seeming to intuit that it was a sore subject, and that she shouldn't press further. 'Well – you're in the room, now. He might be a name, but you're there too. And that's all that matters, in the moment. And the notes I have from other clients are that he's very professional to screen test with, if that helps.'

It didn't help. It didn't help at all.

'Thanks, Nat,' I said anyway, my heart pounding at the thought of seeing him in person, again.

For a hair's breadth of a second, it was almost enough to make me want to call the whole thing off. But I'd wanted this for so long, and this was a bigger chance than I ever thought I'd get. And I had promised myself I'd never let my feelings for anyone mess with my career again.

Especially not Avi Kumar.

I just didn't know whether that would be under my control, or how it would be to see him after all this time.

'So Tuesday, then,' Nat said, clearing her throat. 'I'll email you the details.'

'Looking forward to it,' I half-lied. I still felt like I was about to vomit with nerves – about seeing Avi, or the audition, I wasn't sure.

But even still, excitement coursed through my veins, my hand shaking as I hung up the phone.

Shit.

This could be it. This could finally, finally be *it*.

And in that moment, determination washed over me.

Avi Kumar or no Avi Kumar, I was going to do everything it took to get that part.

A few days later I'm standing outside the building where my screen test will take place in exactly ten minutes' time.

Nat, as always, called me half an hour ahead of my slot to wish me luck, but it didn't soothe me as it usually does.

It's my first screen test, and I'm about to encounter a man who I thought I'd never see again, so the nerves are even worse than usual. Spinning around inside me like a Catherine wheel, setting fire to everything in sight.

Possessed by some force outside myself, I pull out my phone and scroll down to my old text conversation with Avi. Our chat is a meandering thread, peppered with link after link to covers of our favourite songs.

I take a breath and do something in this moment that I haven't considered doing once in the last three years: I delete the entire thread.

A year, trapped in time. All evidence that we ever knew each other gone in a second.

If I am going to work with Avi – if I am going to be able to face him, even – I need to start on the most even footing I can find. He might be attends-the-Oscars-famous, and my greatest screen achievement to date might be an advert for soap, but I've got to go in strong. I'm auditioning for the lead and he's the love interest, not the other way around. It's why I was so attracted to this role – finally, a female character who could hold her own. So I have to hold my own in there, too. No matter how he might make me feel.

I close my eyes, take a breath and enter the building.

'Lara Francis?' a voice calls, the sound of stilettos echoing in the broad, bright corridor. After I entered the building, I was ushered up to the fifth floor and settled in a surprisingly comfortable chair to wait.

This process is a far cry from the usual audition scene. I'm usually crammed in a hot, overcrowded room full of women who look a bit like me. Who I have to make a conscious effort not to compare myself to unfavourably.

But here, there's no need; there's just me and sunlight streaming through a window, a view of London spilling into the distance. It's peaceful, and the lack of distractions gives me enough time to do a few meditative breaths, my eyes fixed on the skyline as the heels approach.

I tear my eyes from the window to find a small, sharply dressed woman about my age, holding a clipboard. Her expression is not unkind, but there's a steel in her gaze that tells me she means business. This industry isn't just brutal for the actors: to make it, you have to have an unshakeable nerve. Or a relative in the industry – that always helps.

She leads me down the corridor to a door marked 'Screen Test Room 1'. I hardly have time to wonder where Room 2 might be before she opens the door and ushers me through. If I thought the meditation breaths had calmed me down, I was wrong: adrenaline kicks through me as the door swings shut and I'm face to face with 6ft 2 of messy dark hair, a chiselled jawline and dark hazel eyes that used to crease at the edges when I told a bad joke.

Shit.

In the half-second before the nausea hits, I manage to see that he looks a little harder around the edges than he used to. Smooth. Polished. As professional as the handshake he's now extending to me.

'Lara,' he says, his voice turning over my name as if it's alien to him. As if he hadn't called it a hundred times across the bar.

'It's a pleasure to meet you,' he continues. The nausea deepens, edged with a flicker of anger and hurt. It makes sense that he'd try and hide the fact that we've met before. He has a new life, now – and he made it very clear he didn't want me in it.

Even still, despite myself, disappointment and confusion cloud my vision momentarily.

I grasp his hand, doing my best to shake it firmly.

'It's a pleasure to meet you too, Avi,' I echo. Something flashes in his gaze for a fraction of a second – something that looks like warmth. Old familiarity. It throws me, completely.

I blink, frozen for a second, my hand still clutching his.

'Lara, thank you so much for coming in today,' a voice from my left says, clearing their throat gently, and I realise how stupid I'm being.

Well done, Lara. Three seconds in the room and you've already screwed up.

The table across the room of producers and casting directors should've been my first port of call, but I was so distracted by Avi that I forgot they were there. I notice the director isn't present – or at least no one that looks like the Google Images I've searched of him – and balk for a second. Perhaps he's in Screen Test Room 2, with another actor. But then you don't get much higher priority than Avi Kumar.

Breathe, Lara, I say to myself as I turn away from Avi and cross the room to shake their hands. A row of people who are about to decide my future, but who aren't registering at all on the Richter Scale of my nervous system compared to the man behind me.

'Alessandro sends his apologies,' the producer says. 'He was held up in Italy, so we'll be handling the screen test today and he'll be reviewing the tapes.'

I swallow, processing the magnitude of his statement. This footage is all the director will have to make the decision that could impact the rest of my life. I'd hoped to at least be able to make a good impression in person, too.

Shit. A flash of nerves arrives so suddenly I almost want to run. This is feeling incredibly, inescapably real.

'Right,' the casting director says, getting up from the table and moving us to our marks. My hand shakes as I take the script from him. 'We'll start with an early scene, half-way through their first meeting. Could you please read from page two to page seven?'

I nod, swallowing as I look down at the script and try to focus my gaze.

'Sure,' Avi says, his tone smooth. His voice makes me jump and I look up, his eye catching mine. I look back down at the script.

Channel it, Lara, I say to myself as the producer returns to his table, breathing out and getting into my body. *He is just any other actor. You know these lines. You know this part. You are Amelia.*

You've got this.

'Okay, and go,' the producer says, and my head snaps upwards again.

'Amelia,' Avi starts the scene.

Miraculously, a calm washes over me as I take my cue.

For the length of a scene, I'm able to detach myself entirely from the fact that I'm currently in the room with Avi, and disappear into the character. The feeling is comforting and familiar, the edges of myself blurring into the background as

I sink into it. This is what I've always loved about acting – its detachment from reality. The possibilities it opens up to live a thousand lives other than your own. The possibilities it's opening up, in this moment, to pretend the man in front of me doesn't make me feel a million things that make me want to leave this room and never come back.

And despite my unease, there's a strange comfort in doing this with Avi. Our rapport is smooth, trading lines like we've been doing it for years, falling easily back into our old rhythm when we'd practise for auditions in the empty theatre above the pub after closing time. It's... easy.

Alarmingly easy.

The feeling comes out of nowhere and jolts me out of character momentarily. Avi falters, watching as I grasp for the next line.

'Sorry,' I murmur, glancing over at the table to my right, that feels suddenly like a courtroom jury, before returning my gaze to the script as a blush of mortification creeps across my cheeks.

'That's OK,' one of the casting directors says, standing up, and for one horrible second I think I might've messed it all up.

But he stays where he is, folding his arms and looking between Avi and me with great interest.

'I'd like to move on to a later scene, now,' he says, clearing his throat. 'The one in the pub.'

Oh, shit. Avi's eyes flash to mine and I can see he's caught the meaning, too: that scene is a kissing scene. A kissing scene in a pub. It's so ironic I almost – despite everything – want to laugh. I swallow instead, my throat suddenly bone dry.

'If you're not comfortable— ' the casting director starts, his gaze flicking to the clock above the door.

'I am,' I interrupt quickly, avoiding Avi's gaze. 'It's fine.'

The casting director says nothing, just gestures for us to start, and we flick through our scripts to the right page, the silence almost unbearable.

Once we've oriented ourselves, we start the scene.

I look up at Avi, his hazel-brown eyes trained on me.

There's a question in them, and I can't tell if it's the part he's playing or if it's him coming through. Checking I'm OK with this. My heart kicks.

A rush of feeling warms my skin and I nod, infinitesimally. Staying in the moment, in the character. Stemming the tide that's telling me that the man in front of me is not his character, but someone else.

He takes a tentative step towards me, and a shiver runs down my spine.

Shit. This is happening. This is actually happening.

He winds his arm around my waist, my skin coming alive at his touch. His hand clenches around the fabric of my shirt and it's a struggle not to gasp aloud.

He leans down and delivers his line, his voice low.

'I know you, Amelia Blackwood,' he says, and my breath catches in my throat.

For a moment, I almost forget myself.

But before I know it, my line slips out, falling off my tongue.

'Do you?' I ask.

And that's his cue: his grip on my waist tightens and he leans in.

Anticipation rushes through me, and I lean towards him, tilting my face upwards.

'Cut!' the casting director shouts, and the breath rushes out of my lungs.

Avi's hand drops from my waist, leaving a ghost of warmth, and he steps away. A crashing disappointment moves through me, followed by a wave of embarrassment that almost knocks me off my feet.

Oh, God. What was I thinking?

There's no way he was actually going to kiss me. Kisses in screen tests require prior warning, these days.

Nat would have given me a heads up, and we'd have discussed it. Cleared it, ahead of time.

But, for just a moment, I had really thought it would happen.

Had hoped it would.

What in God's name is wrong with you?

The casting director is standing in the same spot on the other side of the room, arms still folded, expression as unreadable as before. I hardly dare to look at Avi, my heart is beating so hard.

'Thank you very much for your time, Lara,' he says, finally, after a beat of silence. He returns to his previous position behind the desk and shuffles some papers, then sits down, looking up at me as he does so.

'We'll be in touch,' he says, by way of dismissal.

I swallow, and manage to speak, thanking them for having me and saying some other things I'm not fully aware of — my focus is suddenly on getting out of this room as fast as possible.

I glance at Avi, the nausea from the beginning of this audition rising up suddenly. Half of me is desperate never to see him again, the other half already reliving how it felt to have his hand on my waist. Disappointment flooding through me that even now, after all this time, he still has such an effect on me.

Get your shit together.

I manage a nod in his direction and burst from the room.

I'm downstairs and halfway through reception moving numbly towards the revolving doors when a voice calls out.

'Lara!' it says, again.

I turn to find Avi panting at the bottom of the stairs. The receptionist openly gawks at him from behind her desk – it seems that even for a studio, a huge movie star rushing down to reception to call after a random nobody is an uncommon occurrence. But I can't register Avi as a movie star in this moment.

The flannel shirt might be gone, but everything else is still there: the slight hunch of his shoulders, the half-smile that used to show me he was nervous or having an off day.

The parts that I thought made up a whole – a person I thought I knew like the back of my hand.

Who, as it turns out, I didn't know as well as I thought.

And this means I can't say anything either, apparently. My lips have parted but no words are coming out.

He runs a hand through his hair. 'It...' he falters, looking momentarily as unhinged as I feel. 'It's good to see you,' he finally says, then lets out a breath and swallows, his Adam's apple bobbing.

I'm not sure what to say to this, so I just nod stupidly.

'Anyway,' he continues, 'I, uh...' he glances up at the clock above the reception desk. 'I'll see you, OK?'

I nod, again, suddenly unable to speak.

What is wrong with him? Where are we possibly going to bump into each other?

'See you,' I finally manage, then I watch as he runs to the lift and disappears into it, glancing at me once more over his shoulder before the doors close.

My heart hammers, the old feelings rushing back all at once. Now I'm no longer having to stay professional for the audition, it's like a dam has broken.

Hurt. Confusion. Anger. A headache that feels like it's going to split my head in two.

All of it clearing into one, impossible realisation: until last week, landing this role was my greatest dream.

Now, I have no idea what I'm going to do if I get it.

Acknowledgements

I've been thinking about writing this section almost every day since I found out my book was going to be published. A river of gratitude has been spilling out of me since I signed with my agent and got the news about my book deal, and I don't think it will ever stop. Let me try and do justice to all the wonderful people it flows toward.

First, to Elizabeth Counsell. From the moment we met, I knew you were my agent. For your belief in me, not just for this book but for my whole career. Your love for Andie. Your unflinching commitment to reading everything I send you – even when it's a ten-thousand-word fragment written on a long-haul flight, and you're about to go on holiday. Thank you, thank you, thank you. I am so excited for everything to come, and so immensely grateful.

To everyone at Northbank, Natalie Christopher and Diane Banks and Martin Jensen and Matthew Cole. For your belief in me, and for your work to help me build the career of my dreams. Thank you. I cannot ever say it enough.

To Darcy Nicholson. Sometimes I still have to pinch myself that my book ended up in your hands. You were and are my editorial idol, so to have you now as my editor feels like a wonderful stroke of the universe. I am so grateful for everything you have done to transform this book and me, pushing me to new heights as a writer and investing so much time and care into everything from the edits to making sure I can go on a proof tour that aligns with the cities I'm visiting to see Taylor Swift in concert. Thank you so much. For your faith and patience and kindness and commitment to Andie and her story. I could write pages and pages but I will stop here and just keep sending it to you in effusive emails instead.

To Jeramie Orton. For that first wonderful phone call that could have lasted three days. For loving Andie as much as I do. For everything you did to make sure you became my US publisher. For being there every step of the way—me, you, and Darcy making up an editorial team beyond my wildest dreams. For believing in me, and this book, and answering my emails about cheese positioning even when they come through at eleven p.m.

Thank you so much, for all of it. I am so humbled and grateful that I get to work with you.

To CJ, for everything. To Jonny Bauer, for teaching me to breathe. To Edward Mannix, for lighting the way to a level of healing I could never have imagined.

To my parents, for always supporting my dreams. To my dad, Martin Gillam, for telling me when I was complaining about my school uniform that I wouldn't have to worry about it when I was older because I could wear jeans at Oxford or Cambridge when I went to university. For telling me if I wanted to be an editor one day that he felt sure I could make it happen. For believing I could be a tennis player even when I struggled with every other sport. For always helping me to see every side of a situation. Thank you. And to my mum, Dr. Amanda Gillam, for showing me by example that the sky is the limit for women, always. For doing a PhD in her fifties. For taking a job at a school where she had to teach four different subjects at once and not even flinching at the challenge. For balancing all of that with raising three independently-minded, soft, and kind women. Thank you—for inspiring me. For always, always believing in me. Love you.

ACKNOWLEDGEMENTS

To my sisters, Charlotte Gillam and Lucie Gillam, for being the inspiration for Sara—my forever best friends and two of the bravest people I know. Watching you both pursue your dreams and happiness—whether that's moving across the world or going after an acting career—always inspires me to keep pursuing mine. Grateful to be your sister. Love you more than I can ever say. Thank you.

To Andrew—I am not even sure where to start here. But I will try. Thank you for picking me up off the carpet when I was lying there during the pandemic crying about the fact that I'd never write a book and saying, "Why don't you try?" For always believing I can do more than I think I can. For loving me through some of the hardest times of my life in these last few years. For having the softest heart of anyone I've ever met. For choosing me every day. For telling anyone and everyone you meet that your girlfriend is going to be a famous author. Thank you, for all of it. I feel immensely privileged to spend my life with you.

To everyone at Bloomsbury in the UK and Penguin Books in the US—THANK YOU. Having worked in publishing for the better part of four years, I know how much work goes into making a book, and I cannot tell you how grateful

ACKNOWLEDGEMENTS

I am for every second you have spent on this one. It is an honour and a privilege. Thank you unrestrainedly to the following at Bloomsbury: Fabrice Wilmann, Maisie McCormick, Natasha Onwuemezi, Joely Day in Editorial. Carmen R. Balit and Emma Rogers for the WONDERFUL cover. Beth Maher in Marketing. Ben Chisnall in Production, and Abigail Walton in Publicity. The brilliant rights team: Stephanie Purcell, Hannah Stokes, Helene Navarre, Callum Mollison, Victoria Lawrance, Flora Wood and Ana Paula De La Borbolla. And in Sales – Joe Roche, for being the most amazing colleague at S&S and now for all of this! I can hardly believe how exciting it is to get to work with you again in this capacity. To Caroline Bovey, and David Heathscott, David Smith, Fabia Ma, Finn McQueen, Georgina Ugen-Skeene, Hannah Cronin (and also for all the work you did on my books for Head of Zeus!), Inês Figueira, Karen Sweetland, Lara Morrison, Lauren Elizabeth Moseley, Lily Watson, Lorraine Levis, Lucie Moody, Luke Crabb, Max Bridgewater, Nikky Ward (hi! How cool is this!), Rachel Rees (eternally grateful for everything you have done so far for books that are not my own, which you proudly championed on my behalf and on behalf of my Head of Zeus authors – beyond thrilled that I have the privilege of you selling mine, now. What a dream!), Robyn Enslin, Sarah Knight. In Export: Sarah McLean, Hattie Castelberg, Joanna Vallance, Mariafrancesca Ierace, Rosie Barr, Inez Maria, Rayna Luo, Emma Allden, Ellen Chen, Hannah Rimmington.

And the same to these folks at Penguin Books: Brian Tart, Andrea Schulz, Pamela Dorman, Patrick Nolan, Kate Stark, Mary Stone, Rebecca Marsh, Ivy Cheng, Chantal Canales, Norina Frabotta, Mike Brown, Nick Michal, Jason Ramirez, Dave Litman, Claire Vaccaro, and Andy Dudley and the entire sales team.

To Tamara Acarali, for being one of the first people to read *Bad Publicity*, and for giving me the best beta reader notes ever, which made me cry with joy because you had seen the characters as real people, just like they were in my head. Thank you a million times for replying to my tweet. I am so grateful.

To Kristina Fazzalaro and Annabel Robinson, for taking time out of your busy schedules to tell me about your jobs and helping me take Andie from possibly the worst publicist of all time to an incredibly competent one. In particular, thanks to Kristina for the story about landing the radio show by the stroke of genius of pursuing a journalist who was from the same location that the book was set in. I am grateful that you lent that genius to Andie!

To Sara O'Keefe, for having coffee with me and for being the first person to encourage me to submit my book to agents. For supporting me so much with my career. Thank you.

To Emma Leong, for emailing me on a Saturday to tell me how much you loved my book, shutting my boyfriend up who had just been telling me that no agents would get back to me over the weekend. To Edwina de Charnace, for your love for Andie from the first page. To Laura Williams for your belief that this book could be so much more than it was. To Kiya Evans, for your wonderful notes and your passion for this project. Thank you all for your belief in me and this book. I am so grateful for it.

To Sophie Raphaeline, for founding such a wonderful bookshop in Another Country. To Kim Houde, for being kind enough to share its magic with me.

To my Competent Oddballs Meg Pickford, Charlie Hiscox, Matilda Singer, Peyton Stableford, Sophie Whitehead – thank you for everything you have done to keep me sane while I have gone on this completely insane journey. Special mention to Matilda for telling me when I let her know I had written a book that she was already imagining my launch party. I dreamed of having friends like all of you, and have to pinch myself that I now have them. Love you all.

To everyone at Head of Zeus, who celebrated with me when I got the news at work about the book deal. Madeleine O'Shea and Laura Palmer and Martina Arzu. Ayo Okojie and Yasminn Brown and Becky Clark and Nic Cheetham. Kate Young, for happening to be in the office that day and for being so kind and saying you couldn't wait to do events together. I hope that we make that happen!

To anyone and everyone else who I have come across in this last crazy year—thank you. I am sorry if I have not mentioned you in here, but please know I am forever grateful to all of you.

And, finally, to you – the person reading this book. Thank you so much for picking this up and visiting its pages. I hope you found something in them. Love and light.

Bianca xx